TURN TO DUST

A DETECTIVE KAY HUNTER CRIME THRILLER

RACHEL AMPHLETT

SAXON
PUBLISHING

CHAPTER ONE

The crows should have alerted him.

Ducking and wheeling across a bleak late spring sky, the birds cawed and cackled as they swooped upon the muddy undulating landscape before rising to the air once more.

They seemed distracted, hesitant to leave the field in pursuit of the tractor that rumbled over the adjacent land, dragging a seed drill in its wake. Back and forth, back and forth, following the furrows left behind from the plough only weeks before.

A cold wind whipped across the field, shaking the hedgerows and threatening to tear the ripening buds from a cluster of hazel shrubs that hunkered under a canopy of birch. A second blast of air shoved against the metal five-bar gate, rattling the chain looped between the frame and a wooden post.

Luke Martin blew into his hands and wished he'd worn an extra pair of socks.

Instead, the damp mud oozed around his calf-length rubber boots and chilled his toes, and every breath he took was expelled in a cloud of condensation.

His fingers fared little better.

The thermal-lined gloves he'd purchased had promised on the label to protect his extremities from temperatures down to five below zero Centigrade, but he reckoned now that the claim was overambitious.

He became aware of a vehicle approaching, the purr of the engine running under the crackle and snap of branches and woodland detritus disappearing under its wheels.

Luke turned away from the field to see a battered four-by-four round the corner in the single track.

Its roof caught on low-hanging tendrils of ash and oak while the vehicle rocked from side to side, the suspension groaning under duress.

Sunlight reflected off its dirt-streaked windscreen, obliterating the driver's features, but not the way his hands gripped the steering wheel.

Gesturing to a grass-covered verge to the right of

the gate, Luke walked around to the side of his own car as the four-by-four creaked to a standstill moments before the ratchet of the handbrake reached him, almost as an afterthought.

The driver swung his door open and swore as his boots met the soggy earth.

Tugging his woollen hat over his ears to protect his balding skull, Luke moved around to the front of the four-by-four and stuck out his hand.

'Maybe Sonia was right,' he said. 'Maybe we should have taken up golf instead. That's what most blokes our age do.'

'It'd still be bloody freezing.' Tom Coker took the outstretched hand in a tight grip, then glared at the mud smeared along the side of the vehicle. He jerked his chin at Luke's car. 'How long have you been here?'

'About fifteen minutes. Traffic was lighter than I thought.'

'Had a look yet?'

'It doesn't look too boggy. Hard going, but not waterlogged like I thought it'd be.'

'That's something, at least. Let's get a move on. The longer we stand around here talking, the colder we're going to get.'

Luke wandered back to his car, popped open the

boot lid, and eyed the equipment laid out on a tarpaulin to protect the carpeted lining.

He lifted out the shovel first – an ancient tool passed down to his father by his grandfather, and now his. Since moving to the smaller house in Seal six months ago, he was using it for his hobby rather than tending a vegetable patch any more, and he remembered why when his back twinged as he straightened.

'Come on, old man,' said Coker. 'Dennis said he wants to prep this field tomorrow, so we need to get a move on.'

Luke glanced over his shoulder. 'Any problem with the contract?'

'None at all – if we find anything, he takes a thirty per cent cut and the rest is ours.'

'Sweet.' He tugged the metal detector out from its swaddling of blankets, and shut the car boot. 'Is this the only field we can use?'

'For now. We'll get another go at it towards the end of September after the harvest, and he said there might be another field nearer to the house on the other side of the woods we can take a look at as well.'

'Let's go, then.'

Luke fumbled the chain as he looped it away from the gate, his numb fingers clumsy while his thoughts turned to the flask of hot coffee Sonia had packed alongside two tuna salad sandwiches she'd insisted he take with him. The flask and food remained in the car, and would do so until mid-morning.

Losing track of time was one of the reasons he enjoyed metal detecting.

'Have there been any finds near here?' he said as he fastened the gate back in place and stumbled across the furrows alongside Coker.

'Not on Dennis's land, but then I don't think he's ever had anyone take a look. There were a couple of thirteenth-century brooches found a few miles away three years ago. And lots of musket balls.'

Luke groaned. 'Always the bloody musket balls.'

'I remember when you used to get excited about those.'

'That was before I hit double figures. Honestly, if Charles I's lot wasted that much ammunition during the Civil War, it's no wonder they lost to Cromwell's army. They obviously couldn't shoot straight for shit.'

His friend snorted, then stopped and surveyed the landscape before them. 'It'd be so quiet out here, if it wasn't for those bloody birds. Dennis reckons he can't even hear the A20 unless the wind's blowing in this direction.'

Luke squinted against the cold chill that snapped

at his coat collar, then inhaled the rich earthy air. 'Beats being at work, too.'

'You busy at the moment?'

He wrinkled his nose. 'In between contracts. I spent yesterday sending out quotes, and a couple of those should come through in the next week or two. You?'

'Skiving. I was meant to be rendering a house over at Sevenoaks this morning, but I sent two of the lads instead. Okay, shall we split up?'

Luke turned his attention to the rolling landscape, the noise from the tractor carrying over the hedgerow.

And still, those bloody crows. Caw, caw, caw.

'I think I'm going to head down there. Looks as if it has a slight rise, then an indentation marked on the Ordnance Survey map I took a look at before you turned up. It might yield something. What about you?'

Coker pointed to the hedgerow separating the barren field with the one where the farmer worked. 'I'll start there. There's a ditch system that runs parallel to the boundary. It could be an old trackway or something, so it's worth checking out.'

Luke bumped his fist against his friend's outstretched hand. 'Be lucky. Break in a couple of hours?'

'Sounds good.'

Pulling the headphones up over his head and adjusting the pads over his ears, he switched on the machine and listened to its beeps and whirrs as it nestled into the setting he programmed. Satisfied he was ready, he began to march towards his intended search area, sweeping the metal detector in front of his feet as he walked.

It'd be sod's law if he missed a find in his hurry to reach the contoured land he had set his mind on.

The world contracted around him as he worked, the movement of the metal detector right to left and back almost trance-inducing. Any worries about work deserted him while he focused on what he was hearing.

He moved without purpose, simply staring at the tufts of long grass that were poking through the earth in a last-ditch attempt to claim it before barley seedlings took over for the summer months.

After a few minutes, he raised his gaze to his left to see Coker with his back to him, intent on his own progress. He wouldn't admit it to anyone, but a competitiveness rose in Luke's chest as he turned back to his work.

He wanted to be the one who found it.

The find.

Sonia joked that it was his vain hope of paying off a chunk of the mortgage before their son left home. Of course, his chances were slim – but a man could dream, couldn't he?

The birds grew louder as he approached the rise in the field.

He could hear them over the beeps and squeaks in his headphones.

Luke scowled at the top of the incline, and then stopped.

The field rolled down towards a boundary that Luke knew bordered a stream – it was another of his and Coker's targets for the day's exploring in the hope they'd find traces of a Civil War encampment that was rumoured to have been in the area.

The crows had clustered together – a murder, he recalled – halfway between his position and the boundary. They bickered and called to each other as two or three birds at a time rose into the air, then dived back and noisily shoved their way back into the centre of the flock.

'What the—'

He pushed his headphones off his head, looping them over the back of his neck, and frowned.

He couldn't see what was causing so much

interest for the crows because whatever it was lay in a smaller indentation in the field.

Dead fox?

Badger?

Intrigued, Luke wandered over to where the birds gathered, ignoring their indignant squawks as he drew closer, sending them into the air once more.

The crows landed a few paces away, dark beady eyes watching him, daring him.

A pale-pink form lay stretched out between the furrows caused by the tractor's wheel ruts, muddy tyre tracks creating a zig-zag pattern that reflected his unsteady progress.

Luke frowned as the form became a shape, and then the shape became the outline of a man.

A naked man.

'Are you all right, mate?' He kept his voice jovial, despite the spike in his heart rate.

What was he? Drunk?

He'd have to be, out here exposed to the elements, except—

Luke stopped, then swallowed.

Throat dry, a bitter acidic taste on the back of his tongue, the reality caught up with his brain.

The man wasn't drunk.

His whole body lay contorted within the brown soil, his arms at unnatural angles. His legs – Jesus, what had happened to his legs? – were disproportionate in size to his torso, and mud splashed over his skin as if he'd tripped over without trying to break his fall.

And his face—

Luke turned away, stomach churning, and saw then what the crows had been doing.

The man's eyes were staring at him from another furrow, accusing, bloodied and torn.

And at his feet, all around Luke's frozen toes encased in his useless thermal socks and rubber boots, were teeth.

Lots and lots of teeth.

CHAPTER TWO

A bleak sky laden with rain enshrouded the splashes of light that flashed through the thick canopy of trees above the potholed woodland track.

Detective Inspector Kay Hunter held on to the strap above the passenger window of the mud-splattered pool car, the springs in the worn seat squeaking with every bump as the vehicle rocked from side to side.

Beside her, Detective Sergeant Ian Barnes clenched his jaw and cursed under his breath when a branch twisted and smacked against the windscreen, his hands gripping the steering wheel.

'Should've nicked one of the Land Rovers from Traffic,' he said.

She held her breath as the car went through a deep

puddle, and wondered whether she should raise her feet off the floor in case water began to pool under the door seal.

Barnes accelerated, the mud relinquishing the car with a thick suck of reluctance, and then the trees thinned out, exposing an area of broken ground.

A line of cars were parked haphazardly alongside a bramble hedgerow bisected by a metal five-bar gate, and Kay spotted two patrol cars emblazoned with the Kent Police logo beside a dark-coloured van.

She opened the car door, swung her legs out and reached for a pair of wellington boots she'd thrown behind the passenger seat when Barnes had collected her from home half an hour ago.

Barnes was doing the same, replacing his leather lace-up shoes with a battered pair of boots. He turned to her once done.

'Ready?'

'As I ever will be.'

The wind caught her hair as she rose from her seat and slammed the car door. Peering over the roof, she spotted two white-suited figures moving from the van to the gate, one carrying a silver-coloured metal suitcase.

Beside one of the patrol cars, three men hovered as a police constable spoke with them.

Barnes joined her. 'Witnesses. Hughes said two of them were metal detecting – one of them found the body. The other bloke must be the farmer who owns the land.'

'Let's have a quick chat with them first, and then go and see what Harriet's lot are doing. Is Lucas here yet?'

'His car is over there – behind the tractor.'

'Okay. We'll catch him in a moment. Who was first on scene?'

'Ben Allen, from Tonbridge. He was on a routine patrol when the call came through from the farmer, and nearest to the scene.'

On cue, Ben emerged from the driver's seat of the second vehicle, murmuring an update into the radio clipped to his vest. He nodded when he saw Kay and Barnes heading towards him, and ended the call.

'Morning, guv.'

'Morning, Ben. Everything under control?'

'It's a quiet one – no-one around here, apart from these three.' He jerked his thumb over his shoulder to where his colleague had corralled the witnesses. 'Lucas got here fifteen minutes ago, and already confirmed life extinct. Not that there was much doubt of that.'

'We heard it's the body of a man,' said Kay. 'Unknown to the farmer, is he?'

'Not much of a body left, to be honest, guv. I've never seen anything like it.' Ben wrinkled his nose.

'What do you mean?'

'He's all deformed. And naked.' The police constable shook his head. 'It's a strange one.'

'Can you introduce us?'

'Of course.'

Kay followed him across the slippery mud to where the three men huddled at the side of the patrol car, almost as if they were trying to put as much distance as possible between them and what lay in the field.

Introductions made, the two uniformed officers excused themselves and wandered over to the gate.

Kay turned her attention to the farmer. 'Mr Maitland, I apologise – you may have answered similar questions from my colleagues, but we have to learn as much as possible about what's happened here. How long have you farmed this land?'

Maitland took a shaking drag from the cigarette held between his finger and thumb, and then squinted at her. 'Me personally, about thirty years. It's been in the family for a couple of hundred.'

'What do you farm?'

'Crops, mainly. Barley, wheat. The wife's got me trying lavender this year for the first time. Not sure how that'll work out.'

'When was the last time you'd been in that field, prior to this morning?' said Barnes.

'Last week. Tuesday. I was turning over the soil ready for the seed drill. It was due to be planted tomorrow.'

The farmer broke off, his face glum as he stared at the makeshift cordon of blue and white police tape.

Kay turned to the two men beside him. 'Which one of you found the body?'

'That was me,' said Luke.

'Are you all right?'

The man shrugged. 'Do you know who he is?'

'Not yet. Did you recognise him?'

'No. I've never seen him before. Well, as far as I could tell. His face was all smashed in, and—'

He stopped, covering his mouth with his hand.

Kay reached out for his arm. 'Take your time. It's okay. I know this is hard.'

'The crows had had a go at him, I think. I saw them when I first got here at half eight. I wondered why they weren't following the seed drill in the other field like they usually would.'

'Did you touch anything?'

'God, no. I yelled across the field to Tom, told him to stay back and that there was a dead body, and we got out of there. We put the metal detectors and stuff in the cars, and then went over to tell Dennis. We called triple nine after that.'

'Dennis, did you enter the field with the body in?' said Kay.

'No. Figured you lot wouldn't thank me for that.'

'Good. All right, we've got your statements so you're good to go. Luke – if you need to, speak to your GP about what you've seen, okay? Don't bottle it up.'

He nodded, and then sloped back to his car alongside Tom and the farmer, all three men murmuring under their breath.

'Want to take a look now?' said Barnes.

'Yes, come on.'

They wandered over to the gate, and Kay greeted the police officer who handed a clipboard to them.

'Thanks.' She scrawled her signature across the crime scene entry record.

Barnes lifted up the tape and she ducked underneath, her gaze already taking in the second cordon that had been erected close to where the man's body had been found.

A group of white-suited CSI technicians crouched

in a broken semicircle, each of them working methodically to record any evidence that would help to work out why the man had been killed and how he had died.

The Home Office pathologist, Lucas Anderson, stood outside the cordon, his head bowed as he watched.

'Lucas,' said Barnes.

'Morning,' he said, the paper suit crinkling as he held out his hand. 'Death has been declared. I'll complete the paperwork when I get back to my car so they can move him once Harriet's lot have finished, but it's unusual.'

'Cause of death?' said Kay.

Lucas pursed his lips. 'You know I don't like to posit assumptions, Hunter.'

'Come on, just your initial thoughts. Please.'

At that moment, one of the CSIs stood and moved to the side, and Kay got a clear view of the dead man.

'Jesus Christ.'

'Different, isn't it?

'What happened to him?'

'Good question,' said Lucas. 'Look, I won't give my official opinion on cause of death until I've completed the post mortem—'

'But you do have an opinion,' said Barnes. 'What is it?'

'The only time I've seen vaguely similar injuries like those to his legs is from suicides. Specifically, people who have jumped from buildings.'

Barnes squinted at him. 'He's in the middle of a field, Lucas.'

'I know. I said it was unusual, didn't I?'

CHAPTER THREE

A cacophony of activity filled the incident room as detectives, uniformed police officers and administrative staff jostled for space and called out instructions and good-natured insults to each other.

Kay stood in front of a freshly wiped whiteboard at the far end of the room and stared at the photographs Detective Constable Gavin Piper had pinned to the board moments after Barnes had uploaded the files from his phone upon returning to the town centre station.

Outside, the jangle of mid-morning traffic filtered through the windows, the sounds fading in and out of Kay's consciousness as her mind worked.

She nibbled at a ragged thumbnail, and then

uncapped a pen and scrawled her initial thoughts onto the board.

'Here you go, guv. Soup. Thought it'd help you defrost.' Gavin grinned as he held out the mug to her, and then jerked his chin at the photographs. 'Do you think he died by accident, and someone moved him there?'

'I honestly don't know at the moment, Gav.' She blew across the hot surface, and took a sip. 'Who made this?'

'I did. My sister and her boyfriend bought me a soup-maker for my birthday. First time I've tried it out. That one's spicy parsnip. Is it all right?'

'Yeah, it's good, thanks.'

'I hope one of those has my name on it, Piper,' said Barnes as he joined them, and then smiled as Gavin handed him a mug from the tray. 'Champion.'

'Round up everyone else, Gav – let's get this briefing underway, and then we can get back to work.'

Kay waited while the burgeoning team of police officers joined their admin colleagues and wheeled chairs to the front of the room. Once they were ready, she provided a brief overview about the investigation and who the key points of contact would be.

As Senior Investigating Officer, she would still be

responsible for reporting progress to Detective Chief Inspector Devon Sharp, but at least his role meant she wouldn't have to spend too much time at Headquarters trying to argue her case for more personnel to be assigned to her investigation.

Introduction complete, she tapped her finger on the nearest photograph. 'We've got the first of these printed off, Ian. Fingerprints have been taken but while we're waiting for those results, take a look at this. There's a small tattoo on his bicep here. It's old, but can you make out the letters underneath it?'

'Hang on.' Barnes put his soup mug on the desk next to the whiteboard, then fished his reading glasses from his inside jacket pocket before staring at the image. 'Looks military, doesn't it? The writing's all faded though – I can't make it out.'

'Bet it says "Mum",' said Gavin.

'Very funny.' Kay peered at the photograph. 'Isn't there someone over at Headquarters who knows this sort of stuff?'

'I'll give Joanne Fletcher a call,' said Barnes. 'There might be someone within the media relations team who can assist. Sharp will probably have some ideas too, given his time in the military police.'

'I'll catch up with him when he gets here. Send over the photo to Joanne as well though, on the proviso the media team don't share it with the press. The last thing we need is for that to be broadcast before we've got some answers.'

DC Carys Miles wandered over, notebook in hand. 'Simon Winter just called from DarentValley Hospital – Lucas is going to do the post mortem tomorrow morning, but he says the teeth have been sent over to a specialist orthodontist for examination.' She frowned. 'Were his teeth not in his mouth?'

'No,' said Barnes. 'Most of them were all over the ground next to him. Along with his eyes.'

'Ew.' Carys wrinkled her nose. 'Baseball bat to the face, was it?'

'We don't know,' said Kay. 'Lucas had a few thoughts, but he won't commit to an opinion until the PM has been done. In the meantime, can you get onto Rural Crimes and see if they've had any problems in the area lately?'

'Will do, guv,' said Carys. 'What about the farmer, Dennis Maitland – did he see anything?'

'No, and I don't think he's going to be much help. I had a look online and those two fields are on the outer boundary of his land. He says he ploughed the field last week, and hasn't been back since. I suppose until it's all planted up, he doesn't need to. There's nothing there to steal, is there, Ian?'

The detective sergeant shook his head. 'I guess that's why he was happy for the two blokes to use their metal detectors – it's not as if they could cause any damage at the moment.'

'Why strip him naked?' said Kay, flipping the pen between her fingers. 'Whoever did this could've simply taken any identification off of him.'

'He could've been wearing a uniform, ma'am.' Probationary Detective Constable Laura Hanway's voice carried over the heads of her colleagues. 'Might have been military, or perhaps a private security guard for something. Especially given the tattoo, perhaps.'

Kay wrote her suggestion on the board. 'Good start. Anyone else?'

'Building on from that, perhaps there was something else about the clothing,' said Sergeant Harry Davis. 'If it wasn't a uniform, they might have had some sort of distinctive logos, or labels that could tie him to a certain place or person.'

'Yes, another good point,' said Kay. 'There were the remnants of a plastic zip tie around one of his ankles, so whoever did this restrained him before he was killed.'

She ran her eyes over the man's prone body in the second of the photographs. 'Okay, what about the location? Why there? Harriet's team have taken casts of footprints, but so far they've only matched the boots our witness, Luke Martin, was wearing. They've taken other prints into evidence, but those might take some time to work through – the farmer told uniform there's a footpath running alongside the left-hand boundary to that field.'

'Depends how long he was out there before being discovered, I suppose,' said Carys. 'It rained on Friday night. Maitland reckons he ploughed that field last Tuesday so if our man's body was dumped between then and when it rained, any footprints belonging to a suspect or suspects might have been washed away.'

Kay turned away from her team and ran her eyes over the notes she'd added to the board.

No evidence, no identity, and no witnesses to the crime.

How the hell were they going to solve this one?

'First steps,' she said, facing her team once more. 'House-to-house enquiries within a one-mile radius of the farm, and I want CCTV and Automatic Number Plate Recognition data from all roads passing within a mile of this land as well. Carys – can you get onto someone at Headquarters and have a sketch of our victim's face composed from these photographs so that we've got something appropriate to show homeowners? I'm not letting anyone see these images – they'll have nightmares for months.'

'Will do, guv.'

'All right, everyone. Dismissed. Let's get a move on with this.'

CHAPTER FOUR

Gavin flicked up the collar of his wool coat and pulled the knitted beanie hat down over his ears before shoving his hands in his pockets.

Despite the mid-morning air temperature being reported as almost into double figures on his car dashboard, an aching chill clung to the damp air in the tree-lined lane, and weak sunlight cast a yellow-grey hue to the sky, sparkling in the puddles that lined mud-streaked grass verges.

Up ahead, two patrol cars were parked in a lay-by, the occupants already door-knocking at a cluster of properties huddled at the side of the lane that appeared to be old farmworkers' cottages.

He peered over the roof of the car as Laura

emerged from the passenger seat, swearing through gritted teeth as she zipped up her coat.

'Bloody hell, Gavin. What happened to the early spring we were meant to be having? It's freezing out here.'

He grinned, then gestured up the road towards the nearest cottage. 'Shall we make a start? Think yourself lucky you're not in uniform anymore.'

The probationary detective constable grinned. 'Thank God. February nearly broke me – that last shift scuffing around the town centre in three inches of snow at two in the morning dodging puddles of vomit…'

She shook her head, a sense of wonder in her voice.

Gavin locked the car, checked over his shoulder for traffic, and then led the way towards the houses.

'How are you settling in?'

'Really well, thanks. I think it helps that everyone is going out of their way to make sure I don't feel out of my depth.'

'It probably helps that you're a known quantity after helping out with that kidnapping investigation last year. When is your next exam?'

Laura kicked at a pebble in the road, sending it

flying over to the other side where it bounced and skidded into a deep pothole with an audible splash.

'The week after next. I'm trying to keep ahead on the revision work, but I don't know how I'm going to do that now. I'd imagine we're going to be working some long hours until we solve this one, aren't we?'

'I expect so. I had the same problem a few years ago – we had a couple of big cases one after the other while I was studying.'

'How did you manage? I'm useless at getting up early at the best of times, and by the time I get home the last thing I want to do is sit and study – all I want to do is veg out.'

'The only way I could do it was to put in a couple of hours when I finished my shift and study at my desk, or ask Hughes to book a spare interview room for me if I didn't want to get interrupted. I found that if I did my revision at work, rather than try to do it when I got home, it became a part of my work routine.' Gavin shrugged. 'It seemed to work, anyway. It might be worth giving it a shot.'

Laura smiled. 'I will, thanks. These houses – they back onto the woods near where the body was found, right?'

'Yes.' Gavin pulled out an Ordnance Survey map from his pocket, the edges already creased from where he'd folded it inside out. He held it out and pointed to the countryside depicted below the A20. 'You've got Sevenoaks a few miles to the north here, and we're here on this C-road. These are the farm cottages marked here. The field where the body was found is about here, and these are the woods that back onto the garden of the first property.'

'Okay, got it.' Laura shielded her eyes with her hand as they approached the house. 'Rented, or owned?'

'This one and the one next to it are owner-occupied,' said Gavin, refolding the map and tucking it into his jacket. 'The next-door neighbour owns and rents out the two properties on the end as well, so we'll leave uniform to the rentals and do these two ourselves. That way, we can crack on and get to the next hamlet. Kay's got five other patrols working the other side of Maitland's farm as well. With any luck, we'll have all of the initial statements done by the end of tomorrow.'

Laura shivered as a fresh gust of wind shook the hedgerow to their left, pushing a loose tendril of hair from her face. 'How come we pulled the short straw being out here while Barnes and Carys get to stay in the warmth, then? Who did you annoy to deserve this?'

Gavin grinned. 'I'm still classed as the new kid when it suits them, and you've only just joined. Hence, we get the cold weather work.'

'Let's get on with it then, shall we?'

He pushed against a moss-covered wooden gate into a shallow front garden, stepped aside to let Laura pass, and then wiped his hands together to lose the remnants of lichen that clung to his skin before rapping his knuckles against the front door.

Taking a step back and lifting his gaze, he noticed a handful of missing slate tiles from the gabled roof and paint peeling from the four windowsills that faced the lane.

If it wasn't for the state-of-the-art satellite dish that protruded from the brickwork next to one of the two upstairs windows, he would've sworn that the surrounding woodland was trying to reclaim the property from its owner one season at a time.

The door opened on squeaking hinges after a few moments and a man peered out, his wispy grey hair sticking out in tufts either side of his ears.

'Yes? Who are you? If you're selling something, you can go back and read the sign on the gate.'

Gavin held up his warrant card and introduced Laura. 'And what's your name please, sir?'

The man took the warrant card from him, and

inspected it before handing it back. 'Humphrey Godmanstone.'

'How long have you lived here, Mr Godmanstone?'

'Thirty years in April. Inherited the place from my parents.'

'Does anyone else live here?'

'No. Did away with the wife a decade ago.' He smiled, exposing crooked teeth. 'Don't worry. I didn't kill the old tart. She buggered off. Took the two kids as well. Northampton, I think. That's where her sister lived, anyway. Good bloody riddance.'

Gavin cleared his throat, knowing that Laura would be watching his every move in an attempt to learn from him, and wishing Carys was beside him instead.

He tried to ignore the heat rising from his neck to his jawline. 'We wondered if we might ask a few questions about an incident we're investigating in the area.'

'Such as?'

'Could we come in?'

'No.'

Gavin forced a smile. 'Not to worry. We're investigating the death of a man whose body was found on the outer boundary of Maitland's farm.'

'Is that so?' Godmanstone's hand dropped from the door, and he leaned against the frame, his arms crossed. 'What's that got to do with me?'

'I understand the woodland at the back of your property joins onto that land? We're conducting house-to-house enquiries in the area to try to ascertain whether anyone has noticed any suspicious activity in the past week, or whether you've heard anything.'

'Like what?'

'Strangers to the area, perhaps hanging around in the lane. Any vehicles that have seemed out of place, or anything of yours – garden tools and the like – that might've gone missing in recent weeks.'

'Haven't spotted anything. And if anyone tried to steal anything from the garden shed, they'd have to get past the geese first.'

'Geese?' said Laura.

'Yes, young lady. Geese. Better than guard dogs. Cheaper – and if you tire of them, at least you can eat them.'

Gavin gritted his teeth, then ploughed on. 'Have you heard anything strange at night, anything that seems out of place here?'

'No. Once the light's out, I'm asleep. I don't wake up until the radio comes on at seven o'clock for the news. Mind you, these days I don't know why I bother – only puts me in a bad mood before I've even started the bloody day.'

'All right, Mr Godmanstone.' Gavin snapped shut his notebook and forced a smile as he held out a business card. 'Thanks for your time. If you could—'

The door slammed shut.

Gavin sighed, and pushed the card through the letterbox, then turned to Laura.

The detective constable covered her mouth with her hand, but couldn't hide the creases at the corner of her eyes.

'Not a word, Hanway,' he said over his shoulder as he pushed through the garden gate. 'Not a bloody word.'

A woman stood on the doorstep of the house next door, grinning as they rounded the corner of the low privet hedge that separated her home from Godmanstone's property.

'He's a delight, isn't he?' she said without rancour. 'I don't know why he keeps the geese – he's enough to scare anyone.'

'It takes all sorts, Ms—'

'Mrs.' She held out her hand. 'Beverley Winton.'

Gavin made the introductions, noticing the splodges of white paint that covered the woman's fingers, and then jerked his chin towards the properties to their right. 'And you own these as well, I understand?'

'That's right. We're doing up this one at the moment, and then that'll be available as well. Did you want to come in?'

'If we could, thanks.'

'Sorry about the mess. Don't trip over the dust sheets – I've been painting the stair balustrades this morning. I don't know how paint manufacturers get away with putting "only one coat" on the tin. That's the third lot on there, and I'm still not happy with it.'

She opened a door into a cluttered living room. Curtains billowed at open windows, and Gavin ran his gaze over the packing cases stacked against one wall.

'We just have a few questions,' he said. 'We're investigating the death of a man who was found in one of the outer fields to Maitland's farm this morning. We wondered if you'd noticed any suspicious activities in the area over the past week?'

The woman paled. 'A dead man? No – I haven't noticed anyone new around here. The lane is pretty quiet once anyone living along here has gone to work. It's the same in the evening. Do you think we're in danger?'

'We're inclined to believe this is an isolated incident, Mrs Winton,' said Laura. 'Have you noticed anything that might be considered unusual for this time of year? Or any thefts from your garden shed, for example?'

'My husband, Peter, hasn't mentioned anything. He keeps the shed locked anyway, just through habit after we lived in town for so many years. We haven't got the same trusting nature that our tenants do.'

'Or geese,' said Gavin.

'No, thank goodness.' Winton managed a laugh, then her eyes grew serious once more. 'I'm sorry I can't be of more help. I can ask Peter about it when he gets home, if you like?'

'That would be much appreciated, Mrs Winton,' said Gavin, and handed her a business card. 'Even if you think it might not be significant, it's best to let us know.'

CHAPTER FIVE

Kay looked up from her computer screen as the door to the incident room opened and Detective Chief Inspector Devon Sharp marched across the room, his expression one of consternation.

Several inches taller than Kay, the ex-military policeman kept his grey-flecked brown hair closely cropped and moved with the bearing of one used to a parade ground.

He loosened his tie as he stalked towards his office behind her desk, his attention taken by his mobile phone screen, his brow puckered.

Kay bit her lip as he walked past her, his head still bowed, then gathered up the copies of the photographs she'd collated. Pushing back her chair, she wandered over to the open door of his office, and knocked.

'Guv? I wondered if you had a minute?'

He glanced up from his phone, momentarily surprised, then blinked. 'Sorry, Kay – miles away there. Come on in.'

'Everything all right?' she said, closing the door behind her and taking the more comfortable of the visitor chairs opposite his desk. She eyed the worn threads on the armrest, and wondered if Headquarters were ever going to provide the DCI with some new furniture.

Probably not.

'I've just spent three hours this morning arguing for an increase to our budget for next year.'

'Oh. I presume it didn't go well?'

'I'd have rather had a root canal.' His mouth twisted into a sardonic smile as he tossed his mobile onto his desk and sank into his seat. 'I hear you had a body in a field this morning, over near Sevenoaks?'

'Actually, I was hoping you could help me.' Kay provided him with an overview of the morning's discovery, and then slid the photographs across the desk. 'Barnes took these while we were chatting with Lucas and Harriet. We wondered if they might have some sort of military significance.'

Sharp reached out for the A4-sized images, and leaned back in his chair as he sifted through them. He paused for several moments on each one, turning the photograph at different angles, and then lowered them to his desk and frowned.

'It reminds me of the sort of tattoos some soldiers would get after completing a tour of duty,' he said. 'Sort of a reminder, as a way to prove they'd survived intact. What's the age of the victim?'

'I gave Lucas a call an hour ago to see what he thought, now that he has the body at the morgue. He said he won't be able to narrow it down properly until after the post mortem tomorrow morning, but estimates the man's age to be between early forties and late fifties.'

Sharp ran his hand over his chin, and picked up another photograph. 'That age group would place our victim anywhere from the Falklands conflict if he's in his late fifties, right the way through to the Afghanistan campaigns of recent years.'

'That's a lot of people, guv.'

'I know. I'm not familiar with this particular artwork, though. There's nothing on this that says to me it's one particular regiment or another.'

'What about the writing underneath? Does that ring any bells?'

'Looks like some sort of an abbreviated code. If he was Special Forces or something like that, it might relate to his unit. You know they work in four-man teams?'

'Yes. So, you're saying it might be limited to a small group, rather than have a wider regimental bearing?'

'Exactly. And you say there was nothing else to identify him?'

'No, not by way of clothing or piercings anyway. Lucas has sent off the loose teeth that were all over the ground to a specialist orthodontist. I'm hoping she might be able to glean some more information from those for us.'

'It's going to be bloody hard if they weren't in situ,' said Sharp. 'Unless the dentistry suggests he had work done while he was overseas.'

'Do you think we're onto something with this tattoo being something to do with the army, then?'

'I think it's worth following up, yes.' He pulled a notebook from his pocket and scribbled across a fresh page before pointing the end of the pen at the images. 'Can I have those?'

'Of course.'

'Okay, what I'll do is make some phone calls, speak to some of the contacts I have that have either retired or are still serving. What else is your lot doing?'

'Gavin and Laura are out helping with the house-to-house enquiries around Maitland's farm. Barnes is currently going through the ANPR reports with Debbie West to see if any of those raise any flags. We're concentrating on vehicles owned by anyone with previous convictions for assault and that sort of thing who might have been in the area.' Kay pushed back her chair and stretched. 'Carys has started working through the property searches for a wider radius around the farm in case there's anyone we should be talking to with previous convictions as well. There's no-one within the current house-to-house parameters that appear in the system.'

'Sounds like it's all under control,' said Sharp, and rested his elbows on the desk. 'How's our new recruit settling in?'

'Laura? Really well, actually. It's going to be interesting to see how she balances this investigation alongside her exams, but I've tasked Gavin with mentoring her. Given that he was in the same situation a couple of years ago, hopefully she'll learn from him.'

'Good. All right, keep me posted.'

CHAPTER SIX

Kay hunkered into the thick collar of her woollen coat and checked over her shoulder before crossing Palace Avenue.

Her low heels wobbled on the uneven surface of the pedestrianised lane leading towards the High Street, and, as her calf muscles tightened with the incline of Gabriel's Hill, she concentrated on taking deep breaths to help ease out the stress from the past few hours.

A freshness pinched the air around her, as if winter wasn't yet ready to release its grip from the county, while her breath escaped her lips in a fine mist.

She let her mind wander as she gazed into the shop windows she passed.

On her left, the charity bookshop had changed its display to one focusing on local guides, no doubt hoping that some early season tourists would take advantage of the chance to learn more about the county town and contribute to a good cause at the same time.

She smiled, partially thankful that the door was locked and the sign had been turned in the window to read "closed", otherwise she would have been tempted to browse the paperbacks that lined the shelves.

Adam, her veterinary other half, would have a heart attack if she bought more books. The shelves in their living room were already bowing with the weight of their combined reading passions – not to mention the hefty technical tomes he kept for work.

An old nightclub remained shuttered, and the place appeared forlorn as she walked past its bare concrete steps.

Her mouth twisted at memories of policing the street as a young uniformed constable in the months prior to starting her training as a detective. The lane might be clear at the moment, but at the weekend it would only be a matter of a few hours before the pavements were covered in empty kebab trays, takeaway burger wrappers, and worse.

Midweek, however, the town was quieter, more sedate, and a little less confrontational.

When she reached the top of the lane, she turned left into Jubilee Square and hurried across the road towards the alleyway known as Market Buildings.

She loved the shortcut through to Earl Street – boutique clothing shops and artisan cafés jostled for space alongside vape shops and pubs, with the latter the only one doing business this time of night.

Adam had booked the table for seven – despite it only being midweek, there was a play on at the small theatre further up the street, and they both knew how busy the local eateries could get after a performance as both audience and actors alike poured into pubs and restaurants up and down the street.

She passed a dark-green sandwich board on the pavement at the door to the eatery as a waft of cooking aromas wrapped themselves around her.

The maître d' smiled as he took her coat and hung it on a rack behind the reception counter. 'Good to see you. Your other half is already here.'

'Has he been waiting long?'

He shook his head, and gestured towards the tables set out in a room off to the left of the main door. 'He arrived about fifteen minutes ago. I've got a bottle of Australian Verdelho on its way to the table for you. Nicely chilled.'

Kay stopped in her tracks. 'Really? How'd you get hold of that? We can't find it anywhere.'

He winked. 'It's a secret. The boss would kill me if I told you.'

She laughed as they reached the table.

Adam rose from his seat, kissed her cheek and waited while the maître d' settled her into her chair. As the man walked away to another table, he reached out for her hand and ran his thumb across her fingers.

'You look gorgeous.'

'I'm wearing my work clothes.'

'They're better than mine, which are currently soaking in a bucket of hot water at home.'

'Oh, no – what was it this time?'

'Don't ask. Hopefully the stains will come out.'

She laughed, and then spotted a waiter crossing the room towards them. She quickly ran her eyes down the menu Adam handed to her, and placed her order.

As the man headed off to the kitchen, she emitted a contented sigh.

'This was a good idea.'

'I figured if you had a new case, I wouldn't see

much of you over the next few weeks, so I'd get you alone while I can.'

'That's probably not a bad idea. I have a feeling this isn't going to be an easy one.'

'Grim?'

'Very – and unusual.' She gave him the briefest of explanations, not wishing to put him off his dinner and mindful of the confidential nature of her work. 'We get the post mortem results sometime tomorrow with any luck. Hopefully that will help.'

'Best make the most of tonight, then.'

Their starters arrived; a mixture of olives, bread and dips on a share plate that was placed between them. After their wineglasses were refilled, the waiter wished them a pleasant meal and retreated to the bar.

Kay shredded a slice of bread between her fingers and dipped it into a ramekin of balsamic vinegar. 'We haven't been out properly for ages. Haven't you got a waif or stray waiting at home to be cared for?'

'Not this week – unless you want two very friendly Vietnamese potbellied pigs in your kitchen.'

'Er, no thanks.'

'Didn't think so. Don't worry – they're happily taking advantage of one of our pens at the surgery. If you need a break from the office, you should drop by and see them.'

'I'll try.'

'Things might change next week, though – just to warn you. We got a call from a wildlife rescue place at Thurnham this afternoon. They've received a few calls about a litter of fox cubs that were seen out on the Pilgrim's Way looking worse for wear. If they haven't got anyone to take them in for a few days once they've been captured and given a clean bill of health, I might work from home and do that. I can keep up with the feeding routine in between finishing a paper I have to submit before the end of the month.'

'Fox cubs? Christ, don't tell Carys – she'll move in.'

As she wiped the last of the crumbs from her fingers, the waiter came to remove the plates, and minutes later their main courses arrived.

Kay eyed her steak with relish as accompaniments were brought to the table, a large bowl brimming with steamed vegetables and a dish laden with new potatoes that shone with a buttered polish.

She waited until Adam began to cut through the tender meat of the spatchcock he'd ordered, and leaned closer. 'This is the part I hate about investigations. Waiting, and wondering where we might get the breakthrough.'

'It's still the golden hour, isn't it?'

She wrinkled her nose.

Adam was right, the first few hours of any major crime investigation were the most important, but not always the most fruitful.

'The problem,' she said, lowering her voice as the woman from the next table sidled past and sat, 'is that we don't know when he got there. We don't know how long he was lying out there. It could've been any time between last Tuesday and this morning.'

'I know a few smallholding owners north of that area. If you get stuck, I can put you in touch with them. The smaller property owners tend to look out for each other, especially when it comes to equipment theft or anything like that. They might be able to help.'

'Thanks. Hang on for the time being – I'll let you know if we get to that point.'

'Okay. I'll keep my ears open when I'm out and about on my rounds in the meantime.' He pointed at her steak with his fork. 'Now, eat. I can hear your stomach rumbling from here.'

CHAPTER SEVEN

'Good morning, detectives.'

Lucas Anderson peered over his shoulder as Kay and Carys shuffled through the double doors into the examination room, their protective coveralls rustling in the air-conditioned stillness.

The home office pathologist's place of work at Darent Valley Hospital was a cramped space tucked away on the first floor behind the pharmacy and the radiological department. Despite this he and Simon Winter, his assistant, somehow managed to cope with post mortems requested both through the hospital and by the Kent County coroner.

Kay had never got used to the smell.

As much as she tried, the stench of death would

cling to her nostrils, her clothes, and her skin for at least twenty-four hours afterwards. She wasn't sure whether it was her imagination or scientific fact but talking to her colleagues from time to time, all of them agreed.

Kay didn't know how Lucas coped, but she was glad that he did. So often, her investigation could hinge on the information the pathologist gleaned from the unfortunate souls that found themselves in his company.

'Started without us, Lucas?' said Carys, drawing nearer to the aluminium table. 'Jesus.'

Kay chuckled as her colleague reared backwards at the last minute, bringing the back of her hand close to her mouth.

'I told you it wouldn't be pretty.'

'Even so, guv.' The detective constable blinked, and then turned back to the body laid out before them. 'Poor bastard.'

'Indeed,' said Lucas. He gestured to the twenty-something lanky mortuary assistant who hovered in the background, his gloved hands carrying two aluminium bowls with indeterminate contents. He nodded to the two detectives and then turned his attention to a collection of instruments and equipment on a counter that ran the length of the back wall.

'Simon and I made a start half an hour ago, so you've missed the worst of it.'

Kay let out the breath she had been holding. 'Have you managed to glean any more information as to how he was killed?'

Lucas sighed, and gestured to the body before him. 'It's not straightforward, I'm afraid. He has lacerations to his forearms, several broken ribs, a broken pelvis – you can see here how badly his legs are broken. That suggests to me a large impact injury, but I'm waiting on the X-ray results to clarify that. Simon is conducting some tests on the liver, heart and pancreas over there. There are ligature marks on his wrists as well, suggestive of being bound together with plastic zip ties similar to that found around one of his ankles. On first inspection, we can see compression injuries to the vital organs – all of them, not just those that Simon has been testing. When I'm finished here, I'll make some phone calls to some colleagues of mine in the Greater London area because there are some points I want to discuss with them before I go any further.'

'Have you got a cause of death?' said Kay.

The pathologist gave a mirthless chuckle, and then shrugged. 'It's difficult to pinpoint at the moment. Any one of those injuries would have been enough to kill him. Or, the shock of any of these injuries could have caused a heart attack. We just have to work out the order in which they were sustained. His fingertips and the skin on his hands would lead us to believe he worked as a manual labourer. There were traces of splinters in the palm of his hand, and his fingernails – the ones that aren't broken – appear worn.'

'So, not a white collar worker, then.'

'I wouldn't think so. Even if he was a keen gardener or handyman in his spare time, this sort of wear and tear accumulates over a long period of time, perhaps years.'

'What about any old injuries?' said Carys. 'Is there anything like dental work or titanium plates on any leg or arm injuries for instance that could be used to identify him?'

'There were half a dozen teeth left in his mouth by the time we got him here,' said Lucas. 'Two more fell loose during transportation, and of course Harriet and her team gathered up the remainder at the scene.'

'I've got some of them here,' said Simon, and held up an aluminium tray. 'The rest have been sent off to the specialist.'

Carys wrinkled her nose as the lab assistant shook

the tray and its contents rattled. 'Any clues amongst that lot?'

'He hadn't been to see a dentist in a long while,' said Simon. 'But no, there are no dentures or bridging plates for us to work with.'

'There's an old injury to his ankle bone,' said Lucas, and beckoned them along the length of the table to the man's feet. 'It'll be easier to show you once I've got the X-rays to hand, but you can see the skin is slightly raised here – this has been broken before, and given the way the skin has healed, I'm inclined to think that this injury is several years old. He certainly didn't sustain it at the same time as all of these other ones.'

Kay battened down the frustration that threatened. 'What about his age? Any further ideas on that?'

'I can't narrow it down much more other than to say he is in his late forties to early fifties.'

'And you can't give us a cause of death until you hear from your colleagues in Greater London—'

'I'm sorry, Kay.' He shrugged. 'I've asked Brian or Hugo to give me a call as soon as possible. They know it's urgent – I'm hoping I'll hear back from them this morning. As soon as I do, and if they can shed any light on this, I'll give you a call.'

'Thanks, Lucas. I understand – it's frustrating,

that's all. We know nothing about him. We did wonder if the tattoo on his bicep might be military,' said Kay. 'Sharp is going to have a word with some of his ex-army contacts.'

'Well, given the state of his physiology, he hasn't been in the armed forces for a long time. The muscle definition just isn't there.'

'A real man of mystery then,' said Kay.

As if picking up on the disappointment in her voice, Lucas wagged a finger.

'I'm not giving up on him yet,' he said. 'I have some ideas about this, but I want to make sure I've got my facts right before I send you off down the wrong path with your enquiries.'

CHAPTER EIGHT

Ian Barnes slurped his tea, pushed his reading glasses up his nose, and rolled his chair closer to the desk.

A steady hum of activity filled the room around him, a white noise that fluctuated in and out of his consciousness as he worked. The rattle of the photocopier as it juddered to a halt jarred with the constant ringing of desk phones and mobiles as each of the investigating officers worked through the tasks Kay had given them at that morning's briefing, trying to progress their enquiries.

A thin veil of condensation clung to the windowpanes as the steady hum of traffic on Palace Avenue passed by below. In the distance, a siren wailed and he paused in his work for a moment before gauging that it belonged to an ambulance, and not one of his colleagues' patrol cars.

The door burst open as Kay hurried into the room with Carys at her heels, their excitement palpable.

'Everyone, to the front of the room now,' she said. 'We've had a breakthrough, and I need your full attention.'

Barnes raised an eyebrow at her as she threw her bag under the desk after pulling out her notebook. 'I take it Lucas has struck gold?'

'You're not going to believe this, Ian,' she said, 'but I think he has. Come on, I'll explain everything.'

He locked his screen, shoved his keyboard across the desk and followed the DI as she weaved her way between the gathering police officers and administration staff, their expressions a mixture of confusion and intrigue.

The voices died down when Kay reached the whiteboard and turned to face them, and Barnes nodded to Gavin in thanks as he took a spare chair beside the detective constable.

Carys hovered at the perimeter of the group, her focus on Kay. Barnes could sense his colleague's impatience as the last of the investigation team joined them, jostling for space.

'Okay, everybody here?' said Kay. 'Carys and I

attended the post mortem of our victim this morning, whose identity remains unknown at the moment. Lucas Anderson's report has been emailed across to Debbie – is that in HOLMES2 yet?'

'I'll do it straight after this briefing, guv,' said the police constable.

'Please, do – it'll help if everyone has a read through to familiarise themselves with the extent of our victim's injuries and what I'm about to tell you.' Kay rapped her knuckle on the photograph in the middle of the whiteboard, an image that showed the victim spreadeagled amongst the muddy furrows of the field. 'Lucas was waiting to hear back from one of his colleagues in the Greater London area before he was willing to give his final opinion on cause of death following the post mortem, but he rang me while we were travelling back. According to his contact – and Lucas has confirmed that as far as he's concerned, the victim's injuries fully support his assertions – our man here fell from an aircraft.'

Barnes jumped in his seat as voices exploded around him.

Shocked faces turned to one another, the cacophony reaching a crescendo before Kay's voice cut through them all.

'Quiet, please. Settle down and I'll go through what we've learned in the past half an hour.'

He shuffled in his seat and turned to a new page in his notebook, keen to find out what his colleagues knew, and almost – *almost* – wishing he'd been the one who'd gone to the post mortem instead.

Carys leaned against a filing cabinet as her gaze swept the room, a knowing smile on her lips as she gauged her colleagues' reactions.

'Before I take you through the news we've just received, I'll run through the basics of the report. Our victim is in his late forties to early fifties, weighs about ninety-four kilograms – that's just under fifteen stone for those of you already reaching for your calculator apps – and before he hit the ground, Lucas estimates his height to be about six foot tall or about one hundred and eighty centimetres. The impact broke his legs in several places, which is why in the photographs he appears to be shorter.'

'He wasn't a small bloke, then,' said Gavin.

'Right,' said Kay. 'Lucas's contact in Central London reviewed his findings and said that the only time he's seen injuries such as those found on our victim was in a case where a stowaway fell from the undercarriage of an aircraft as it descended into

Heathrow. That stowaway landed in a skate park, and luckily didn't kill anyone who was in the park at the time. However, in that instance the victim would've suffered from lack of oxygen and hypothermia first, then fallen because he would've been unconscious – if not near death – when the undercarriage was lowered. The other issue we have is that in addition to the injuries the London-bound stowaway had, he was covered in ice – and a lot of it, because of the aircraft's cruising altitude before coming in to land. So, we're close, but there are still gaps in our knowledge of the facts.'

The DI crossed her arms as she began to pace the carpet. 'I have three problems with Lucas's findings. I'm not saying he's wrong, but the implications for this investigation are going to test us. First, unless there was a major issue with an international flight last week that hasn't been released by the authorities at Heathrow or Gatwick, no aircraft would lower its undercarriage this far out from those airports. Second, we would've received hundreds of complaints from residents if a commercial aircraft was flying that low over Kent. It's bad enough when the air shows are on. Third, our victim was naked. Where are his clothes? Lucas's contact in London says the only instance he's seen where bodies have fallen from the sky in that state is when the airliner they were travelling in broke apart mid-flight. The sudden effect of wind speeds at altitude or a slipstream can strip the clothes from bodies.'

Laura Hanway raised her hand. 'Guv, sorry to state the obvious, but if our man was hiding in the undercarriage and froze to death, surely any ice would've quickly melted. Did Lucas find any traces of frostbite in amongst the victim's other injuries?'

'No, he didn't. Nor did he find any traces of hypothermia, which would've been consistent with those extreme temperatures.' Kay's face was grim when her eyes locked with Barnes's. 'There's no easy way to say this, but Lucas states categorically in his report that given the facts and evidence available to him at this time, our victim wasn't unconscious when he fell. His lungs contained particles of soil that match the samples taken from the field where he was found. He took his dying breaths face down in that mud.'

A stunned silence greeted her words, and Barnes swallowed.

'Poor bastard,' he said.

'I know,' said Kay. She cast her eyes over the assembled officers. 'So, we have a dead man, with similar injuries to that sustained by a stowaway last year, with no signs of frostbite that would indicate he fell from an identical height to known stowaway incidents, and we've had no reports from local residents of large aircraft passing overhead last week. That leaves me with one conclusion at present – that our victim fell from an aircraft, but not one as large as a commercial airliner, and not from such a height that he'd pass out before hitting the ground. And, given that we've received no reports from members of the public of seeing it happen, it most likely happened at night. As for his clothes, I have no idea.'

'Do you think it was an accident?' said Barnes, tapping the end of his pen on his knee. 'Perhaps some sort of skydiving club prank gone wrong?'

'Maybe,' said Kay. 'I'm certainly not ruling it out until we know otherwise.'

'There was nothing reported from the search teams in the adjacent fields, guv,' said Carys. 'And Harriet's CSI team didn't find anything like a parachute in any hedgerows or undergrowth near where the body was found.'

'Well, if anything changes, make sure it's reported,' said Kay. 'In the meantime, these are your actions for the remainder of this week, everyone. I want you to contact local skydiving clubs and parachute clubs, to find out if there have been any reports of extra-curricular activities in the area. I want a record of all registered airfields in the area collated and made available to the team, and I want our search to include anyone with a pilot's licence, to include ultralights and microlights. We also need to establish what the rules are regarding night-time jumps, because I can't imagine anyone not noticing a bloke falling through the air in daylight. Flag anything unusual for each briefing and we'll make a decision when and how to follow it up, especially if those activities include anyone deciding to jump from a plane with no clothes on.'

When she ran a hand through her hair, Barnes could see his colleague's efforts not to let the swift turn of events overwhelm her, and a surge of pride rose in his chest.

'That's all, everyone,' she said, and forced a smile. 'I didn't say it was going to be easy, did I?'

CHAPTER NINE

Kay returned to her desk and exhaled as the team dispersed around her, pairing up or working in smaller groups to disseminate the information and tasks she'd set them for the next forty-eight hours.

She sent a text message to Adam to let him know she'd be home late, and then looked up as Barnes walked over.

'That was a hell of a result, guv.'

'Wasn't it just? Everything else okay here?'

He nodded. 'All under control. Debbie's got all the house-to-house statements into the system, and she and Phillip will cross-reference those once she's uploaded Lucas's report. Gavin and Laura have moved on to reviewing the remainder of the CCTV footage we've received this morning from a couple of motels in the area, and I'm dying for a coffee. Coming for a walk?'

She slipped her phone into her bag and smiled. 'You know what? That sounds like a bloody good idea. God knows when we're next going to get a break, so let's find something to eat as well. My treat.'

Barnes's face lit up. 'I knew I liked you for a reason, guv.'

'Ha ha.'

Five minutes later, Kay and Barnes had crossed Palace Avenue and were strolling up East Street past a row of solicitors' offices spread out the length of the busy road.

'Good timing, Ian. Another half an hour and we'd have had this lot to contend with,' said Kay. 'Where do you fancy going?'

He checked over his shoulder, and then led the way over to the pedestrianised zone of Bank Street. 'It's not too cold. Shall we get something from the café along here and go and sit by the river? Less chance of being overheard.'

'Sounds like a plan. Is half an hour all right with you? I wanted to check in with Gavin to see how Laura's getting on before I try to catch up with Sharp.'

'No problem. Here you go.'

'Thanks.'

Kay stepped through the door he held open, the aroma of freshly baked savoury pastries, herbs and spices wrapping itself around her as she eyed the menu on the blackboard nailed to the wall. She cast aside the plan to have a meagre sandwich and ordered one of the pasties, almost salivating as the café owner used tongs to place it in a paper bag before handing it over.

Once her colleague held his takeaway lunch of a chicken pie, and their coffees were ready, they set out for a favourite spot on the river towpath only a short walk away.

By the time Kay lowered herself onto the wooden bench behind the Archbishop's Palace, the pastry had grown cool enough to eat and she groaned with pleasure as she took the first bite.

'Good call, Ian. I haven't had one of these for ages.'

'Don't tell Pia, for goodness' sakes. I'm supposed to be losing weight before we go on holiday in June.'

'Your secret's safe with me.'

'What time are you heading over to Headquarters?'

'About two o'clock. Sharp was going to have a

ring around some old army contacts about that tattoo, and I'm hoping he might have some news for me about our victim. Anything would be a help at the moment, even if it's a particular regiment or group of people we could contact. I don't fancy the prospect of having to trawl through all the personnel they must have on record living in Kent. And that's if our victim is from this area. If he was living further away, I don't know what we're going to do.'

'Why do you think he fell into that field, then?' said Barnes, using a napkin to dab at the gravy that had dribbled onto his chin. 'You must have some sort of theory you weren't willing to put forward to the team, in case that's all they focused on.'

She shrugged, finished her mouthful and then squinted along the waterway to where the tourist boats were moored. 'I don't know, to be honest. There's part of me that wonders if it's something like a stag night dare gone wrong – I mean, let's face it, we've seen enough stupid naked drunks who've ended up in the Accident and Emergency department over the years, or dead.'

'All skydiving clubs and that sort of thing have to be registered though, don't they?'

'Yes. That's why I wanted all pilots' licences in the area checked and accounted for, not just the ones relating to clubs. If it is the case it's an accident, then a private party rather than one through an established club might've been flouting the rules and so it'd make sense they'd keep quiet about an accident.'

'That'd take some doing.' Barnes finished his pie, held out his hand for Kay's discarded paper bag, and walked over to the bin beside the path. He was frowning when he returned. 'Guilt isn't an easy emotion to hide, and a secret like that within a group of people would be hard to contain. Someone will break eventually.'

'I know.' Kay rose from the seat and dusted off the back of her trousers before falling into step beside him.

She tipped her head back until she could take in the ornate stonework of All Saints Church as they passed. She enjoyed this pocket of stillness within the busy town centre, and savoured the lush green surroundings that softened the concrete and asphalt architecture beyond the landscaped gardens.

Pausing, she turned to her colleague who was checking his phone. 'Ian, if it wasn't an accident, what sort of person would push a man from an aircraft mid-flight? And go to all that trouble removing all his clothes and any identification first?'

He took a deep breath as he ran his gaze over the

ancient gravestones to their left. 'I hate to say it, but if you're right, then I'm inclined to think they've killed before. It's too calculated; too well planned.'

'I know. Comparing the two scenarios, I'm sort of hoping it's simply an accident that hasn't been reported, and whoever's involved is trying to distance themselves from whatever went wrong.'

'You could say our victim flew under the radar, then,' said Barnes, dimples appearing in his cheeks.

Kay narrowed her eyes at him. 'Next time you're buying lunch.'

CHAPTER TEN

Carys fell into step beside Sergeant Harry Davis, and buttoned up her jacket.

The steady drone of a light aircraft reached her, and she turned in time to see it trundle along the grass runway before lifting into the air.

There was an engineering hangar over on the far side of the car park behind a chain-link fence, the double doors wide open and the sound of machinery carrying across to where they walked. The whole aerodrome buzzed with a frantic activity, as if everyone was making the most of the break in the weather before a forecasted rain squall set in.

'You all right?' said Harry, shoving the car keys into his pocket. 'You were a bit quiet on the way over.'

She smiled. 'Yes, fine. Thanks – just thinking about the case, that's all.'

'It's a weird one, isn't it? Do you think Lucas is right, and our man took a tumble out of an aircraft?'

'If that's what the injuries point to, and his contact in London reckons it matches that stowaway from a few years ago, then I'm inclined to believe him.'

'Horrible way to go.' The older sergeant shivered, then brightened. 'Mind you, it gets me out of uniform for a few days while I help you lot, so I'm not complaining.'

'It's crazy at the moment – I overheard Kay and Sharp talking last week, and Headquarters can't provide them with any personnel. There aren't enough graduates coming through the recruitment and training process, and there's a freeze on promotions in West Division – or so I've heard.'

'It's the same in uniform,' said Harry. 'Too many shifts, and not enough of us to cover them. I'm going to have to go back and check the roster for the weekend as it is.'

Carys tilted her head and sniffed the air. 'I can smell something cooking.'

'There's a café on the side of the main building there. Do you want to get a bite to eat before we make a start on the interviews?'

She eyed the picnic tables and umbrellas flapping in the cold wind that swept off the airfield beyond, and shook her head. 'Afterwards. It smells good, doesn't it?'

Harry held open the door into the aerodrome's reception area for her, and she ran her eyes over the cork board fastened to the right-hand wall.

Colourful brochures depicted grinning tandem skydivers, arms outstretched as they tumbled through an azure sky. Next to those, a series of health and safety notices had been pinned side by side with more brochures offering flying lessons, air shows and more.

'Morning – can I help you?'

She turned her attention to the man who stood behind the reception desk, his face eager. He was in his late thirties with straw-coloured hair a little on the long side, and his delight at the prospect of new customers dwindled when she withdrew her warrant card and made the introductions.

'And you are?' she said.

'Michael Childs. I'm one of the instructors here. Is there a problem?'

'Actually, we were hoping you might be able to help us. It's regarding the parachuting club here. Is there anyone we could talk to about that?'

'I might be able to answer your questions. I do

some flying for the tandem skydivers at weekends if they're a pilot short.'

'Great, thanks.' Carys pulled out an artist's sketch that had been created using a composite of images of the victim's face, and handed it over. 'Do you recognise him?'

Childs took the sketch from her and raised an eyebrow. 'Can't say I do. Is he a pilot?'

'We think he was a parachutist,' said Harry. 'Or a skydiver. At the moment, we're trying to identify him.'

'I don't think he's been here. I've been flying here for going on six years, and I know most of the regulars.'

'Would you be able to provide us with a note of their names?' said Carys.

'I'll have to check with the boss, but give me your email address and if he says it's okay with him, then I'll send them over.'

'Thanks.' She handed him one of her business cards and tucked the sketch back into her bag. 'What about casual parachutists?'

'You mean the ones that have gift cards and things for tandem jumps? Yes, we're obliged to keep a record of all of them as well. We have to – they can't jump without a medical certificate that's been signed off by their usual doctor. No form, no fly, as we say.'

'Is that right?' Carys glanced at Harry, then back to Childs. 'Look, this is going to sound strange, but what about people who want to do something a bit different when they jump?'

'Like what?'

She felt heat rise to her cheeks under the green eyes of the flying instructor, but pressed on. 'What if someone wanted to jump out of a plane naked?'

Childs let out a bellow of laughter, a guttural noise that echoed off the thin walls of the office. He wiped at his eyes, and smiled at her. 'It'd be a brave man who tried that, let alone at this time of year.'

'Never heard of someone doing that?' said Harry.

'No,' said Childs, his face sobering. 'And we wouldn't allow it either. In fact, I wouldn't imagine any club allowing that – not if they wanted to keep their licence. What's all this about, anyway?'

'I'm going to have to ask you to keep this confidential for the time being, as until we can identify him, we can't let his family know, but we're investigating the death of a man whose body was discovered in a field a couple of miles south of Sevenoaks,' said Carys. 'The last thing we want is for this to be leaked to the press – it'd be traumatic for his relatives.'

'Not a problem, you can rely on me.'

'Thanks. If you could let me know when you'll be able to send over that list of club members, I'd appreciate it.'

'No problem.' He waved her business card at her, and smiled. 'I've got your phone number and email.'

'Cheers.' Carys returned the smile and moved towards the door.

'How tall did you say he was?'

She stopped and turned, her fingers on the door handle. 'Just over six feet.'

'Do you know what he weighed?'

She frowned, caught Harry's quizzical expression, and then moved back to the counter. 'Yes, nearly fifteen stone. Why?'

Childs frowned. 'If that's the case, then he wouldn't have been allowed to jump. No pilot in their right mind would let him.'

'Why not?'

'We have weight restrictions in place – anyone over fourteen and a half stone is too heavy. He'd unbalance the aircraft when he jumped, and that can have catastrophic consequences for the pilot because it upsets the centre of gravity. It's too dangerous.'

'Is that the same at every club?'

'It's a British Parachuting Association rule. No getting around it, unless he was part of a private club.' He wrinkled his nose. 'Hell of a risk, though.'

'Last question,' said Carys, her pen poised over her notebook. 'What about parachuting at night?'

'God, no, not here – out of the question.' Childs winked. 'We leave that sort of malarkey to the Paras.'

CHAPTER ELEVEN

Kay rubbed at tired eyes and managed to smile as her investigation team swooped on the bacon and egg butties Debbie West had ordered from the café up the road.

One look at the volume of information that had been collated by the time their shift ended the night before, and she'd made the decision to call an early start in order to brief the team and sort out a roster for the weekend.

'Bribing us, guv?' said PC Phillip Parker. He lowered himself into a seat near the front of the semicircle of chairs that had been arranged near the whiteboard, and sank his teeth into the greasy snack.

'As always,' she said. 'How did you get on yesterday?'

He swallowed, and licked his fingers. 'We've finished collating the list of airfields, including anyone using private land to fly microlights and ultralights. We'll get those into HOLMES2 this morning.'

'Thanks, Phillip. Sounds like you have all the information under control.'

'We're getting there, guv.'

Kay rose from her perch on the table next to the whiteboard as the rest of the team began to crowd together. She nodded to Sharp who emerged from his office holding his mobile phone, and called the briefing to a start.

'First of all, did anyone get a positive identification for our victim or a hint of who he might be from the statements you took yesterday?'

A rumble of negative responses met her question.

'Never mind, I guess it was a long shot,' she said. 'In the meantime, I've received an email from Lucas Anderson this morning. Simon Winter has been running some tests on our victim's vital organs, and had some interesting results to report. Apparently, our man was suffering from a degree of cardiovascular disease that could have contributed to chest pains or shortness of breath — as he was a large man anyway, he would've been starting to show signs of heart disease that, left untreated, could have proven fatal within two to three years without medical treatment.'

Carys raised her hand.

'Yes?'

'Guv, when we spoke to the receptionist at Headcorn aerodrome yesterday, he said that our victim was too heavy to be allowed to do a parachute jump. Given that he had a bad heart as well, and wouldn't have been issued with a medical certificate to jump—'

'It doesn't appear to be the case that he left the aircraft of his own volition,' said Kay. 'What we now have to establish is whether he got into the plane by choice, or whether he was coerced or forced.'

'He was a big bloke,' said Barnes. 'I can't imagine he'd have got in the plane if he knew how it was going to end for him.'

Kay picked up the copy of the post mortem report she'd been reviewing. 'Lucas does note in here that there were traces of fibres under the victim's fingernails, and tears to the skin around his palms and fingertips. If there was a struggle, or he tried to cling on before falling to his death, then you might have a point there. Debbie – can you make sure you cross-reference that in HOLMES2? If we get to a point where we have enough evidence to support what

Barnes has suggested, then we're going to have to pull all the records for aircraft that have logged flight plans across this area and take a look at which interiors might match these fibres. Hopefully if we get to that point, the manufacturers will be able to help.'

'Will do, guv.'

As the team dispersed back to their desks, Kay saw Sharp beckon to her.

She hurried over, and followed him into his office. 'What's wrong, guv?'

'Shut the door, Kay, and take a seat. This could take a while to explain.'

The detective chief inspector wore a harried expression, his brow knotted in concentration as he collated briefing notes, meeting minutes and reports and then shoved them into the tray next to his computer screen.

His battered leather-upholstered chair creaked as he sat, and he leaned back, resting his hands on the pitted surface of the desk, and brushed imaginary dust from its surface.

Kay knew his army discipline meant he kept a cleaning cloth and furniture polish in the bottom drawer of the filing cabinet, but said nothing as he gathered his thoughts.

Finally, his gaze met hers.

'Some of what I am about to tell you can't be shared with the team,' he said. 'So, I'm trusting you to hear the whole story, and then we'll decide between us what we can divulge in order to advance this investigation. Understood?'

'Of course, guv.' Kay placed her notebook and pen on the desk before folding her hands in her lap. 'What is it?'

'One of my old army contacts managed to trace the origins of that tattoo. As we suspected, only a handful of soldiers were thought to have had it, and because of that, it's been pure luck we've got this lead.' He drummed his fingers on the desk, then stopped. 'I'll try to keep it brief. Back in 1999, a team of specialists from an infantry regiment decided to infiltrate a known enemy stronghold in a town in Kosovo. I don't know how much about the conflict you might recall, but it was a bloody mess.'

He blinked, and then exhaled. 'Sorry. It was a while back, but—'

'I didn't know you were out there, guv.'

'Only briefly, as part of an observation group.' He shook his head, a sadness clouding his eyes. 'So frustrating, not being allowed to do anything to help.'

Kay bit her lip, and lowered her gaze to her hands. After a few moments, Sharp cleared his throat.

'The men who got that tattoo were rumoured to have had enough of what they'd seen. One night, they set out from a makeshift camp and headed for a mountain base that was one of three strongholds belonging to one of the organised crime gangs running loose.

'Needless to say, the gangs had very little to do with the armed forces in that fractured country, but everything to do with black market goods that were being smuggled in and out including sex slaves – women and children – through Europe and into the Middle East.'

Kay's jaw clenched. 'The bastards. Did the soldiers stop them that night?'

Sharp shook his head and picked up a loose paperclip on his keyboard. 'No, that was beyond their capabilities – there were only six of them against a contingent of at least twenty. My contacts can't verify all the facts – after this many years, it is hard to decipher what's true and what has descended into myth and legend. What is known is that those six men rescued fourteen women and children from that mountain base, escaped with no loss of life to that six-man team, and insisted that the refugees be convoyed out under cover of darkness the following night. Smuggled over the border to safety.' He managed a smile. 'As you can imagine, the shit hit the fan once the top brass found out, but there wasn't a lot they could do about it by then. They couldn't exactly hand back the refugees to their captors – we all know what went on over there during that time.'

'What happened to them?' said Kay.

'They were transported out with a convoy of medical supplies that morning – the base commander couldn't wait to get rid of them. By then, it was pretty well known that the camp would be under surveillance by the cartel once word got out those refugees had been rescued and taken there, and the commander's duty was to keep his men safe.' He unwound the paperclip as he spoke, twisting the thin wire around his thumb. 'Luckily, they got word through the network of translators and informants that the crime gang had moved on, and that they believed the women and children had tried to escape on their own but perished in the conditions on the mountain. They never knew the six-man team had been there.'

Kay's shoulders relaxed. 'Thank God. What about the men? The six soldiers who rescued them?'

Sharp cleared his throat and reached out for a glass of water beside his desk phone. Taking a sip, he contemplated her over the rim of the glass before setting it down.

'That's where it gets interesting,' he said. 'Obviously, the camp commander couldn't afford to let the word get out about what they'd done – it would be inviting retaliation on the base and the rest of his men. By the same token, he couldn't be seen to condone what the six men under his leadership had done – otherwise they'd have all been off doing their own rescue missions, and putting the whole of the tentative ceasefire talks at risk.'

'So, what did he do?'

'The only sensible option open to him, and one that he knew would be supported by his superiors. He discharged all six of them. Set them packing back to the UK three days later. Rumour has it that they were debriefed at Brize Norton on arrival, ordered not to speak about their mission to anyone under threat of prosecution, and told that they had lost all their rights to their army pension for insubordination and putting their colleagues' lives at risk.'

'Bloody hell,' said Kay. 'But they were heroes.'

'Maybe, but they couldn't be trusted to follow orders,' said Sharp. 'Think of it this way – what if the enemy's men did see those women and children in a British Army camp? What would have happened then?'

'What happened to the soldiers?' said Kay. 'Did they simply go their separate ways?'

'Eventually, according to my contact. They were allowed off base after the debriefing sessions, until all the paperwork was signed off. That's when he thinks they got the tattoos – to remind them of what they'd done. Despite everything, they believed it was the right thing to do.'

Kay ran a hand through her hair. 'Jesus, guv. That's a hell of a story, but how does it help us? Did your contact have a note of their names?'

Sharp's mouth narrowed. 'Unfortunately, not. Like I said, it's hard to fathom how much of the story has become urban legend, rather than fact. However, he was able to ascertain that one of the men came from the Thanet area, and that he was in the infantry regiment for a time before being discharged.' He held up his hand. 'And, before you ask, no – we don't have a name or contact details because the file is sealed. No-one is looking at that for at least another fifty years.'

'But does he think he came back to the Kent area?' said Kay.

'That is his view, yes.' Sharp reached out his computer mouse and clicked to open a search engine. 'There are a few veterans' associations in the area, so while the rest of the team are working their way through that list of airfields this weekend, I'd like you to make a start talking to these. Carefully, mind. Let's see what you can find out over the next couple of days, and then we'll discuss the next steps.'

'Will do, guv.'

'I'll email you this list.'

'Thanks.' Kay rose from her chair, picked up her notebook and pen, and then frowned. 'Guv, do you think our victim was killed as retribution for that rescue mission all those years ago? Perhaps one of the warlords survived the conflict and has decided he wants payback.'

Sharp paused, his finger hovering over the "send" button on the screen.

'I sincerely hope not, Hunter. That would be one hornets' nest I could do without.'

CHAPTER TWELVE

Ian Barnes glared at the radiator under the windowsill in the incident room, peered at the brown sodden mess within the crumpled pages of paper kitchen towel in his fist, and then lashed out with his foot.

His shoe met the corrugated metal surface with a satisfying clang, but did nothing to fix the central heating system.

'Does that work?'

Carys wandered over, a bemused expression in her eyes.

'No. Nor did bleeding the bloody valve.' He held up the rust-coloured evidence. 'They only fixed it a couple of years ago, for goodness' sake.'

'I'm bringing in an extra sweatshirt or something

tomorrow.' She shivered. 'This is ridiculous. I can't feel my fingertips.'

Barnes lobbed the paper towel into the waste bin. 'No point reporting it. Nothing will get done, and then it'll be summer anyway.'

His phone began to ring as he sat. 'What've you got, Hughes?'

'There's a bloke down here says he's got some information about your investigation,' the desk sergeant told him. 'Apparently, Gavin and Laura spoke to his wife on Thursday while he was at work.'

'Well, they're out exploring airfields this weekend,' said Barnes. 'Do you want to show him into one of the interview rooms while I have a quick read through the wife's statement?'

'No problem. Number four is free, so he'll be in there when you're ready.'

'Cheers for that.'

Barnes replaced the receiver, and then logged into the HOLMES2 database, scrolling through the entries until he found Beverley Winton's statement.

'Anything interesting?' said Carys.

'Might have some more information from one of the residents who lives in a property that borders Dennis Maitland's farm. Are you busy, or do you want to tag along?'

Carys scowled. 'I'm cross-referencing pilots' licences.'

'Come on, then. Sounds as if you could do with a break.'

He led the way down the stairs, swiped his security card across the panel next to the door leading to the interview rooms, and held it open for her. After bringing her up to date with the meagre details from Beverley's statement, he entered interview room four and introduced himself to Peter Winton.

The man was dressed in a long-sleeved chambray work shirt with the familiar logo of a local tyre fitting company embroidered over the breast pocket. He wore his ash-coloured hair short and contemplated the two detectives with piercing blue eyes.

'I hope I'm not wasting your time,' he said, and scratched his right earlobe, 'but Beverley told me I should come and see you, just in case.'

'Not a problem, Mr Winton.' Barnes unbuttoned his jacket as the man returned to his seat, and pulled out a chair opposite him as Carys settled to his right.

'Please, call me Peter.'

'Thank you. Now, I've had a read of your wife's statement. You own the cottage next to Humphrey Godmanstone, and you rent out the two properties on the other side of yours, is that correct?'

'Yes. They're a couple of hundred years old. They were originally farmworkers' cottages. They're not listed, though, so we've been able to do what we want with the renovations.'

'That's good,' said Barnes, and smiled. 'Now, what did you want to tell us in relation to our investigation?'

'Right, well.' Peter leaned closer and clasped his hands together. 'The thing is, I don't sleep very well at night. I suffer from insomnia, you see. I used to work as a continental truck driver, so all those years doing late shifts must have messed up my biorhythms or whatever they're called.'

He cleared his throat, then lowered his eyes. 'I've been suffering from a bit of stress lately, too – not that I'd tell Beverley, because I wouldn't want her to worry. It's just that we overstretched ourselves buying these houses to do up a couple of years ago, and then I lost my job and it was a few months before I got taken on at the tyre place. Anyway – yes, I don't sleep much.'

'And I understand that you heard something on one such night last week?' said Barnes, in an attempt to bring the man's rambling thoughts back on track.

'Exactly. Sunday night, in fact.' Peter's face became more animated, the tension lines that were etched under his eyes easing. 'Beverley had gone up to bed, and I'd tried to sleep but by five past one, I was tossing and turning and, well, I didn't want to wake her up. She works so hard. I came downstairs, and thought I'd make a cup of tea and sit in one of the armchairs to read. That's the only good thing about this whole insomnia thing, I suppose – I'm getting through all the books I've bought over the years. Anyway, I heard a van or something drive past the cottage and turn in.' He frowned. 'We don't get a lot of traffic passing over our way, not at that time of night, and I think that's what made me stop what I was doing and take notice.'

'Can you remember what time that was?'

'Yes, because I looked at the clock on the mantelpiece. It was just after two-thirty by then.'

'And what makes you think this might have something to do with our investigation?' said Carys. 'Why were you suspicious about this particular vehicle?'

'It sounded like it was going down the side of Humphrey's place. None of our neighbours own a van though, so I went upstairs and took a look through the curtains but I couldn't see anything. I thought someone might've driven round to the back of the gardens where our sheds were. I think they must've driven down the track to the back of Maitland's farm instead. Mind you, I couldn't see any lights.'

'Did you see or hear the van return?'

Peter nodded. 'About twenty minutes later I heard the engine, but they didn't come back past the cottage – they continued along the lane. I mean, it might not be anything to do with your investigation – it could've been poachers. They're a pain in the backside around our way, always cutting through wire fences to pull dead deer through, and things like that. But when I mentioned it to Beverley, she said I should tell you, just in case it helped.'

Barnes finished writing in his notebook, and then removed his reading glasses and raised his head. 'We'll let you know if it does, Peter. Thank you.'

CHAPTER THIRTEEN

Gavin grinned at his colleague as she tied her long hair back into a ponytail and raised her eyes to the sky, her gaze full of wonder.

'Fancy jumping?' he said.

'Not bloody likely, said Laura. 'Crazy, all of them.'

He turned his attention to the people tumbling from the aircraft several thousand metres above them. 'I always thought I might be up for it, but not after seeing the photos of our victim. I think I'll stick to surfing.'

'Sure,' said Laura. 'You've only got sharks, jellyfish and rip tides to worry about there. What could possibly go wrong?'

'Ever tried it?'

'Hell, no. You might be an adrenalin junkie, but I'm not.'

'You go horse-riding in your spare time, don't you?'

'So?'

'Well, that's just as bad – those things have a mind of their own.'

He held his breath as he watched the freefalling figures tumble in the air, his throat dry. Although they seemed to float gracefully, he knew they were travelling at several metres per second.

'I can't imagine how terrified he must have been, knowing he was going to die,' said Laura, her voice barely audible. 'I mean, even if it was dark he'd have seen lights from houses, wouldn't he? He'd have known when he was going to hit the ground.'

She shivered, and Gavin watched as one by one, the skydivers' parachutes opened.

The bright rectangles of coloured nylon did nothing to lift his dark mood, and he clenched his fists.

'Let's go and find someone to talk to about the flying schedules here,' he said.

Laura traipsed alongside him, the hem of her suit trousers swishing against the long grass growing between the car park and the two-storey concrete building that stood beyond a chain link fence.

A radar array spun on its axis on the flat roof, and Gavin jumped as a tannoy system fixed on the wall above a ground-floor window spat to life, announcing the time for the next jump scheduled to take place that afternoon.

Inside the building, men and women's changing rooms were signposted to the left of the entrance doors, while a warning notice stuck to the wall advised patrons that the airfield's owners took no responsibility for personal items left in lockers.

The remainder of the ground floor seemed devoid of anyone else, and Gavin turned his attention to the concrete stairs that led upwards.

'This place feels like it's been here since the Second World War,' said Laura, her voice echoing off the bare walls as they climbed.

'I heard the bunker look was all the rage in home decor this season.'

'Very funny.'

When they reached the top of the stairs, a set of heavy wooden doors blocked their progress and Gavin pressed a doorbell that had been retrofitted under a security keypad.

'Hello?'

The same voice from the tannoy crackled through a credit card-sized speaker above the doorbell.

'Detective Constable Gavin Piper, and my colleague DC Hanway. We wondered if you could please answer some questions about an ongoing investigation.'

'Hang on.'

A buzzing noise reached him, and Gavin felt the door give under his touch as the lock disengaged.

It opened inwards, and a man in his forties pulled it the rest of the way.

'I need to see your ID.'

Gavin and Laura held up their warrant cards.

'Thanks. Come and sign in over here. You'll need to complete the health and safety questionnaire, too. Do you want tea, or a glass of water?'

'We're fine, thanks,' said Gavin. He ran his eyes over the lines of text beneath the airfield's logo, agreed that he undertook every responsibility listed, and that he would follow staff instructions in the case of an emergency, and scrawled his signature where indicated before handing the pen to Laura.

'Sorry, I'm Carl Brightwater,' said the man and stuck out his hand. 'My colleague over there running the control tower this afternoon is Len Walters.'

An older man with white hair peered at them

over central console, raised his hand, and then adjusted the headset he wore before turning back to his work.

'Let me run through the weather forecast for our pilots, and then I'll be with you,' said Brightwater. 'There's a table and chairs over by the window if you want to take a seat while you wait.'

Gavin sidled past a cheap office furniture assemblage strewn with documentation, and wandered over to where Brightwater had indicated.

Four metal chairs – none of which looked comfortable – had been placed around an old plastic patio table, the round corners scratched and chipped. Beyond the table, floor-to-ceiling windows provided a view of the airfield where a mixture of gliders, microlights and propeller-powered aircraft were dotted around the edges or parked close to a single large hangar over in the corner near the car park.

The whole place teemed with activity.

As he watched, a light aircraft came in to land, the pilot correcting his position moments before the plane bounced onto the grass runway and taxied to a standstill at the end of a line of similar models.

'That's the flying school that runs out of here,' said Brightwater. He sipped a glass of water as he moved to the window beside Laura. 'It only has three aircraft, but they've been in business for nearly ten years and have a fantastic reputation.'

He turned and gestured to the chairs. 'I'm presuming you're not here about flying lessons, though. What is it you wanted to talk to me about?'

Waiting until Laura had settled, Gavin made sure she was ready and paying attention before he started his questioning. He knew how important these first few months were for anyone studying to become a fully-fledged detective, and given the support he'd received from Kay, Barnes, and Carys, he was determined to ensure his new colleague received the same level of help.

After all, he would be relying on her investigative skills one day.

'How long have you worked here, Mr Brightwater?' he said.

'Here in the control tower, about six years. I was one of Matt's early pupils when I learned to fly here.' He jerked his thumb over his shoulder to where the flying instructor was now walking towards the control tower with his latest charge. 'When I was made redundant in the City, I approached the owners of the airfield to see what openings were available. I had to let go of my dream to own my own plane one day, but I figured I could still do something here. I started eight months after walking out the door of the financial institution I worked for on Cheapside.'

'How many pilots use this airfield on a regular basis?'

'There are eight private owners, then there are two timeshare groups – they share the use of an aircraft to save on running costs, same as you would a holiday home – and then we have a dozen pilots who rent one of two aircraft we have available for hire. On top of that, there are six microlight owners that use the airfield and of course anyone visiting this part of Kent is welcome to use it too. They might park here for one or two nights while they hire a car to explore the area or catch up with friends.'

'And you keep records of all of these?'

'Absolutely.'

Gavin took a moment to check his notes, pacing the interview so that Brightwater wouldn't feel bombarded by questions, and determined to keep the man relaxed in order to glean as much information as possible.

'I see you've got some skydivers here today – is that a regular occurrence?'

'Yes. The owners of the airfield worked with the British Parachute Association to open it up to enthusiasts eighteen months ago. We've got two pilots

– Matt Pendergast, the flying instructor being one of them, and Clive Asher, one of the two owners, is the other. You can see the aircraft over there – the one with the blue stripe down the length of the fuselage.'

'How many of the pilots registered here are allowed to fly at night?'

'Only Matt. He hasn't logged any night flights for a while, but he keeps his licence up to date because he can be asked to teach the Night Rating course from time to time.' He rose from his seat and beckoned Gavin and Laura to the windows as the Cessna began to taxi towards the runway. 'Here you go, the next skydiving group are about to take off. Clive is flying this group up, and then they'll do a tandem jump.'

The aircraft sped along the runway, lifting into the air as it drew alongside a dilapidated shed at the far end of the airfield, before arcing gracefully away over the trees as it gained height.

'What about night-time parachute jumps?' said Gavin. 'Do you offer those here?'

Brightwater shook his head. 'We haven't got the staff coverage to do that, and to be honest I don't think the owners want the additional risks that come with that – not to mention the insurance costs.'

'What sort of things would an airfield need to be

mindful of, if it did offer night-time jumps?' said Laura.

Gavin glanced at her and nodded. It was a good question, and he didn't mind if she interrupted. At least she was confident enough to do so.

'Well, the parachute area would need to be clearly marked out,' said Brightwater, turning back to the room. He crossed his arms over his chest. 'All and any obstructions would be illuminated so they could be seen from the air, and every jumper would have to carry at least one light so they could be tracked from the ground – and by others in the air with them. It's a logistical nightmare, to be honest.'

'Do you know of any local clubs or airfields who offer night jumps?' said Gavin.

'No, not at the present time. In fact, I don't know of anyone who's done that around here, not since I've been flying.'

Laura closed her notebook as Gavin shook Brightwater's hand.

'Thank you for your time, we appreciate it.'

He waited until they had left the building and were walking back to the car, and then turned to his colleague.

'There were no discarded lights or anything like that found near our victim's body, was there?'

'Not that I recall from the reports Harriet and her team sent over, no.'

'No parachute… and, no clothes, either.' He pulled the car keys out of his pocket and aimed the fob at the door. 'So, either he jumped during the daytime and nobody saw him fall, or he jumped at night with no lights.'

'Maybe if it was a private jump, something secret for a laugh like a stag night or something, they might have used a friend's airplane or something like that,' said Laura. 'If they had jumped before, they might have their own equipment. We'll just have to find out if you can buy that sort of stuff online or locally around here.'

'Okay, let's head back to the incident room and start making some phone calls.'

CHAPTER FOURTEEN

The next morning, Kay sipped coffee from a stainless steel travel mug and watched a cluster of people who had gathered at the end of an asphalt driveway leading to a local community hall.

Fresh buds covered the ornamental hedgerow that bordered the pavement to the left of her parking space, and a magnolia tree shot out tentative leaves from its lower boughs in the garden opposite.

She reached out and turned down the radio, wearied by the number of advertisements that belted out enthusiastically between the latest pop songs, three of which seemed to be on permanent repeat every hour, but reluctant to listen to the political wrangling on the other channels.

An A-frame sign had been placed at the end of the

driveway, advertising a voluntary support group for local veterans whose regular meeting had started at nine o'clock.

Impatient for answers, but mindful that she couldn't rush her investigation for fear of scaring potential witnesses away or having them clam up when a stranger approached them, Kay had opted to wait until the group dispersed and she could chat to the volunteers alone.

She scrolled through the search results on her phone and located the two-page website for the group.

According to the home page, it met on Sunday mornings between nine and eleven, with the last hour given over to coffee, cake, and casual conversation. The second page of the website listed support organisations and suicide helplines.

Checking the clock on the dashboard, she saw the meeting had fifteen minutes to go.

She raised her gaze to the group hovering outside the hall, all smoking proper cigarettes, not vaping like many of their younger contemporaries might.

Roll ups, too. Cheaper.

Her heart sank at the sight of some of the men – as far as she'd seen there were no women apart from those volunteering this morning.

Two of the older ones, pensioners by the look of

it, huddled off to the side, a younger man stooping to listen. He wore faded jeans, battered cheap-looking walking boots and a black anorak, and seemed to sway on his feet a couple of times before one of the older men reached out to steady him.

Four others stood with their backs to him, their heads turning to the road as a bright red motorbike throttled past, appreciative expressions on their faces. One man gestured as the rider disappeared into the distance, and Kay could hear the others' raucous laughter.

Gradually, a handful of others left the church hall, paused to shake hands or scrounge a cigarette, and began to disperse in pairs or alone.

When she was sure only the volunteers remained, Kay checked her mirrors, wound up her window, and stepped into the road.

Peering down the length of the street, she saw the last of the veterans' group – four men who had jostled and laughed their way out of the hall – stop outside a pub on the T-junction with the main road.

They seemed to debate whether to wait another hour until the doors opened, then thought better of it and disappeared around the corner.

Kay locked the car and made her way over to the hall as a woman bustled past two parked cars on the driveway and bent over to fold up the A-frame sign.

She smiled as Kay approached. 'Morning. Can I help you?'

Kay waited until she was closer, and then showed her warrant card. 'I didn't want to interrupt the meeting, but I wondered if I could have a word?'

'We're in the middle of tidying up, but you're welcome to come in if you don't mind me answering your questions while I wash up. We have to give the keys back at half past so the football club can use it from twelve. I'm Janice Crispin, by the way.'

She manhandled the sign into the back of a russet-coloured two-door hatchback, then gestured to the open double doors of the community hall. 'Come on through. There are only two of us working today. Luckily, a few of the veterans offered to help stack all the chairs away before they left, so we don't have much to do.'

'Who does the other car belong to?'

'The cleaner – she lives next door but, with two adult children at home, I think it's easier for her to leave her car here at the weekend.'

As Kay followed her into the single-storey building, she ran her eyes over the line of cork boards that filled the entrance hallway advertising all manner of social and sports clubs, support groups, and a community library.

'You can see why the committee insists on good timekeeping,' said Janice. 'It's a popular venue.'

'How long have you been here?'

'About three years. We used the hall over at Seal before this for a couple of years, but it was difficult for some of our veterans to get to, especially for those who couldn't afford to drive. The bus service is atrocious on Sundays. Here we are.'

Janice led the way into a brightly lit kitchen that had cabinets along both sides, a stainless steel-topped workbench in the middle, and modern appliances.

'This is my husband, Andrew.'

Kay shook hands with a stout man in his late sixties who wore a striped apron over jeans and a sports sweatshirt.

'Detective Hunter wanted to ask us some questions,' said Janice. She plunged her hands into a sink full of soapy water and began working her way through a pile of dirty coffee mugs with gusto.

Her husband flicked a tea towel off his shoulder and dried the crockery while he leaned against the counter.

'Problems with one our attendees?' he said.

'I'm after some information, actually. I said to

your wife that I thought I'd be better off speaking with you both first, rather than causing any issues for the men who come here. I'd imagine they have enough to be dealing with.'

'You're not wrong there,' said Andrew. 'Thanks for your consideration. What did you want to know?'

Kay placed her bag on the table in the middle of the kitchen and unfolded the artist's sketch of the victim.

'This is a composite from a series of photographs. I'm afraid I'm investigating the death of this man. Do either of you recognise him?'

Andrew took the sketch from her and held it so his wife could see it at the same time.

'I don't think I've seen him before,' said Janice, water dripping from her fingertips. 'Did he do something wrong?'

'I don't know. That's what I'm trying to find out. Look, this has to be treated in the strictest confidence—'

'You can trust us,' said Andrew. 'I was an ambulance officer for thirty years, and Janice here worked as a mental health counsellor. We're used to keeping things private. It's why the men in our group trust us.'

'Thank you. I appreciate it.' Kay pointed at the

sketch. 'We don't have a name for him, but he does have a tattoo on his arm that gives us reason to believe he was posted to Kosovo in ninety-nine. We're hoping that might help someone recall what his name might be, and who we might talk to about what he's been up to since then.'

Andrew frowned. 'I don't think any of our regulars were in that conflict. A couple of our older ones were involved in the tail end of the Korean War, then there's one who was in the Falklands—'

'Most of them are Gulf veterans, except for Robin – he's our youngest attendee. Afghanistan.' Janice pulled the plug from the sink and picked up a second tea towel as the water gurgled down the drain. 'Oliver Townsend over at the centre near Riverhead – the other side of Sevenoaks – might know someone who could help, perhaps?'

'Oliver?' said Kay.

'He's an Afghanistan war veteran himself,' said Andrew. 'Runs a smaller group, but a different age bracket to a lot of our attendees. You might have better luck there. Hang on, I've got his number in my phone.'

He handed the sketch back to Kay and pulled a mobile phone from his back pocket while she retrieved her notebook.

'Will he still be at the centre?' she said, eyeing the clock on the wall above the sink.

'No – they meet on Monday evenings.' Andrew recited the phone number and checked she'd written it down correctly, together with Oliver's name and the address of his support group. 'But I'm sure if you give him a call, he'll be happy to see you today. Just tell him you've been talking to us.'

'That's great, thanks for your help. I'll let you get on.'

'No problem. Do me a favour, though?'

'What do you need?'

Andrew's eyes softened. 'When you find out who your victim is, if he has no family to pay their last respects, let us know. We try to do something special for those who have no-one to say goodbye.'

Kay swallowed, fighting down the emotions that surged through her.

'I will. I promise.'

CHAPTER FIFTEEN

Oliver Townsend had his head lowered over a tabloid newspaper when Kay climbed from her car and wandered across the pub car park to a motley collection of picnic tables spread out across a threadbare lawn.

It had to be him; there was no-one else around, and the pub didn't open for another ten minutes.

In his early thirties, he sat with his chin in one hand, stubble covering his jawline as he yawned and ran a hand over a mop of chestnut-coloured hair.

'Oliver?' Kay held out her hand as she approached. 'Detective Inspector Hunter.'

The man rose slightly from the picnic table, his grip firm. 'Have a seat. I know the landlord – he'll let us in once he sees us waiting out here.'

Kay glanced towards the warm-coloured render of the pub, spotted a few lights on inside, and hoped the landlord took pity on the pair of them. She shoved her hands into her pockets and turned her attention back to Townsend.

He began to fold up the newspaper, before tucking it into a canvas courier bag on the seat next to him. 'What can I help you with?'

'I've been over to see Janice and Andrew Crispin at the veterans' support group, and they suggested you might be able to help me.'

'Yeah, you said on the phone. You've got a missing man, right?'

'I've got a dead man.'

'Oh.' Townsend rocked backwards, and blinked. 'That explains why you didn't want to say much earlier, then.'

'I thought it'd be better if I explained the situation face to face. I'm trying to do this without raising a flag at the moment, not until I know what – or who – we might be dealing with.'

'Fair enough. And you think he was a soldier?'

'Yes.'

She peered over his shoulder as the door to the pub swung open, and a man beckoned.

'Come on in, folks. It's too cold to be sat out there.'

'I could've told you that fifteen minutes ago,' said Townsend. He swung his leg over the seat and grinned at the publican. 'Pint of bitter for me, and whatever the lady here is having.'

'Orange juice, thanks.'

'On duty?'

'Always.'

'Come on, then. Hopefully, the tight git has turned the heating on as well. You never know your luck.'

Kay's eyes fell to the man's legs as he led the way into the pub, noticing he walked with a pronounced limp.

He glanced over his shoulder, as if reading her thoughts. 'Landmine. Afghanistan.'

'Sorry.'

'Not your fault. Hurry up, you'll let a draught in.'

Kay thanked him as he held open the door for her, and stepped into a low-beamed room.

A fire burned in a grate to the far left of where she stood, and a bar ran along the right-hand side. Tables and chairs, as well as a couple of comfortable-looking sofas, had been dotted through the length of the space while local artwork adorned a wall next to a door signposted for the toilets. Horse brasses had been nailed to an enormous oak beam above the fireplace, glinting in the glow from spotlights strategically placed along the ceiling.

'I'll bring your drinks over,' said the publican. 'Take a seat.'

'Thanks, mate.' Townsend gestured to a table near the fire. 'Might as well make the most of it. He doesn't light it that often.'

'Piss off,' came the response from the bar.

Kay smiled. 'I take it you're a regular here.'

'How'd you guess?' Oliver pulled out a seat for her, and then took one facing the room, his back to the fire. He hung the courier bag on the back of the chair, and then thanked the publican as the drinks were brought over to the table before turning his attention to her once more. 'All right. How can I help?'

'How long have you been running your veterans' support group?'

'About two years. I'd been attending here and there anyway, just to get myself out of the house once I was discharged. I did okay on my own for a while, and got lucky – I landed a job with my father-in-law at his garden centre, so money wasn't a problem. It was just hard to find someone who could listen to me when I needed to talk. My wife's brilliant, she really is, but she wasn't there, you know? And it's not fair on her having to listen to me going over what happened all the time. We both wanted to move on.'

'How are you? I mean—'

'Mentally and physically? Better than most.'

'That's good.'

'It is, thanks. Yeah, so when the last person who ran the group decided to retire a couple of years ago, I offered to step in. I'd been studying various bits and pieces to keep my mind active while I was going through recovery and physiotherapy, and I thought I could put some of that to good use.'

'Do you enjoy it?'

'I do, yes. Gives me a sense of focus, and if I do need to speak to someone then I can within that group. It's a real mix of people who turn up, but we've all been through something. It's not good bottling it up – I tried that, and it didn't work.'

'What's the sort of age group that you see turn up?'

Townsend sipped from his pint, and smacked his lips before answering. 'It's a younger demographic to that of the Crispins' group. I'm sort of in the middle – I'm thirty-one. There are a couple of younger ones than me, and then the rest are probably upwards in age to about late fifties. Gulf veterans, a couple from the Balkans who have had ongoing health issues, and one bloke who was badly injured in a fire on base here in the UK eight years ago.'

'As you say, a right mix of people.'

'It makes for some interesting conversations. Speaking of which, what've you got?'

Kay gave him a précis of the case to date, careful to eliminate any information that might allude to myth or unsubstantiated evidence, and then showed him a sketch of the victim's face. 'Do you recognise him?'

His brow furrowed. 'Can't say I do, no.'

She slid a photograph of the victim's tattoo across to Townsend. 'We think he might have got this on his return from Kosovo. Have you ever seen anything like it before?'

He turned the photograph around and held it up to the firelight behind him, his eyes narrowed. 'I don't think so. What is it? Some sort of memorial tat?

'Memorial tat?'

'Yes, you know – a tattoo to commemorate an event, or a mission. Something like that.'

'What makes you say that?'

He smiled, and tapped his finger on the lettering under the tattoo. 'Because of this. It's unusual, that's all.'

'Have you seen it before?'

Townsend shook his head. 'No. Not that one. It just reminded me of one or two I saw out in Afghanistan when blokes came back off leave. They'd survive a firefight or something like that as a group, and then they'd all go and get the same tattoo, sort of like a badge of honour. Or a memorial if one of them had died.'

'Okay, I get it. Yes – we think it might be something like that. It's the only identification we have for our victim at the moment. He wasn't carrying any ID on him when he was found.'

Wrinkling his nose, Townsend placed the photograph on the table between them. 'How did he die?'

'It wasn't suicide.'

'I kind of guessed that.'

'I'm sorry, I can't say much more at the moment.' Kay swirled the remnants of her juice around her glass. 'Do you know anyone who might be able to shed some light on this?'

Townsend drummed his fingers on the table, and then pointed at the photograph of the tattoo. 'Can I take that?'

'Can I trust you?'

'Scouts' honour.'

'All right. What are you going to do with it?'

'I'm still in contact with the bloke who used to run the volunteer group, plus I can ask our two regulars who served in the Balkans if they know anyone in the area who was in Kosovo and had a tattoo like this. I'm presuming it's a limited edition?'

'We think there were six of them.'

'That makes it easier. Okay, let me check around over the next few days and I'll get back to you. Got a phone number?'

Kay reached into her bag and passed him one of her business cards.

'Good.' He grinned, drained his pint, and pointed at her empty glass. 'In the meantime, it's your round.'

CHAPTER SIXTEEN

When Kay entered the incident room early the next morning, the space hummed with activity.

Despite it being half an hour until the shift started, most of the investigating team – the ones who weren't making last minute dashes to get children to school or concluding tasks on their other caseloads – were in attendance, and the atmosphere was one of industriousness and grim determination.

A bitter aroma of coffee, instant noodles, and energy drinks soured the air and she wrinkled her nose as she switched on her computer to log in.

Barnes placed a mug of tea next to her keyboard before moving around to his side of the desk.

'Productive weekend?' she said, running her eyes down the emails that had multiplied in her absence.

'Yes, hope so – you?'

'I think we'd better set aside more than an hour for the briefing. According to the HOLMES2 alerts, I can see updates here from every member of the team.'

'It'd be good to get some progress this morning. Is Sharp coming over?'

'Not this time, no. He phoned me on the way in – he's headed to Headquarters for a meeting with media relations. We'll see what comes to light during the briefing and over the course of today, and then I'll have a chat with him about whether it's time to issue a public appeal for information. Anything happen elsewhere over the weekend?'

'No – I've been through the logs from downstairs, and it was a quiet couple of nights. No major incidents on the roads, either.'

'Well, at least if we do an appeal it won't be overshadowed by anything and we might get some extra personnel from uniform to help with the phone calls.' She leaned back in her seat and blew across the surface of her tea before taking a sip, and watched as Gavin and Laura stopped beside Debbie's desk to speak with the police constable. 'How did those two get on over the weekend?'

Barnes peered over his shoulder. 'Good, from

what I'm hearing. Gavin said Laura's not afraid to jump in and ask questions, and I think they're all getting on fine. I've noticed she looks to Carys for the day-to-day processes, but that's understandable seeing as she's the more experienced of the two. Laura seems to be fitting in well, anyway.'

'That's one less thing to worry about, at least.' Kay drained her tea. 'All right, let's get started, shall we?'

Ten minutes later, a crowd of uniformed officers and plainclothes detectives created a semicircle around where Kay stood in front of the whiteboard. Each member of the investigating team held a copy of an agenda produced by the HOLMES2 management database. A silence fell as Kay held up her hand.

'Thanks, everyone. We've had a busy weekend, and we've got a long way to go over the next few days, but let's see if we can find a way forward and see some justice for our victim. Ian, do you want to start us off, please? I see on the report here you've had a follow-up conversation regarding the house-to-house enquiries from last week.'

'Thanks, guv.' Barnes moved to the front of the room and loosened his tie before bringing his colleagues up to date with Peter Winton's interview.

'I've spent the rest of the weekend going through the CSI reports that were emailed over from Harriet's team on Friday afternoon, particularly in relation to vehicle track marks at the crime scene. We know it'd rained heavily since last Sunday night when Peter said he'd heard the van, so any trace evidence would've been washed away, but I decided to go for a walk along the track when I was out with Pia yesterday, and there are definite vehicle markings. I put some sticks in the track next to them to mark them out – it was starting to get dark by then. I organised a uniformed team to seal off the track before we left, and I left a message on Harriet's phone when I got home. I'm hoping she's going to get a team over there this morning to take some samples.'

Kay updated her notes as he spoke, and then raised her head as he wandered back to his seat. 'Ian, that's great work – thank you. If Harriet doesn't get back to you by ten o'clock, can you let me know? Those samples need to be a priority now. The van might not be connected to our case, but we need to rule it out if it isn't. Keep me posted.'

Her colleague nodded in acknowledgement, and she turned to Carys. 'How've you been getting on?'

'I've made further enquiries about night-time parachute jumps, guv. If our man was the victim of an accident, he had to have had at least fifty previous jumps to his name before being allowed to go up at night. I've also been told he would've needed to hold an endorsed "B Licence". I've gone through the records of everyone locally who does have one of those licences, and spoken to parachute clubs about it, but no-one recognises him from the image we've got.'

'That elimination process is an enormous help though, Carys. Thank you,' said Kay.

'Guv?' Gavin raised his hand and gestured to Laura. 'What Carys is saying ties in with what we heard chatting to airfield personnel on Saturday. If anyone was planning to do a night-time jump, it would've had to have been lodged with the Parachute Association, Civil Aviation Authority, and the local police station. We've spoken to all of those, and there are no records for such a jump between the Tuesday when Dennis Maitland ploughed that field and last Wednesday when our victim was found. In fact, there haven't been any night-time jumps in that area for quite a while.'

Kay waited until the assembled officers had finished updating their notes, and then gestured to the list of bullet points she'd updated on the whiteboard.

'I think it's quite clear that our victim wasn't killed in an accident,' she said. 'The focus of this investigation now is to ascertain who he is, and why he died in such horrific circumstances. Ian – I want you to take Laura with you and head back to the track next to the Wintons' house. Arrange for uniform to provide continuing assistance in sealing off access to it until such time as Harriet has processed the evidence you've identified.'

'Guv.'

'Carys – can you and Gavin go and interview Dennis Maitland again to find out what he knows about public usage of that track, or whether he's had cause to use it over the past couple of weeks? Ask him about aircraft sightings over his land, too. Perhaps he heard something last Sunday night that will tie in with Peter Winton's statement.'

'Yes, guv,' said Carys.

Kay finished delegating that day's urgent tasks, and then held up her hand. 'Before you all go, I can confirm that we've received some information to indicate that our victim was a member of the armed forces based on the tattoo on his arm. At the moment, we still don't have any identification for him, and that part of the investigation could take a while. With regard to motive – keep an open mind while you're working through your enquiries. Until we have more information, we can't rule out anything, is that understood?'

A murmur of assent filled the room.

'All right, thank you, everyone. You've got a lot to work through so unless there's something urgent, the next briefing will be at four o'clock tomorrow afternoon.'

CHAPTER SEVENTEEN

Barnes wrinkled his nose at the stench arising from a stagnant pool of water beyond the bracken and rotten leaf litter that peppered the woodland to his right, and then cast his gaze across the line of blue and white crime scene tape that had been tied between two poplar trees.

Beyond the striped plastic barrier, a pair of uniformed officers stood with their backs to Barnes, their attention taken by the group of six crime scene investigators who crouched on opposite sides of the waterlogged track, talking in low tones.

Wind rustled through the branches above him, an eerie sound that muted conversation and set the hairs on the back of his neck on end.

His feet were getting cold.

He shuffled across to where Laura stood, her expression one of fascination as she watched the white-suited figures move back and forth.

She glanced up at him as he joined her.

'I never had time to watch what they do when I was in uniform,' she said. 'I was always the one with the clipboard, making sure no-one came near the crime scene who wasn't supposed to be there, or dealing with the public and their bloody mobile phone cameras.'

'How're you finding major crimes, then?'

Laura exhaled. 'If I said I was loving it, it'd sound really crass, wouldn't it?'

'But all of us would understand. It's what keeps us going. Kay always says it's about justice. Justice for the victim, and justice for whoever is left behind. I wouldn't be anywhere else.'

He smiled as her shoulders relaxed, and then turned to his left at a loud whistle.

Barnes had tasked four uniformed constables with searching the surrounding woodland for any other trace evidence and PC Aaron Stewart now held his hand aloft from his position several paces away amongst the thick undergrowth.

'What've you got?'

'Rabbit.' Stewart bent down for a moment, then

straightened and held up a dead rabbit. 'There's a trap here.'

'Poachers?'

'Looks like it.'

'Shit.'

'What's wrong?' said Laura.

'It puts a different angle on this vehicle, doesn't it?' said Barnes as Stewart tossed the dead animal aside and began to pull apart the snare. 'Here's us, hoping that van has something to do with our victim's death, and yet we've now got evidence of poaching.'

He broke off as Stewart clambered over a fallen tree to join them, a tangle of wood and wire between his hands.

'Nasty,' he said. 'I'll report this in to Rural Crimes.'

'Thanks,' said Barnes. 'Warn the others that there could be more – the last thing we need is someone getting injured amongst all this undergrowth.'

'Will do, guv.'

While Stewart radioed through the message to his colleagues before returning to his search quadrant, Barnes peered at the track disappearing into the distance beyond the CSIs' position.

He'd been careful staking out the vehicle tread marks, ensuring the twigs he'd used as markers were inches away from the potential evidence so that the forensic experts could take photographs and casts as necessary without worrying about contamination.

The markers had been cast away to the tangled verges as the CSIs processed the scene, starting at the taped-off boundary and moving forward towards the field boundary beyond the woodland.

'Where does this lead?' said Laura. 'To the field where the victim was found, or one next to it?'

'One next to it – if you imagine the gate to the field where he was found, then this goes to the field to the right of that. Maitland was ploughing the one to the left of it last Wednesday.'

'How far?'

'About six hundred yards from where we're standing. Just around that curve.'

Laura pivoted, staring back in the direction from which they'd walked after parking the car in the lane. 'So, only about a quarter mile in length in total. And if Peter Winton hadn't been sleeping badly—'

'We'd have never known.'

'Do you think it has something to do with the dead man?'

'Professionally speaking, I'd say we wait for the evidence before making a conclusion, especially given that dead rabbit.'

'Personally?'

'My gut feel is yes. Why would someone drive a van down here in the middle of the night? I don't think a poacher would take that sort of risk, not the sort who traps a rabbit here and there, and anyone killing deer wouldn't get too close, either. They usually park away from their hunting ground. It's why farmers around here are always complaining about barbed wire fences being cut and horses or cows getting out – it's because the poachers drag the carcasses across the fields to their vehicles and don't care what happens to the livestock.'

He glanced across at his colleague, who seemed fascinated by his insights. 'Tell you what, though – get onto Rural Crimes when we're back at the station and ask them if there have been any reports of poaching around here, just to rule it out, okay?'

'Sure.' She pulled out her notebook, then pointed at the snare Stewart had left on the ground next to his vehicle. 'Is there any use trying to get fingerprints off of that?'

'Stewart will try, but if it's anything like the ones that have been found before, we won't find anything. They usually wear gloves.'

Half an hour later, the forensic team were packing away their equipment, and the four uniformed officers had collated a small pile of snares, discarded aluminium drink cans, one shoe, and a bundle of rags that were indistinguishable.

'We'll have to process all of this as well,' said Patrick as he stood next to Harriet and peeled off his protective paper suit. 'It'll be a couple of days before we've got anything to report, though.'

'Thanks,' said Barnes, battening down his disappointment. He began to walk back to the car, Laura at his side. 'I bloody hope Carys and Gavin have more luck speaking to Maitland.'

CHAPTER EIGHTEEN

Carys eased off the accelerator as the car rumbled across an iron cattle grid, then weaved the vehicle around a cluster of chickens that were pecking at the mud-covered concrete apron of the farmyard.

There was an open barn off to the left of where she parked. A variety of well-used machinery cluttered its floor while a tractor with enormous wheels blocked access to a gated entrance at the back of the yard. Two sheds and a dilapidated lean-to took up the right-hand side, their contents obscured by a musty gloom.

When she unclipped her seatbelt and opened her door, the stench of manure assaulted her senses and she turned to Gavin with a grimace.

'Did she give us this one on purpose?'

Her colleague grinned. 'You must've done something really bad.'

'I was joking.' She slapped his arm. 'I thought Kay said they were growing lavender here?'

'Maybe that's what the manure is for. Give it a boost before the summer.'

'That's bull—'

'Exactly.' Gavin pointed at the house that stood in the centre of the U-shaped mixture of buildings. 'Shall we start there?'

'It's a good a place as any. I can't see anyone out here.'

She skirted around the mud, wondering fleetingly if it was all dirt – or worse – and then brushed aside the tendrils of a tangled and naked wisteria that clung to a wooden trellis next to the front door, before pressing the bell.

The door opened after what seemed an age, and a man of Gavin's height stood on the threshold, his greying hair flecked with nicotine-yellow stains and a shabby long-sleeved rugby shirt that had seen better days.

'Dennis Maitland? I'm Detective Constable Carys Miles, and this is my colleague DC Gavin Piper. Could we come in?'

'I'm in the middle of doing the wages, but all

right. I presume you can't wait.'

Carys forced a smile. 'You presumed right, thank you.'

Maitland stood back to let them in and pointed down a wide hallway to a door at the end. 'Make yourselves comfortable in the office – it's the door down there on the left. I was going to make myself another cup of coffee. Do you want one?'

'We're fine, thanks.'

'All right. Be with you in a minute.'

Carys followed Gavin into the room Maitland had directed them to, and eyed the pile of paperwork stacked on the farmer's desk beside an ashtray.

An old computer whirred next to a dust-laden keyboard, and she recognised a popular book-keeping software package displayed on the screen. A bookshelf against the left-hand wall overflowed with farming magazines, almanacs, and a few dog-eared spy thrillers, while a four-drawer filing cabinet teetered next to the window, the top drawer open and more paperwork strewn over the hanging files inside.

She took a seat next to Gavin at the sound of footsteps in the hallway and Maitland reappeared with a steaming mug of coffee in one hand and a plate of cake slices in the other, which he proceeded to place on the desk between them.

'The wife'll never forgive me if I don't offer you some of this,' he said, a smile brushing his mouth.

'I'm never going to say "no" to homemade fruitcake, Mr Maitland,' said Gavin, taking a large wedge.

Carys rolled her eyes and pulled out her notebook. 'You said you were doing the wages, Mr Maitland. How many people do you have working for you?'

'Please,' said Maitland between mouthfuls of cake. 'Call me Dennis. I've got eight workers now. I took on a part-time lad last summer and he works here in between university terms to get some experience before he graduates. The others have been with me for years. One of them even worked for my father – he refuses to retire. I think his wife scares him.'

'We're trying to get a better understanding of the land around your property,' she said. 'In particular, a track that runs from the field next to where our victim was found and the lane that connects with one of the C-roads into Sevenoaks. We've got a witness statement from someone who says they heard a van using that track a few nights before that man's body was discovered.'

Maitland frowned. 'I'm surprised anyone got a vehicle down that at this time of year. Hang on.'

He brushed crumbs from his lap, wiped his hands on the back of his jeans, and then strode across to the bookshelf. Running his hands over the contents, he pulled out a document and returned to the desk, pushing the plate out of the way before unfolding a map.

'This shows more detail than your average Ordnance Survey map – it's nearly a century old, so it's not cluttered with all the information on modern maps. It's easier if I show you the boundaries on this, rather than try to explain it,' he said. He tapped the map with his finger. 'Here's the farmhouse here, and this is the field where Luke and Tom were metal detecting. This one is where I was working on Wednesday, and you can see the track marked here at the back of the other field.'

'Any idea why someone might use it?' said Gavin.

'Poachers, I'd expect,' said Maitland, 'but what they were hoping to catch, I don't know. Nothing big, that's for sure. I haven't seen deer on that side of the property for a few years now, not since we replaced all the hedgerows and fencing. Could be kids, I suppose? Hiding away for a spot of nookie?'

Carys smiled at the farmer's turn of phrase. 'Could be. How far does your land extend?'

Maitland sketched out the boundary with his

finger. 'Not too far. Manageable, at least. That's what helps to keep the costs down, although this idea of Liz's to put this field down to lavender over the next couple of years will eat into our profits for a while until we find out if there's a market for it.'

'Do you have an aircraft, Dennis?' said Gavin.

The farmer raised his head and blinked. 'An aircraft? What would I need one of those for?'

'It's just a routine question as part of our ongoing investigation,' said Carys. 'Do you?'

'No. Never seen the point of them, unless I'm going on holiday. Mind you, haven't had one of those for three years, either.'

'The neighbouring farms that abut your land – what do they farm?' she said.

'Down here on this edge of my boundary are the Ditchens family,' he said. 'They have an orchard – lots of different fruit crops. Been around for a couple of centuries. Off to this end here, nearest the road, they have a couple of strawberry fields. On the other side of my property are Adrian and Helen Peverell. They're farming rabbits for commercial purposes – you know, pet food and the like.' He scowled. 'Never been a fan of battery farming myself but they switched from barley and wheat to the rabbits about ten years ago and have been going great guns. I think they sold some of the unused land to the Ditchens, come to think of it.'

'Do either of those families own an aircraft?'

'Not that I know of.'

'Going back to the week before the body was found in the field,' said Carys. 'Have you heard any light aircraft overhead at night, or anything else that has seemed unusual to you?'

'Honestly, detective – no. The minute the bedside light goes out, I'm asleep until the alarm goes off at five. Liz reckons an earthquake wouldn't wake me.'

'Do you socialise much with your neighbours?' said Gavin.

'I see them at local events from time to time,' said Maitland, 'and we sometimes borrow equipment from each other if we need to. The problem is, we're all so busy running the day-to-day stuff, we don't get a lot of time to socialise. Speaking of which, if you haven't got any more questions, I need to finish these wages before three o'clock so I can transfer the money online.'

Carys tucked her notebook into her bag. 'No, no more questions. Thanks for your time, Dennis. If you do hear anything about someone using that track, could you give us a call?'

'Will do.'

CHAPTER NINETEEN

Kay tapped the volume control on the steering wheel as the traffic ground to a halt on the Ashford Road and eyed the silver hatchback that executed an eight-point turn in the driveway of the Turkey Mill archway before shooting past her in the opposite direction.

She wondered how many other drivers would be tempted to do the same and try to find another route into the town centre.

After checking the clock on the dashboard, she cringed as a motorcyclist risked life and limb to weave between the stationary vehicles on a dilapidated scooter that probably wouldn't pass its next MOT test, and wondered if she should phone Sharp to ask him to run the briefing that morning.

She had another forty minutes before she was due

in the incident room, and crossed her fingers as the queue of cars surged forward.

Earlier that morning, a knock on her front door had thrown her morning routine into disarray as the woman from the wildlife refuge delivered four fox cubs into Adam's care and hurried away to get her children to school on time.

Leaving the house ten minutes later than her normal time wreaked havoc on Kay's commute, but Adam was struggling to feed the four hungry foxes on his own, and she had taken pity on him, holding each cub as he'd administered the next specialised portion of food.

She smiled. If she were honest, she enjoyed the opportunity to share some time with him and the latest temporary additions to their household – after all, it wasn't everyone who could say they had a litter of fox cubs in their kitchen.

At some point, she would have to invite Carys around to meet them before they were moved back to the wildlife rehabilitation centre and released, otherwise her detective constable would never forgive her.

As she eased her foot off the brake, the car picked up speed as the traffic eased, and she exhaled as the road curved past the carriage museum and Archbishop's Palace.

She had fifteen minutes to spare, which gave her enough time to check through any correspondence, new leads and reports Debbie would have processed out of HOLMES2 and left on her desk before the shift began in earnest.

As she turned the car into the asphalt driveway next to the brick-clad police station, she leaned out of the window and swiped her security card and slowly drove forward to avoid four uniformed police constables who ran out of the side door and over to their cars.

She frowned as she drew closer to a spare parking space, recognising Carys's figure huddled beside her own car, a worried expression etched across her fair skin as the two patrol vehicles launched past the barrier, sirens blaring.

The woman lifted her chin at Kay's arrival, then hovered near the bonnet as she reverse parked and snatched up her handbag from the passenger seat.

'Morning, Carys,' she said, locking the door. 'Everything all right?'

'Could I have a word, guv? Before you go inside?' She held up a takeout cup. 'I got you a coffee.'

'Thanks.' Kay raised her eyebrow. 'What's going on?'

Carys moved until she was closer to Kay before her shoulders sagged. She turned her own cup between her hands. 'I'm sorry, guv. There's no easy way to tell you this, and it's been going around in my head since I got the call on Friday because I know how much you've got on at the moment, and what with this investigation and all—'

Kay took a sip of coffee and peered over the rim of the takeout cup at her.

The detective constable's nervousness was palpable; an energy that emanated from her as she shuffled her feet and cast her gaze to the pitted surface of the car park.

Lowering the cup, Kay tilted her head to one side. 'Carys? Whatever is the matter?'

Carys swallowed, then cleared her throat. 'I don't know how to say this, guv but I've been offered an interview.'

'Interview? What for?'

'A promotion. Detective sergeant.'

'Oh. I didn't know there were any openings available in West Division. I—' Kay's heart skipped a beat as her world shifted, an inexplicable feeling that what happened in the next few moments would have a monumental impact on both of their futures. She bit her lip as the full implication of what Carys was telling her struck her in the solar plexus. 'Where?'

'Glamorgan, guv. Cardiff.'

'Wales?' Kay blinked. 'That's miles away.'

'I know, right?' Carys managed a sad smile.

'Bloody hell.'

'I-I just didn't want you to find out through hearsay, not after everything you've done for me. You've been so good to me, giving me a chance and everything over the years.'

'Morning, guv!'

Kay glanced up at a shout from across the car park and held up her coffee cup in greeting to Phillip Parker, who was heading towards the entrance with Debbie, and then turned back to Carys. 'Does anyone else know?'

'No. I wanted to tell you first.'

'When's the interview?'

'Friday. I've got to go up Thursday night though, because it's at ten o'clock in the morning in Bridgend. I'll never make it if I try to leave early, and—'

'No, that's fine. I'll speak to Barnes. We'll work it out. Wow. Cardiff, eh?' Kay smiled, shock turning to pride as she placed her hand on Carys's arm and began to steer her towards the station. 'Do they know what they're letting themselves in for?'

Carys smiled, her shoulders relaxing. 'I was worried, guv. I didn't know what you were going to say. I thought you'd be angry with me.'

'Angry with you? No – not at all. It's just a shock, that's all.' She paused at the door, wrapping her fingers around the handle before looking across at her colleague. 'You do realise if they interview you, you're going to beat the competition? Seriously, you've got what it takes. Are you sure this is what you want?'

'I want to be a detective sergeant, guv. I'm ready. And let's face it, with the budget cuts around here lately, I'm not going to get another chance at a promotion around here any time soon, am I?' Carys brightened a little. 'At least I'll be able to afford my own place in Wales. I could get a cat.'

Kay nodded, unable to voice an argument to the woman's observations, and tugged open the door.

'I'm going to bloody miss you.'

CHAPTER TWENTY

Kay reached out blindly for her desk phone as it began to ring, and thumbed through a report she had meant to read four days ago in relation to personnel limitations on West Division, her thoughts tumbling over the conversation she'd had with Carys.

The briefing had passed in a blur of loud conversations and paperwork, together with a sense of dread that a change in personnel with no likely replacement to match the detective constable's skillset would have a ripple effect through the team.

'Detective Inspector Kay Hunter.'

'Detective? It's Oliver Townsend. We met on Sunday.'

'Good morning, Mr Townsend. What can I do for you?'

'Actually, it's about what I might be able to do for you. I had a chat with Brian last night – he's the bloke who used to run the veterans' group over here in Riverhead that I told you about.'

Kay pushed the report aside and reached for her notebook. 'That was quick, thanks. Was he able to help?'

'He wasn't, but one of the regulars overheard me talking to him and might have some information to help you. The thing is, I thought it might be best if you spoke to him in person, so I wondered if now was a good time?'

'I've got a meeting at two o'clock this afternoon, but if I leave now—'

'No need,' said Townsend. 'Stephen had to come into Maidstone for something or other anyway and I gave him a lift, so we're here. We were going to get a coffee and wondered if you might want to join us. Saves you the trip.'

'That's brilliant, thanks. Where are you?'

'We're eyeing up that café just around the corner from all the banks on the High Street. It's not too crowded by the look of it.'

'Perfect – I'll be there in five minutes.'

She ended the call, plucked her coat off the hook

next to Sharp's office and hurried down the stairs to the reception desk.

'Hughes, if anyone wants me I'm popping out for an hour. Call me if anything urgent comes through.'

The desk sergeant raised a hand in acknowledgement, and she flew out of the door.

Risking life and limb to zig-zag between the traffic that poured along Palace Avenue, Kay reached the café on time and spotted Oliver Townsend sitting at a table laid for four at the back, facing the room.

He rose as she approached, shook her hand and gestured to the man beside him.

'Detective Hunter, this is Stephen Halsmith. As I said on the phone, he might be able to help you.'

Kay raised her chin as the man pushed back his chair.

He was several inches taller than her, his forearms emblazoned with fading tattoos and a four-inch scar over the back of his right hand. His grip was firm and his gaze steady. Like Oliver, he wore his hair longer than he would have done in the armed forces, and his physique was a slender build rather than one of muscle and brawn.

'Detective Hunter.'

Halsmith spoke with a soft Northumbrian accent seasoned with a smoker's growl.

'Thanks for asking me to come along,' she said. She ordered a coffee from the waitress and then folded her hands on the table. 'I presume Oliver's filled you in about my investigation?'

'He has,' said Halsmith. 'I don't know if what I can tell you will help, but I figured I should give it a go. You never know, right?'

'Right. What did you do in the army?'

'Infantry. Served two tours in the Balkans, one in Kosovo, and one in the first Gulf War.' His gaze drifted to the window over her shoulder. 'Saw too many friends killed, and the others – well, let's just say their health was never the same afterwards.'

'What do you do these days?'

'Crosswords, and competition archery.' He smiled. 'And I look after my grandkids during the week while my daughter and her husband are at work.'

'Doesn't sound too bad.'

'They're both a handful, but yes – I love it.'

Kay thanked the waitress who appeared with her coffee, then turned back to the two men as a couple of pensioners sat a couple of tables to their right. 'All right. What've you got for me?'

Halsmith scratched his short beard, then wrapped his hands around his tea mug and lowered his voice.

'Olly showed me the photograph of the tattoo after I overheard him talking to Brian. I'd never seen it before, but I'd heard things. Back in the old Kosovan days.'

'Like what?'

'Something to do with a six-man patrol who went AWOL and rescued some women and children.' He shook his head. 'I don't know – sometimes you hear stories like that and there's a whiff of bullshit about it. Urban myth, that sort of thing. But this one gathered momentum for a while before it died out. I'd heard the men all got shipped back home and discharged. I forgot about it for a few years, until I got into a bit of trouble.'

'Trouble?'

He held her gaze. 'Drugs. Not much. But I was stupid. I should've just tried to talk to someone. Luckily, my missus found out about Brian's support group and dragged me along to it. I haven't looked back since.'

'How long ago was that?'

'About ten years now. These days I go along to help out, listen to the younger ones. We've all been there, so it's good to do something to support others in a similar situation. Anyway, one day – must be five years ago – a bloke turns up at one of the Monday night meetings. It was obvious he'd been sleeping rough. Brian's good with the new folk, so he sorted him out with some fresh clothes, a shower kit, things like that. The place we meet at hosts a cricket club and has changing rooms so he was able to have a wash and stuff while he was there.'

'Any idea where he'd been staying?'

'Wild camping, I reckon. There are a lot who do it – it's safer these days, and was back then as well. I'd never seen him around town before that, not in Sevenoaks or Tonbridge anyway. No point going to the smaller places – you won't make enough money begging.'

'Did you see the tattoo?'

'No, never. I just thought of him when I heard Olly talking and put two and two together. I never asked him what he did in Kosovo, but I latched on to the fact he'd been there from some of the comments he made. He sort of opened up more towards me after that, knowing I'd probably seen some of the things he had.'

'How did you figure out he was one of the six men?'

'He mentioned he'd helped to rescue some refugees back in ninety-nine. Given the location where he'd been based and the fact he admitted he was sleeping rough because he had no army pension, I put two and two together. I was in awe of him, to be honest. Hell of a thing to do.'

'Can you remember his name?'

'Yes. Ethan Archer. He must've been in his early forties when I last saw him.'

Kay rummaged in her bag and pulled out the composite sketch. 'Is this him?'

'Yeah, that's him I reckon.'

'When did you last see Ethan?'

Halsmith drained his tea, glanced at Townsend, then back to Kay. 'Well, that's the thing, see. That's what I was telling Olly. I haven't seen Ethan for going on three or four years.'

'What do you mean? What happened to him?'

'Nobody knows. One day, he left the group and we never saw him again.'

'Did you check with any other contacts you had?'

'Yes, and I asked around for a while but it's like he disappeared into thin air. No-one knows anything.'

CHAPTER TWENTY-ONE

Pushing open the door into the incident room, Kay stuck her fingers between her lips and whistled.

After apologising to the police constable at the desk nearest to her who jumped in his seat at the sudden interruption, she raised her voice.

'Everyone, briefing now please. We've got a breakthrough regarding the identity of our victim.'

She clapped her hand on Barnes's shoulder as she passed his desk. 'I'll need your help coordinating all this. Are you able to delegate some of your other casework elsewhere?'

'I can try,' he said. 'Another detective over at Headquarters owes me a favour for that burglary job the other month.'

'Do your best. Is Sharp in?'

'Yes.'

'Could you let him know he might want to join us? I think he'll be interested to hear this.'

'Will do.'

Sidestepping one of the administrative staff who nearly collided with her, his arms laden with reports, Kay crossed the room to the whiteboard and wheeled it closer to the back wall onto which a long cork board had been fixed.

Their victim's photograph was the first item to be pinned to it, and, as the team found seats and settled, she began to create a spider web of known facts to date. When she turned, a sea of faces stared back at her with eager expressions.

Sharp leaned against the photocopier, his gaze glued to the board.

Kay cleared her throat. 'Thanks, everyone. If there's anyone missing, anyone out following up leads, can someone make sure this information is passed on as soon as the briefing is finished?'

Debbie West raised her hand. 'I'll take care of that, guv.'

'Thanks. I've received confirmation in the past hour that our victim is Ethan Archer. He was known to attend a veterans' support group at Riverhead until three or four years ago, at which point he disappeared.

Prior to that, he'd been in the British Army and served in Kosovo. One of the support group members, Stephen Halsmith, recalls that when Ethan first turned up at the group, he'd been sleeping rough – Halsmith thinks he'd been wild camping based on some of the comments Ethan made to him over the time he attended the group.'

She gestured to the two displays of information. 'Now that we have a name, I want us to focus on identifying next of kin, any traces of him within the social services system, and whether he's known to local charities. Where's Laura?'

A hand was raised at the back of the group. 'Here, guv.'

'Can you follow up with the Borough Council's housing department and have a word to see if anyone recognises the name or his photograph? Halsmith reckons if Ethan was begging from time to time, then he'd head into Sevenoaks or Tonbridge. You can liaise with police constables Ben Allen and Nigel Best over that way if you need extra hands.'

'Yes, guv.'

'Check Maidstone as well, and extend your search as you need to. Does anyone here have contacts within Kent County Council's housing schemes?'

'I know someone,' said PC Dave Morrison. 'If she

can't help, she might be able to tell us who we can speak to.'

'Good, thanks. I'll leave that with you. On to yesterday's activities – Ian, is there any news about that van or the tread marks in the track?'

Barnes stepped forward. 'Patrick is processing the prints he and his team took yesterday. We found evidence of snares and dead rabbits but we're not sure if those are linked to the van yet.'

'So, we could be looking at a poaching angle rather than something to do with Ethan's death?'

'It's a possibility, guv. I'll be following up with the Rural Crimes division this morning to get their thoughts on that.'

'All right. Carys and Gavin, what did Dennis Maitland have to say?'

'He thought maybe it was poachers that used the track, but thought it more likely it was kids,' said Carys. 'He reckons anyone poaching around there is going for the bigger stuff, like deer. He did give us the details for the owners of the neighbouring farm properties, though. I've put those in the system and we'll organise interviews with them over the course of tomorrow.'

'He did mention that, as far as he was aware, none of his neighbours own a light aircraft,' said

Gavin. 'And he confirmed he doesn't use one either.'

Kay thanked them as they retook their seats. 'Given the status of forensics with the tyre marks, Ian, can you liaise with uniform to carry out additional enquiries with residents along that lane again? We need to corroborate Peter Winton's statement that he heard a vehicle on that Sunday night. If anyone's got a security camera fixed to their property, see if you can get hold of any footage as well. It's a long shot, I know but we need to close out that line of enquiry if it has no bearing on Ethan's death.'

'Will do, guv.'

Kay exhaled. 'Okay, that's plenty to be getting on with. You're dismissed, but you know where to find me if you have any questions. Thanks for your time.'

She gathered her notes together as chairs scraped backwards and the team dispersed.

Sharp beckoned her over as he wandered back to his office. When she entered, he closed the door and turned to her.

'We need to make a decision whether we tell the team about Archer's involvement with rescuing those women and children in the Balkans.'

'You mean in case the killer's motive was revenge for the rescue mission, even after all this time?'

'Exactly.'

She sighed, ran a hand through her hair and moved across to the window before leaning against the sill. 'I don't know if it's the right thing to do yet. I mean, it could colour the investigation if we tell them.'

'Do you want to exhaust any other possibilities first?'

'I wouldn't mind, just to be sure. Otherwise, it's just you and me interpreting what happened back in ninety-nine as a motive, isn't it? We've got no evidence to suggest that's the case. There are so many unknowns at the present time, aren't there?'

'All right. I'm happy for you to continue running the investigation on that basis but if you think any evidence that comes to light points towards that military incident, you let me know straight away.'

Kay nodded, and moved across to the door. 'Don't worry, I will – especially if anyone threatens my team.'

CHAPTER TWENTY-TWO

Gavin caught sight of his reflection in the mirrored wall of the lift and hurriedly tried to smooth down his hair while Laura pressed the button for the third floor.

She grinned at him as the doors closed. 'I've got some hairspray in my bag if you want it.'

He dropped his hand and turned his back to the wall, running his eyes down the text of the poster above the control panel. 'Very funny. Who are we meeting?'

'Valerie Hayes. She's a liaison officer between the council and the local homeless charities. I'm having trouble getting hold of people at a couple of the charities – they're part-time volunteers. I figured if Valerie could act as go-between, it'd free us up to follow some of those other tasks Kay gave to us.'

'Sounds like a plan. How do you know her?'

'I don't – she's Dave Morrison's contact that he mentioned in the briefing. He's still dividing his time between us and a court hearing this week, so I offered to meet with her instead.' She frowned. 'You don't mind, do you?'

The lift juddered to a standstill, and Gavin put out his hand as the doors opened.

'Not at all – I'd much rather be doing this than being stuck in the incident room.' He unbuttoned his jacket as they walked along a short corridor towards an unmanned reception desk. 'It's warmer in here, for a start.'

Laura stifled a snort as he rang a bell on the desk.

Moments later, a young girl barely out of her teens and wearing copious amounts of eye make-up appeared from an open doorway to the left of the desk and tilted her head.

'Can I help you?'

'Detective Constable Laura Hanway and my colleague, DC Gavin Piper.' Laura tucked her warrant card back in her pocket. 'Valerie Hayes is expecting us.'

'Hang on.'

The girl spun on her heel and disappeared, but

Gavin could hear her talking to someone in the next room.

Footsteps sounded across the thin carpeted floor and then an older woman with shoulder-length brown hair entered the reception area, a black lever arch file under one arm. She held out her hand to Laura first.

'I'm Valerie Hayes. I'm afraid we don't have a dedicated meeting room on this floor, so we'll have to use my manager's office instead.' She brushed past Gavin and headed along the corridor, then called over her shoulder. 'He's in a meeting in Chatham until four o'clock and the traffic coming over the hill this time of day is usually dreadful, so we should be all right.'

She stopped at the end and pushed open a door, standing to one side to let them pass.

'Take a seat. I'd offer you a drink, but the plumber's had his head under the sink in the gents' toilet for the past hour, and I don't think the water is coming back on any time soon.'

As Gavin sat in one of two visitor chairs beside a cheap imitation oak desk, he took in the clutter of paperwork strewn across it and the reminders written on sticky notes plastered around the edges of the computer screen. He wondered how Valerie's boss had managed to escape with so many other commitments clamouring for his time.

The whole room resembled utter bedlam.

'You should see it on a bad day.' Valerie shoved the lever arch file into a gap between two others on a filing shelf next to the window and then sat opposite them. 'You mentioned on the phone you had an urgent query with regard to a homeless veteran, Detective Hanway.'

Gavin caught Laura's sideways glance, and waved her to continue.

If she had already established a basic rapport with the woman, then he was happy to let his colleague manage the interview.

'We're trying to find out more about a man by the name of Ethan Archer,' she said. 'We're investigating a suspicious death, and we understand from people who knew him that he disappeared from the area three to four years ago. We're hoping you might be able to help us work out where he's been living during that time.'

Valerie blew out her cheeks. 'Blimey. That's a big ask. Do you know anything about his background?'

'We believe he may have been ex-infantry, potentially the Parachute Regiment,' said Laura. 'He was known to have been sleeping rough, and had been attending a veterans' support group in Riverhead before his disappearance. We wondered whether he was in touch with this department at any point during that period he hadn't been seen, or whether you have a last known address for him.'

'It would take me a day or so to go through our database,' said the housing officer. 'Do you have a date of birth for him?'

'We're still waiting for confirmation from the British Army,' said Gavin.

'Right, well, it might take time to find him without it, but I can have a go.'

'Thank you.'

Valerie finished writing a note to herself, and tore off the page from the pad next to her manager's computer keyboard. 'Do you know when he left the army?'

'We have a date of ninety-nine.'

'That's a long time ago.'

'We realise this isn't going to be easy.'

Grimacing, Valerie folded the note and tapped it with her fingertips. 'It's not. I mean, unless he was specifically referred to this department – or an earlier iteration of it, then we'll be lucky to find a record for him.'

'What sort of problems do these veterans experience?' said Laura.

'Apart from the physical and mental issues we

typically see in veterans who have experienced conflict, it's often when they return to civilian life that the problems manifest,' said Valerie. 'A lot of them joined up at an early age – late teens or early twenties – so the army, for instance, is the only life they know. I think in recent years they've started to give them a bit of a hand when they leave, sort of a transition from one to the other, but it's not enough. It's a huge shock to the system going from having your life organised on a daily basis down to the tiniest detail to having to plan for yourself. In my experience, I've seen the same issues arise when prisoners are released after long sentences.'

'How does your department support them with finding sheltered accommodation?'

'If they come to us, then we put them in touch with the organisations who can assist with housing and associated services. It's about arming them with information so they can make the right choices.' She paused and gestured to the rows of files lining the shelves. 'We're stretched beyond capacity though, and local councils are being squeezed by the government with regards to funding. Unfortunately, the mental wellbeing of our growing homeless population isn't top of their priorities, despite the fact ours is growing because they're encouraging them to leave the cities. It hasn't been a priority for them for nearly a decade, despite all the evidence that we desperately need the money in order to manage the problem.'

'Our victim could have been sleeping rough in the countryside – wild camping,' said Gavin.

Valerie sighed. 'In that case, he might never have registered with us in the first place, or if he did and then ceased all contact, we would have lost track of how to find him.'

'What happens if people like him do disappear, or move on to other locations?'

'Well, nothing. If they don't tell us where they're going, we can't help them.'

'Surely you have to do something for them if they do that?' said Laura, 'I mean, what happens to any benefits they might be entitled to?'

Valerie gave the young detective constable a sad smile. 'That's the problem. Some of these people don't care about that. They don't *want* to be found.'

CHAPTER TWENTY-THREE

Kay flicked through the pages of the free newspaper that had been shoved through the door that afternoon, chin in hand and with a heavy heart.

She didn't read the words.

She didn't focus on the photographs of local sports competitions or fundraising activities.

Her mind kept returning to her conversation with Carys earlier that morning, and the ramifications on the team if the detective constable left Kent Police to pursue her career ambitions.

A mewling from the wire cage in the corner of the kitchen broke the spell, and she lifted her head to peer over the edge of the worktop to where Adam sat on the tiles, checking one fox cub at a time and ensuring each got a fair portion of the food he was administering to them.

Since they'd arrived that morning, he'd been feeding them every hour and would continue to do so during the night.

'Carys is leaving,' she said, hearing the wonder and sadness in her voice.

His head jerked up as his gaze locked with hers, the cub in his lap forgotten. 'When?'

'I don't know. Soon, I suppose. She's got an interview in Bridgend with South Wales Police on Friday. If she gets the job, she's moving to Cardiff.'

Adam ruffled the cub between the ears before placing it on the blankets in the cage alongside its siblings, and then straightened. He washed his hands, and pulled a towel off its hook below the sink.

Wandering over to her, he dried his hands and then sat on a bar stool opposite.

'When did she tell you?'

'This morning, when I arrived. She collared me in the car park.' She managed a small smile. 'I don't think she got much sleep last night, worrying about it.'

'Are you okay?'

'Yeah, just sad really. I mean, I know I can't keep

them all with me forever but I've just come to rely on her so much. She's my most experienced DC.'

'Why Cardiff?'

Kay shrugged. 'It's a damn sight cheaper than here to live. And I think it's simply the case of that's where the job is. The DS role, I mean. It's not like she'd have to stay there forever if she didn't want to, although I think she might have friends in that part of Wales, so...'

'This might've always been on the cards for her.' Adam folded up the towel and placed it on the worktop beside him. 'When will she have to start?'

'Four weeks' time, if she gets the job—'

'Which she will, because it's Carys we're talking about.'

'Exactly.'

'You've still got Gavin, and there's that new probationary DC in the team now.'

'Laura? Yes, I think she's got a lot of promise. A bit less ambitious than Carys, perhaps.'

'That's not a bad thing.'

'Maybe, although I'm going to miss the dynamic.'

'Do the others know?'

'I've brought Barnes up to date, just so he's prepared for the extra workload. I can't imagine we're going to get the funding to recruit a fully trained DC to take her place – we'll have to wait for the next intake from uniform or the fast-track programme.'

'But Gavin doesn't know yet?'

'No. I figured it's probably best to wait until we have confirmation she's actually going before worrying him about it.'

'It'll do his confidence good, I'm sure.'

'You're probably right.'

He reached out and squeezed her hand as the doorbell rang. 'I am. Do you want to get the plates ready? That'll be the Indian takeaway.'

Kay slid off her stool and pulled plates from the cupboard above the cutting board, set cutlery beside them on the worktop and had uncapped two cold bottles of beer by the time Adam appeared with a carrier bag of food.

'God, that smells good,' she said, and laughed as the four fox cubs raised their noses in the air. 'And you're not having any of it, you lot.'

'I'll shut the door so they don't wander out while we're eating,' said Adam, fastening a loop of wire around the bars.

Moments later, they were eating in companionable silence, a foil container of rice between them and another with a mixture of leftovers they picked at after the main meal.

Kay took a swig of beer and gestured to the foxes. 'They're looking better already. Not quite as rough around the edges like they were when they first got here this morning.'

'Amy's going to be popping by early next week if they keep improving. At this rate, they can deal with them better at the rescue centre once they're out of immediate danger.'

'What will happen to them when they're released?'

Adam spooned another scoop of rice onto his plate and smushed it into the juices from his curry sauce before responding.

'The rescue centre has a list of friendly farmers,' he said. 'Ones who don't allow hunting on their land, and who don't have livestock to worry about. These four will probably end up somewhere near the Ringlestone – it's close to where they were found, and not on top of previous releases. There'll be plenty of land for them to split up and roam about on for a few years.'

'I don't know how Amy does it,' said Kay. 'I'd find it so hard to let them go, not knowing what will happen to them.'

'It'd be crueller to keep them.' Adam smiled. 'Besides, she's only got so much room at the centre, and there are always other animals needing to be cared for. We should invite Carys around here before they go back if she has time. She'd never forgive you if she didn't get to hold one.'

Kay tipped her beer bottle against his. 'Sounds like a good plan, Mr Turner.'

He winked and pointed his fork at the rest of the food. 'If you're going to have more, take it – otherwise I'm finishing that off.'

CHAPTER TWENTY-FOUR

Barnes pulled his wellington boots from the back of the car and let out a huff of air as he perched on the passenger seat to put them on.

Beside him, Carys teetered on one foot while she tried to put the other into a boot, cursing under her breath.

'You'd better get used to this, Miles. Where you're going, it's sheep farming everywhere.'

'I'm not there yet, Ian. I've got to get the job first. Besides, it's Cardiff – not the countryside.' She straightened and gave him a sad smile. 'Kay told you, then?'

'Yes.' He gave his foot one last shove and the boot slid on. 'Thank bloody goodness. I'm sure these shrank when I hosed them off the other morning.'

'Got them on the right feet?'

He grinned, stuck up two fingers at her, and then stood and eyed up the fields beyond the yard where they'd parked, inhaling the fresh air.

Rows and rows of gnarly fruit trees stretched as far as he could see.

Carys followed his gaze. 'It's different along here, compared to Maitland's farm, isn't it? Flatter.'

'Doesn't feel quite so desolate this time of year, either.' He stood with his hands on his waistband and turned to survey the rambling property. 'I don't know how people do this for a living. It's bloody hard work, especially now they can't guarantee any harvesting help from abroad.'

'I heard it was pretty bad here last year. A lot of the fruit pickers didn't bother coming over.' Carys stepped around a deep puddle that stretched between a flat-bed trailer and a battered four-wheel drive vehicle. 'Who are we meeting?'

'Him,' said Barnes, and raised his hand as a man appeared on the doorstep to the farmhouse and ambled towards him. 'Hugh Ditchens?'

'That's me.' The fifty-something farmer shook hands with Barnes, then Carys and gestured to a low-slung brick building that hugged one side of the yard.

'Come on over to the office. It won't matter if we get mud on the floor, and it's warm. I switched the heating on in there an hour ago. You all right for drinks?'

'We're fine, thanks. Are you busy here at the moment?'

'In a bit of a lull,' said Ditchens, as he strode towards his office and led them inside. 'Don't worry about leaving your boots at the door – nobody else does.'

His voice was cheerful, matter-of-fact.

As Barnes cast his eyes around the walls and took in the yearly planners and amateur watercolour paintings that jostled for space alongside three faded aviation prints, each depicting a Second World War aircraft in flight, and children's drawings tacked beside those, he sensed that Ditchens wasn't a man led easily to stress.

'This about the bloke that was found in Dennis's field?' said Ditchens, gesturing to an overstuffed armchair and a rickety camping chair. 'Sorry about the furniture. I'm planning on getting some newer bits and pieces nearer the summer.'

Barnes eyed the camping chair with suspicion and ignored the sly glance Cary shot him as she sank into the armchair and crossed her legs. He eased onto it, half expecting to land on the floor, and then turned his attention to the farmer.

'It is. Just a few routine questions to help us understand how he might have got there in the first place. Have you noticed any unusual activities over the past couple of weeks?'

'Can't say I have. Obviously with the tourist season a few months off yet it's not as busy around here – that can be a pain with fly-tippers, particularly in the field that borders the cherry orchard. It's the nearest to the road, you see. Bastards pull up and throw all their rubbish over the fence and then drive off.'

'We're particularly interested in anything you might have seen or heard at night,' said Barnes. 'Vehicles, things like that.'

Ditchens tugged at his earlobe. 'To be honest, I'm usually asleep by ten-thirty most nights so I don't hear much.'

'Do you own a light aircraft, Mr Ditchens?' said Carys.

He chuckled as he saw her look over his shoulder at the aviation prints. 'No – can't afford one.'

'Those paintings look old.'

'They were my father's. He always had a soft spot

for World War Two fighter planes, the Spitfire in particular.'

'Are you aware of any private airfields in the area?' said Barnes. 'For crop spraying and the like?'

'I'm not, and I can't imagine anyone around here needing to use one – we just don't have the land mass like some of the bigger cereal farms do.'

'Where do your workforce come from? Are they local?'

'Mostly from the village, yes. It gets busier at harvest time, of course, so we bring on casual labour to assist even though most of the fruit picking is done by machine these days.' He smiled indulgently. 'There are still some jobs people are better at.'

'Any travellers turn up wanting some work?'

'Occasionally.' Ditchens shifted in his seat. 'Mind you, that's a Kentish tradition, isn't it? Everyone used to come down from London in the old days to help with the fruit and hop harvests. Make a holiday of it.'

'And how do you pay them?'

'Cash.' The farmer's neck reddened. 'But I clear all that with my accountant when I do my tax return.'

Barnes smiled. 'Noted, Mr Ditchens. Very commendable of you. Have you had any issues with people sleeping rough on or near your land?'

'No, thank goodness.' Ditchens leaned back in his

chair and folded his hands in his lap. 'I've heard it's happening more and more, except the government won't do anything about it. They're only interested in the homeless people that they see in towns, aren't they? I figured I'm lucky not to have to deal with that sort of thing around here.'

Barnes rose from the chair, the legs wobbling as he straightened. 'I think that's all the questions we have at the present time, Mr Ditchens. Thanks for your help.'

'Not a problem, detective. I hope you find whoever killed that man. Whoever he was, he didn't deserve to have his life ended like that. It's just not right.'

CHAPTER TWENTY-FIVE

'This is the place. Peverell Pet Food Supplies,' said Laura, turning left off the B-road and following a cracked concrete driveway that weaved between thick pine trees.

Gavin flicked through the pages he'd printed out from an Internet search as she braked to a standstill. 'Says they've been here for ten years, providing quality meat to the cat and dog food industry. Rabbits.'

'I couldn't do that job.'

'Me neither.' He folded the print-outs and dropped them into the footwell. 'I suppose someone has to, though. Fido won't get his grain-free preservative-free kibble otherwise, will he?'

'My sister has a cat. Won't eat anything except one particular brand of food. The expensive sort that comes in one of those sachets, of course.'

'Not an animal lover, then?'

'I like animals – just not that one. Vicious bastard of a fur ball. I only offered to babysit it once. Never again, not unless they give me gauntlets to wear.'

She braked next to a battered grey estate car with mud splashed up its wheel arches.

Dread shivered across Gavin's shoulders as he followed Laura between a series of deep potholes and ran his gaze over the low slung buildings that hugged the fence line beyond the yard.

Muffled noises came from within, a thrum of movement that was pierced with a single shriek – and then, silence.

'We should've insisted on the orchard place,' Laura muttered.

Gavin didn't respond, but turned his attention to the bungalow that had been built to one side, its position such that the windows faced away from the outbuildings and provided a view of a well-established vegetable garden and freshly dug flower borders.

A terracotta bird bath took centre stage in the

middle of a lawn in need of a mow, while a bag of potting compost and a lightweight spade had been left on the grass beside a neatly cut furrow of earth.

The vista provided a stark contrast to what surely lay within the buildings over his shoulder.

Seeing no-one outside the house, he rang the bell.

He didn't have to wait long.

The door opened, and a woman in a blue anorak and skinny jeans appeared, her light-brown hair sweeping her shoulders.

'Yes?' she said, green eyes quizzical.

Gavin held up his warrant card and introduced Laura. 'Helen Peverell? We're conducting enquiries in the area in relation to an incident on Dennis Maitland's property. Can we have a word?'

The woman's brow creased a moment before her eyebrows shot upwards. 'Is this about the dead man we heard had been found? Adrian was going to call Dennis to find out what was going on.'

'It is. Is your husband in?'

'He's in the kitchen. Do you want to come through?'

'Thank you.'

He wiped his shoes on the coir mat and followed her along a plain hallway devoid of any artwork or bric-à-brac and into an airy kitchen at the back of the bungalow.

A man rose from a table beside a large refrigerator, his newspaper opened to the horse racing pages. He held out his hand. 'Adrian Peverell. Did I hear right? You're the police?'

'Yes,' said Gavin. 'We wanted to ask you and your wife a few questions about a man whose body was found in one of Dennis Maitland's fields.'

Adrian gestured to a pair of sofas that took up one side of the kitchen space next to a low table. 'Come and take a seat over here. Hot drink?'

'No, but thanks.'

He let Laura go ahead and ran his gaze over the wax-streaked candles and books that took up most of the table's surface, and glanced up as Helen Peverell sat next to her husband.

She smiled. 'We spend most of our time in here, as you can probably tell. It's often warmer than the living room in the winter. How can we help you?'

Gavin passed across the sketch of Ethan Archer. 'Have you seen this man before?'

Helen bit her lip, and angled the sketch so her husband could see. 'He doesn't look familiar. No, I don't think so. Is he the man who was found in the field?'

'Yes. We're trying to establish if he might have been wild camping in the area. Have you experienced any theft from your farm, or noticed any indication of a break-in in recent months?'

Adrian handed back the sketch and shook his head. 'I haven't, but we have CCTV cameras around the farm, and the boundaries to the yard have alarms set at night so if anyone tried to steal anything or break in, we'd know about it straight away.'

'That's quite an extensive security arrangement, Mr Peverell,' said Laura. 'Have you had trouble in the past?'

His mouth twisted. 'Animal rights campaigners, about two years ago. People don't like to know the truth about where their pet food comes from.'

'You don't sell the rabbits for human consumption?'

'No – only pet food. There are a couple of well-established businesses in the area who sell quality game meat, including rabbit. We saw a gap in the market for cheaper meat for pet food, so we're not in competition with them. Helen comes from a farming family, and my dad was a butcher—'

'—But I have to say, rabbits are a lot easier to deal with than a beef herd,' said Helen.

'I didn't know rabbits were battery farmed,' said Gavin.

'It's common practice over in Europe. That's where we got the idea from,' she said. 'Most British pet food suppliers import the rabbit meat, but we figured we could undercut the import prices and provide a cheaper alternative.'

'Is the business doing well?' said Laura.

'Extremely well,' said Adrian. 'Bit of a relief, actually – we took out one hell of a bank loan to buy the farm.'

'How many people do you have working here?'

'Not many. We have a handful of part-timers come and help when we're slaughtering the meat and getting it ready to be prepared for distribution but most of the time it's just the two of us. We can feed and maintain the battery cages and cope with the day-to-day running of the place.' Adrian shrugged. 'It helps to keep the overheads down. That's why we've been so successful – we don't employ that many people.'

'What about casual labour, backpackers, people like that?' said Gavin.

'We've had a few turn up and ask for work over the years,' said Helen. 'More so people down on their luck and looking for a bit of cash-in-hand work, but we've always turned them away. We do everything by the book here, so the part-timers go through the payroll system.'

'We simply can't afford for an inspection to have any excuse to close us down,' said Adrian. 'This is our livelihood. So, as Helen says, everything is documented and accounted for, including our workers.'

'Do you own an aircraft?' said Laura.

Adrian laughed. 'No – can't afford one for a start. And it's not like we need one farming rabbits.'

Gavin checked his notes, and then rose from the sofa and handed a business card to Adrian. 'Thank you both for your time today. I think that's everything for now, but if you think of something that might help us, or you overhear someone mentioning anything that gives you cause for concern, I'd appreciate it if you'd give me a call.'

'No problem.' Adrian stood, tucked the card into the back pocket of his jeans and gestured to the door. 'I'll show you out if you like.'

As Gavin followed Laura and the rabbit farmer out of the front door, his eyes found the low buildings opposite the house.

'Did you have any farming experience before buying this place?' he said.

'Helen does – like she said, her parents have a beef herd in Shropshire. I'd helped out at a few places while I was backpacking in Australia,' said Adrian. 'That's where I met Helen – I'm originally from Suffolk. We saw this place on the market when we got back, and it was going cheap. Still pricey – hence the bank loan – but cheaper than it would've been if the bank hadn't been about to foreclose on the previous owner's mortgage. That building over there where we keep the rabbit cages was almost falling down, but we got that fixed in the first year. The business expanded quickly after that, so we had to build another.' Adrian stuck his thumb over his shoulder at the second outbuilding. 'We use that one for processing the rabbits – slaughtering, skinning and then preparing the meat for shipment out to the pet food companies. Did you want to have a look around?'

Gavin shook his head, wondering what sort of horrors he'd have to face if he went through the double doors the farmer indicated. 'That's okay, Mr Peverell. I think we've got enough to be getting on with. Thanks for your time.'

'No problem.'

As he turned back to the car, Laura fell into step beside him and exhaled.

'Thank God,' she said. 'I thought you were going to say yes. Those poor rabbits.'

'I know, but it's how chickens are reared over here, too.'

'They're not as cute.'

'Don't tell Kay's other half that.'

CHAPTER TWENTY-SIX

A palpable frustration hung in the air as Kay's team congregated for the afternoon briefing.

Grumbles and a tendency to snap at each other had replaced their enthusiasm, and she tried to recall how Sharp had chivvied them along when she was a detective sergeant reporting to him.

She took a deep breath, and tried to keep her tone light.

'Let's make a start, everyone. I realise this is a difficult case, but we're making headway. We owe it to Ethan Archer to maintain our focus.'

She sensed it then; a change that rippled through the assembled officers and administration staff as they began to sit up straighter in their seats.

The click of pens popping, notebooks being

turned to fresh pages reached her, and then a gradual silence settled on the room.

'Thank you,' she said. 'By now, I hope you've had a chance to read through the reports from the interviews with Hugh Ditchens and the Peverells. Neither of those landowners recognised our victim, and no-one has reported any thefts or signs of wild camping on their land, either. Debbie – how did you get on with trying to locate next of kin?'

The police constable rose from her seat and raised her voice.

'I've gone through all the records, guv. His parents died thirteen years ago, and Ethan never married.'

'Any siblings?'

'I'm unable to find that out. Ethan was adopted by the Archers when he was three years old. They had no children of their own, and I can't find anything to suggest he had any natural siblings.'

'Okay, thanks.' Kay paused to check the agenda. 'Barnes – what's the latest regarding the van?'

'All house-to-house enquiries along the lane have been completed,' said the detective sergeant. 'No-one else can recall hearing a van that night – one or two residents at the far end of the road stated that they do hear vehicles driving along the lane late at night from time to time, but can't specifically identify a van, or a particular date.'

'Anything on CCTV?'

'Nothing, I'm afraid, guv. No-one along there has any security cameras – they're all private residences. There aren't any businesses along that road. The nearest one is over on the main road heading towards Hildenborough. We've checked the footage from there, but no van shows up on the evening Peter Winton mentioned.'

'What about the tyre tread marks?' said Kay. 'How are you getting on with those?'

Barnes turned to Laura and raised an eyebrow.

'We're still waiting to hear back from Patrick, guv,' she said. 'I called him a couple of hours ago, but there's a backlog. He says it might be next week before he's got anything for us.'

'What about light aircraft in the area?' said Kay. 'Anything?'

'All the registered aircraft and pilots in the area are accounted for,' said Phillip Parker. 'None of them recorded a flight that coincides with the night in question.'

Kay paced the carpet. 'Okay, in the circumstances we'll leave the van for the time being. In the absence of any corroborating evidence to support Winton's claim he heard a van that night, we're in danger of wasting time on what could have been something he dreamed up. We need to turn our focus to where Ethan Archer might've been staying before he was killed. Has anything come back from the local homeless charities, or the council?'

'No-one has a record of him,' said Gavin. 'They're struggling with a lack of funding, and it sounds like that's having an impact on the ability to keep track of homeless people in the area. He certainly didn't apply for assistance with regard to housing, according to the people we've been speaking with.'

'So, we have to start considering other options.' Kay turned and tapped the map displayed on the wall. 'In the circumstances, Gavin, I want you to work with uniform to coordinate a search of the wildlife reserve that includes the reservoir to the south of the farming land here.'

'Do you think he'd manage to camp there without being seen, guv?' said Carys.

'Possibly, at this time of year,' said Kay. 'It's been a harsh winter, so that might have contributed to low visitor numbers – only an avid birdwatcher or fisherman would have been brave enough to face these temperatures. Conversely, that could be something Ethan could have taken advantage of – it would be less likely someone would have spotted him.'

Laura raised her hand. 'Guv? Do you think he could've been deliberately hiding out in the countryside, rather than simply wild camping as an alternative to finding shelter in town? I mean, if he was scared, or hiding from someone?'

'I do, yes. We also need to consider the possibility that he wasn't staying in the area at all. If that's the case, then why did he come back here? If he's been hiding for all this time, what brought him out of cover?'

'Someone must've dangled a bloody big carrot,' said Barnes. 'Something to draw him out. When you spoke with Stephen Halsmith, did he say anything about why Ethan might've disappeared in the first place?'

'No,' said Kay. 'I don't think they were close. He said Ethan just stopped turning up at the support group, and I'm guessing he had no way of contacting him.'

'THAT WAS good work with the veterans' associations, Kay,' said Sharp, as he speared a tiger prawn with his fork. 'I don't think the council were going to provide the breakthrough we needed there.'

'Thanks, guv.' Kay took a sip from her bottle of beer, then scooped up another mouthful of rice. 'God, I'm going to have to start a diet or something at this rate. We had takeaway at home last night, too.'

'Are you still running?'

'Not enough.'

Sharp ran his thumb across the label on his beer bottle. 'We need to find out where Ethan's been these past three years or so since Halsmith said he went missing.'

'I've had Laura contact veterans' agencies within a two-hundred-mile radius this afternoon,' said Kay. 'It's taking time, but so far his details haven't raised a flag with any of them.'

'Do you think he went to ground for all that time?'

She shrugged. 'If he managed to stay healthy, find enough to eat, and had shelter, I think he could've done. Especially given his background and training.'

'And especially if he was determined not to be found.'

'Well, we've got nothing for him through the

DVLA, so he was travelling on foot – or bicycle, unless he had an unlicensed vehicle.'

'Harder to hide that.'

'I know.'

'I suppose you've already tried all the local contacts we've got in various drug programmes?'

'Yes, but I don't think Ethan would've been a habitual user anyway. Nothing was picked up on the toxicology report that Lucas appended to his post mortem findings, and he didn't note that there was any damage associated with long-term drug use.'

Sharp used a paper towel to wipe noodle juice from his chin. 'He wouldn't have been able to stay in hiding for so long if he needed a regular fix.'

'Exactly,' said Kay.

Sitting back in his chair, Sharp slid his beer bottle in circles on the desk, condensation creating a path across its surface.

'I think it's time to release his details to the public,' he said. 'It's been a week, and we've only just managed to identify him thanks to Halsmith – and that's yet to be corroborated.'

'I did ask if he'd be willing to go over to the mortuary with Barnes to verify that it is Ethan,' said Kay. 'He's agreed, but it won't be until tomorrow morning.'

'All right, so in the meantime let's get his photo –
or the sketch at least – onto the breakfast news, and
see if anyone comes forward with more information.'
He leaned forward and scrawled in his notebook.

'I'm going to ask Barnes to follow up the
Kosovan angle,' said Kay. 'I'm not aware of any
problems from within the community here in Kent,
but someone might have overheard something that
could help us.'

'Good, yes – do that. Barnes can be trusted to be
discreet.'

Kay sighed, and dropped her fork into the empty
foil container.

'And if all of that doesn't turn up anything, then
we're screwed, aren't we?'

CHAPTER TWENTY-SEVEN

A fine mist cloaked the street as Kay left the police station, heading down the steps and turning left along Palace Avenue.

She clutched the strap of her handbag over her shoulder and hugged the collar of her wool coat at her neck with her other hand, wishing she'd worn a scarf – or at least a coat that left her less exposed to the elements, such as the waxed jacket she'd left hanging on the newel post in the hallway in her haste to leave the house that morning.

Her breath fogged the damp air as she picked up her pace and turned into the short stay car park behind the Carriage Museum.

Despite her having no plans to work late, Sharp's suggestion of catching up over a meal after everyone else had drifted away made sense, and they'd spent some time mulling over Carys's decision to move on as well as the case in hand.

She appreciated that despite his elevation through the ranks to DCI, Sharp remained a good listener – and a friend she could rely upon to see problems in a new light that she might not have considered.

He had been more stoic about the fact they were about to lose their most experienced detective constable, and pragmatic about what Kay saw as disruption to the team.

Besides, until they knew what additional funding or staffing decisions could be taken by those in charge of such matters at Headquarters, they could do nothing anyway.

Kay tried to shake off her glum mood as she walked behind the vehicles that remained in the car park and headed towards the pavement that hugged the road opposite the Archbishop's Palace.

Traffic was light at this time of night, and she jogged across the one-way street behind a passing bus rather than stand and wait at the pedestrian crossing.

The path separated from the road once she passed the Registry Office and cut through the Palace grounds, the mist creating an eerie softening to the occasional noise from a passing car and shrouding the ancient gravestones that stood solemnly outside All Saints Church.

She had no fear of the dead.

It was the live monsters that crossed her path that gave her nightmares from time to time.

Suppressing a yawn, she nodded to an elderly man who walked past in the opposite direction with a terrier cross on a lead, the dog stopping to sniff at the base of the rowan and yew trees that lined the path.

The doors to the fourteenth-century church remained resolutely closed; the next service wouldn't be held until Sunday and the place wasn't open to visitors after four o'clock. Ahead, the path dog-legged right then left, past a clutter of gravestones that huddled under the trees, shrinking away from sight as they aged.

She enjoyed walking the short cut through to the College Road car park – it was reasonably well-lit, despite the street lamps resembling white blobs in the mist swirling off the river, and it gave a little respite from the concrete mass of the town centre after a day's work.

Approaching a crossroads in the path, she automatically glanced to her right and smiled.

A number of years ago, the borough council had installed Victorian-style lanterns along the Horseway leading down to the water, and in the chill night air she was reminded of a childhood story about a wardrobe and places beyond.

A split second later, she stumbled as someone barrelled into her from the direction of the car park.

Crying out from the shock, Kay tightened her grip on her handbag and wheeled around, the shout of alarm still on her lips.

'Sorry, lady. Sorry.' A hooded figure held up her hands, backing away, her face in shadow and her tone apologetic. 'I didn't mean to frighten you.'

'Watch where you're going,' Kay snapped, her heart racing.

'Sorry.'

The figure shoved her hands in her pockets, turned and jogged away through the churchyard, leaving behind a stench of unwashed clothing and body odour.

Exhaling, Kay felt heat rise to her cheeks as she looked around her, reassessing her surroundings.

No-one else was around; no-one else to witness her guilt and embarrassment at her reaction to the other woman bumping into her.

Several shelters for the homeless were nearby, and she had donated to local charities via their websites from time to time.

Yet here she was being scared out of her wits by someone who had probably just left such a place after receiving help.

'Stupid.' She berated herself under her breath, and then picked up her pace and walked under the stone archway that cut through a drystone wall and led into the car park.

By the time she reached her car, her heart rate had returned to normal.

Rummaging in her handbag, still cross at herself, she swore as she tried to angle the bag to see inside to find her keys, and failed. Exasperated, she shoved her hand in her coat pocket.

Her fingers touched the familiar metal surface of her house keys alongside the plastic fob for the car, but also something else.

Frowning, she extracted her hand and stared at the folded piece of paper in her grip.

She had no recollection of putting it in her pocket – she'd only collected the coat from the dry cleaners two weeks ago, and today was the first time she'd worn it.

Feint blue lines crossed the white page and, as she ran her thumb over the creases, she peered over the top of the car to the churchyard beyond the drystone wall.

There was no sign of the hooded woman who had bumped into her.

'Dammit.'

Kay unlocked the car, threw her bag onto the passenger seat and sat behind the wheel. Leaving the door open, she unfolded the paper under the beam from the interior light.

Her heart missed a beat as she read the writing scrawled across the page.

I know what happened to Ethan. Meet me tomorrow. 7am – amphitheatre. Come alone.

CHAPTER TWENTY-EIGHT

Kay adjusted the thick woollen scarf at her neck, cursing the fact she had forgotten to cut away the label that had been scratching against her skin.

She peered through the early morning gloom towards the town centre.

The towpath was deserted this morning, save for a pair of ducks who had swum up to her when she'd arrived five minutes ago before turning their backs in disgust at the lack of food she offered.

She checked her watch.

Two minutes to seven.

A pair of matching takeout coffee cups stood on the first of the low concrete walls that created the amphitheatre behind the Hermitage.

She had purchased them from a takeaway wagon

running a brisk trade from a lay-by on her way into town, its usual customers a gaggle of construction workers in high visibility vests.

She had laughed and joked with them as she waited in line, the aroma of bacon sandwiches too much to resist, which was why a bundle of greaseproof paper perched on top of each of the coffee cups.

Now, she wondered if the woman was going to turn up.

She sighed, and turned from the river to face the amphitheatre.

The modern structure blended into the sloping landscape up from the watercourse and towards the back of the Hermitage. Its semi-circular concrete walls were interspersed with thick lush grass in the summer that filled with people as impromptu picnics accompanied organised plays or concerts over the warmer months.

She cast her gaze over the damp muddy turf that had been churned up over the winter, and shivered.

Somewhere within the hedgerow that bordered the Hermitage, a blackbird scolded before falling silent and a robin bickered a response. The traffic was starting to build beyond the building now, the rumble of lorries thundering along College

Road as a weak daylight began to lift the darkness.

She spun around at the sound of footsteps to her right.

The woman wore an anorak, scruffy jeans and shoes that had seen better days but Kay recognised her from the night before.

She walked towards Kay, her dark eyes peering left and right, shoulders slumped as she drew near.

'I was beginning to think you'd changed your mind,' said Kay.

'I had to make sure you're on your own.'

The woman's voice was thin; reedy, as if unused and unsteady, tinged with fear. 'You are, aren't you?'

'Yes.' Kay picked up one of the coffee cups and a warm sandwich. 'I haven't had breakfast. I figured you might like something, too.'

The woman snatched the food from her, then eyed her warily.

'I haven't done anything with it,' said Kay, impatient. 'It came from the van up on the Sittingbourne Road. If you don't want it, I'll have it.'

She unwrapped the other sandwich, sank her teeth into it, and then wandered over to one of the sets of steps built into the amphitheatre's walls and sat. Standing her coffee cup on the step beside her, she watched as the woman licked grease off her fingers and bolted down the food.

A flicker of a smile flitted across her face as she scrunched up the paper bag, walked across to where Kay sat and took a sip of coffee. She wrinkled her nose.

'Sorry – I didn't know if you took sugar, so I had to guess,' said Kay.

'Doesn't matter. It's warm. Thanks.'

'You're welcome. How did you know who I am?'

'Saw you on the telly in the shelter. Asked one of the volunteers.'

'Are you local?'

'For now. I'm not hanging around, though.'

'What's your name?'

'Shelley.'

'Shelley…?'

'Just Shelley.'

'How did you know Ethan?'

The woman blinked, lowered the coffee cup and stared at the horizon as weak sunlight began to lend a warmth to the air. She swallowed. 'He saved me. Got me away.'

'From who?'

'Them.'

Kay drained the last of her coffee and pushed

herself to her feet before brushing off the back of her coat.

Shelley was about four inches shorter than her, stick thin with hollow cheekbones and a sickly pallor to her skin that was amplified by the long dark hair framing her face.

Her eyes never stopped roaming their surroundings, and she visibly jumped as a brightly clothed cyclist shot past on the towpath. The whirr from his wheels receded into the distance as she turned her attention back to Kay.

'I shouldn't have come here,' she said.

'But, here you are. What did you want to tell me about Ethan? Do you know who killed him?'

Shelley bit her lip, then shrugged. Said nothing.

'Where did you meet Ethan?' said Kay.

A sadness filled Shelley's eyes. 'Here. In Maidstone, I mean. At a shelter.'

'When?'

'I don't know. About three and half years ago. Christ – feels like a lifetime ago,' she said, her tone wistful.

'Can I ask why you were there?'

Shelley flinched. 'I wanted to get away from my boyfriend. He scared me. I had nowhere else to go.'

'Your accent – it's not Kentish.'

'Liverpool. Moved down here with my mum and dad when I was thirteen. They went back a few years ago when my nan got ill.'

'And you didn't want to go back with them?'

Shelley shook her head, her top lip curling.

'How old are you?'

'Twenty-five. You?'

'Thirty-seven.' Kay smiled. 'Probably sounds ancient to you.'

'Why did you join the police?'

Kay took the rubbish from Shelley's hands before wandering over to a nearby bin and shoved the cups and sandwich wrappers through the hole in the side. Wandering back to where the woman waited, she sighed.

'Because I wanted to help people. Because I wanted to try to make a difference.'

'And now?'

'Because I love what I do. What happened to Ethan, Shelley?'

'I told him it was too risky. I told him they'd find out.'

Kay rested her hand on the woman's arm, then pointed out a bench seat tucked away under the trees. 'Come over here, and you can tell me all about it.'

Shelley shuffled to one end of the seat, and

hugged her arms around herself as she stared across the amphitheatre. It was several moments before she began to speak, but when she did, it was as if it were a relief to get the words out.

'We were broke, all right? I'd got talking to Ethan at the shelter – a different one; the church one up the path there wasn't around back then. He seemed okay, not like some of the blokes you meet on the street. He sort of started to look out for me.' She gave a sad snort of a laugh. 'He was old enough to be my dad, but better than my dad ever was.'

Kay crossed her legs, and said nothing, waiting to understand where the conversation was going.

'We'd been hanging around for a couple of months, I suppose,' said Shelley. 'It was autumn by then, and starting to get bloody cold at night. We'd found some cash work, picking fruit for a place up near Snodland but that was all gone and I was starting to panic about how I was going to get through winter. Then one morning – must've been a Saturday – we were hanging around while the market was being set up and this bloke came up to us. Said he could give us some work. Indoors, too. Told us if we were interested to be there the next morning at four o'clock and he'd drive us.'

'Where to?'

'I don't know the name of the place.' Her gaze fell to her hands, which she twisted in her lap. 'It was dark, and I'm not good at remembering stuff like that. It's why I didn't bother with school much.'

'You went with him?'

'Yes. So did Ethan.' Shelley's bottom lip trembled. 'I figured if I was with him, I'd be safe.'

'What happened?'

'We went. We never came back.'

'What do you mean?'

The woman turned to face her. 'They kept us there. Indoors. Working all hours. I-I thought I was going to die there.'

Kay leaned back as the realisation hit her. 'You were kept as slaves.'

'Yes.'

'But you got away. How?'

'Ethan. He planned it. For years. Kept chipping away at it, trying to work out all the things that could go wrong. And then one night he came up to me and told me where to wait. Said that was it. We were going.'

'What happened, Shelley? What went wrong?'

Tears spilled over the woman's cheeks, and she wiped at them with the sleeve of her anorak. 'I got away. He didn't.'

'Where was this, Shelley? Who was keeping you captive?'

Shelley's head snapped around at a shout from the pedestrian bridge further down the towpath. Rising to her feet, she sniffed, and then looked down at Kay.

'Shelley, where were they keeping you? What were you doing for them?'

'I can't stay here. I've got to go.'

'Shelley, wait!' Kay rose from the seat, but the woman was already running towards the towpath, her pace surprisingly quick. 'Bloody hell.'

She watched as the woman disappeared from sight, and wondered how the hell she was going to explain what she had learned to Sharp.

CHAPTER TWENTY-NINE

Six hours later, Kay followed Sharp into a conference room that looked like it had been subjected to a tornado and was taking a while to recover from the shock.

'Sorry,' said Michelle, an administrative assistant who had met them at reception and shown them up the stairs and along a dingy corridor. 'Traffic had a briefing in here this afternoon, and it ran over. We haven't had time to tidy up yet.'

Kay noticed Sharp's mouth narrow. Evidently his old military habits were being battened down for the sake of politeness, because he ran his gaze over the discarded cups, paper plates and screwed-up napkins and then forced a smile.

'Not to worry, it happens,' he said. 'Do the others know we're here?'

'Yes, they won't keep you long.'

She hurried from the room without a backwards glance, and Kay grinned.

'If you fetch the wastepaper basket from under the window, I'll make a start.'

'You read my mind.'

'I thought you were going to have a coronary.'

She rolled up her sleeves, swiped a couple of clean napkins from a dispenser next to a coffee urn on a table to the side of the room, and began to sweep crumbs from the conference table before lobbing them into the bin Sharp held out. While he tipped the leftover food and paper plates into it, she gathered up the discarded mugs and lined them up on the table, turning to survey their efforts.

'Not bad.' She turned her attention to the corridor at the sound of voices outside.

Sharp dropped the bin back under the window and grinned. 'It'll have to do – hopefully Michelle will sort out fresh supplies.'

Kay rolled her eyes. 'I thought it was us lot who were understaffed at the moment, not the admin team as well.'

'The cuts are hitting everyone. I heard they were

having trouble getting temporary staff in to provide holiday cover this year, too.'

'Jesus.'

She straightened her jacket as two men entered the conference room, Michelle behind them.

'DCI Sharp, DI Hunter, this is Detective Sergeant Colin Maxwell from the Serious and Organised Crimes division, and PC Mark Weston from the Rural Task Force. I'll leave you to sort yourselves out while I refill the coffee urn.'

Kay shook hands with the two men before they all took their seats, and Sharp opened the meeting.

'Gents, thanks for coming at short notice.'

'Not a problem,' said Maxwell, easing back into his seat. 'You mentioned on the phone you've got an investigation underway?'

'Yes. We have an ongoing murder enquiry that, based on recent intelligence, suggests to us that we may have an active modern slavery problem that's gone unnoticed for a number of years.' He handed over photographs of Ethan Archer, as well as copies of Kay's statement regarding her meeting with Shelley earlier that day and waited while Maxwell and Weston read through the details. 'To date, we've ascertained that Archer was sleeping rough in the Sevenoaks area but also frequented Maidstone –

especially in the colder months, as there was more access to shelters here. Three to four years ago, he disappeared without a trace and if we're given to believe Shelley's claims, both of them were coerced into forced labour at an agricultural establishment of some sort. Archer has a military background but was demobbed in ninety-nine.'

Kay unfolded a map of the area where Ethan's body had been found and turned it so the two officers could see. 'Archer's body was discovered here, and we've spoken to three landowners to date: the farmer whose field Archer's body was found in, and the two adjacent properties. We've currently got a search team working their way through the reservoir, here.'

'At first, we thought Archer's death might have something to do with his rescue of some women and children during the Kosovan war,' said Sharp. 'Retaliation by one of the warlords, perhaps.'

'I was approached by someone – Shelley – out of the blue on Wednesday night, and met with her this morning. She was extremely nervous, but did state that Archer helped her to escape from their captors.' Kay placed her hand on Ethan's photograph. 'According to Shelley, Archer didn't make it. He was recaptured, and she suspected the worst.'

'Does she know where they were being held?' said Maxwell.

'She says it was dark when they were picked up, and she can't remember any names of places they passed through. Something spooked her while we were talking, and she took off before answering my questions about the location where they were held and the work they were doing. We've tasked our team with going around to all the shelters in the area to see if we can locate her.'

'Do you think her life is in danger?'

'Yes. Yes, I do. Her story corroborates the timeline we've got from other witnesses regarding Archer's original disappearance, and she seemed frightened enough that she ran off when she heard someone shouting while I was talking to her – she's very skittish.'

'I don't recall anything coming through on the Country Eye,' said Weston, frowning.

'Country Eye?' said Sharp. 'What's that?'

Weston pulled his phone from his vest and spun it around on the desk until it faced Kay and Sharp, then tapped an app on the screen. 'It's an app we developed with some partner organisations so that people in rural areas can report suspicious activity and ongoing crimes. The staff who monitor the reports lodged on the app have been trained by Kent Police so that if anything gives them cause for concern, they can escalate it and we'll investigate.'

'And you've had nothing about an agricultural slavery gang?' said Sharp.

'No – a couple of car washes were reported recently but turned out to be legitimate, although lousy working conditions so they did receive a warning from one of the partner organisations, but nothing like a slavery gang.'

Sharp frowned. 'Based on the location of Ethan's body, I'm not inclined to think they were used by a nail bar or a car wash outfit. If they were kept hidden for over three years, then they've been kept out of sight and are working indoors—'

'Or at night,' said Weston.

'How might the slavery gang have kept it from us finding out?' said Kay.

Weston looked across to Maxwell, who gestured to him to continue.

'Well, often it's similar to any other slavery cases such as the nail bars. A gang might set up a business as a recruitment agency that looks legitimate on the outside, but then they use it to organise cheap labour.'

'The farming industry is one of the high-risk areas

we monitor on a regular basis,' said Maxwell. 'Especially around here – you've got seasonal workers coming from all over to work, and they're desperate, so they'll take the crap wages and working conditions. It's a growing problem. We're seeing a dramatic year-on-year increase for slavery in the food and farming industry.'

'Which particular sectors are you seeing these cases in?' said Sharp.

'Fruit and vegetable picking, any of the animal production sectors,' said the detective sergeant. 'It used to be the case that we'd see a lot of Eastern European forced labour, but now we're finding it's people from the UK as well who are trapped in these circumstances, simply because they're desperate for work and then it's too late to get out. It's more lucrative than drug trafficking, and more and more victims are British. We should have the same resources as a kidnapping case to combat the problem, but it just doesn't happen.'

'How does your team try to stop this happening?' said Kay.

'Often, it's based on us being told,' said Weston. 'Certainly from the rural aspect, anyway – it's harder to monitor what goes on in the countryside compared to urban areas.'

'So, unless someone comes to you for help, you can't do anything?'

'Exactly,' said Maxwell. 'We've got our own intelligence officers working undercover, but you know what the budget cuts are like – we can't be everywhere, and we've got limited resources to act on what information we do come across.'

Kay drummed her fingers on the desk for a moment, then glanced at Sharp. 'What if I could persuade Shelley to talk to you, to tell you what she knows?'

'That's a start,' said Maxwell. 'You'd also need to widen the parameters of your investigation, if you don't mind me saying so. You'd want to start looking at all the farms in the area, not just those close to where Archer's body was found – including searches of the outbuildings.'

Sharp scratched his chin, and wrote in his notebook. 'That's going to take a considerable amount of time and manpower, Colin.'

'I realise that, guv, but unless this Shelley person approaches DI Hunter again, I think it's your best way forward. You don't have any way of contacting her, do you?'

'No.' Kay sighed, then rolled her shoulders. 'What happens if she does talk?'

'We'd be able to put her in touch with one of the partner organisations to give her some support,' said Maxwell. 'Typically, that means a roof over her head for ninety days and a care worker to help her adjust and get back on her feet. It's not much, but some of the charities are working with government organisations to try to offer a longer housing period. And, of course, we'd offer her protection while we work with you to prosecute the gang masters and bring them to trial.'

'How successful have you been at trial?' said Sharp.

'Working with the Crown Prosecution Service, we reckon on a sixty-seven per cent conviction rate.'

'We could use some help working this investigation to make sure we hit that percentile.'

'Anything you need.' Maxwell pointed at Ethan's photograph. 'Whoever did this to him deserves to be put away for a long time.'

CHAPTER THIRTY

Gavin stepped to one side, held open the door for Laura and then followed her into the brightly lit community hall.

Food aromas mixed with the smell of damp clothes drying out, and the whole space thrummed with low voices in conversation.

Temporary beds had been laid out in lines along two walls, a screen separating the women from the men to allow a modicum of privacy, while bundles of sleeping bags, blankets and pillows were being gathered by volunteers from those beds whose occupants had already left the shelter for the day.

Laura paused next to a desk that had been set up near the door, a shocked expression crossing her features.

'I didn't realise it'd be so busy.'

'This is only one of them,' he said. 'There are another two near the town centre. And it's still winter – I'd imagine they're going to be packed at night for a few weeks yet.'

'You the police?'

Gavin turned to see a wiry man in his late forties eyeing them from the end of a camping bed, one boot on, the other poised ready and an unlit roll-up between his lips.

His features were cracked and lined, hardened by the winter chill, but his tone was light, interested.

'We are. We were hoping to speak to one of the volunteers.'

The man shoved his foot in the boot and rose to his feet with a groan. He stretched, and jerked his chin towards the far end of the hall. 'They'll be serving breakfast for another half an hour or so.'

'Ta.'

'No problem.' He bent down to pick up a battered sports bag and began to throw his belongings inside. 'Someone in trouble?'

'I hope not. We're trying to find her to help her.'

'Oh?' The man paused, a paperback book in his hand, and raised an eyebrow. 'Who?'

'Shelley. Do you know her? Has a Liverpool accent. Mid-twenties.'

'Rings a bell.' The man tucked the cigarette behind his ear and stuck out his hand. 'I'm Jeremy.'

'Nice to meet you.' Gavin introduced Laura, and then gestured to a cluster of tables near the desk where others were gathering with mugs of hot drinks. 'Got a minute to have a chat?'

Jeremy grinned, exposing a missing upper tooth. 'My schedule appears to be clear this morning, so why not?'

'I'll get the drinks,' said Laura. 'How'd you take yours?'

'Milk, no sugar, love, thanks. Sweet enough already.'

Gavin waited while the man swept up the last of his clothes and zipped the bag before leading the way over to a table in the far corner, away from the rest of the people.

'This a regular place for you to stay?' he said as Jeremy sank onto the chair next to him.

'Yeah. As long as you get here early in the evening, you can usually get a bed for the night.' He winked. 'They don't take block bookings.'

'Can I ask why you're on the streets?'

'Fell out with the missus.' He shrugged. 'I lost my

business when the crash happened a few years ago. Slept in the car for a bit, then sold it 'cause I needed the money. It all went downhill from there.'

'I'm sorry to hear that.'

'It is what it is. I'm hoping to hear that I'm going to get a flat in the next few weeks. I've never been in trouble with you lot, so that works in my favour. Problem is, there are so many others who need a roof over their head. Women, children. Us blokes tend to have to wait.'

Gavin let his gaze wander over the heads of the groups sitting around the tables and spotted Laura at the far end of the hall, chatting to three volunteers who were manning the tea urns and doling out breakfasts.

'Why'd you want to be a copper, anyway?' said Jeremy.

'My dad was one.' He turned his attention back to the man. 'Seemed like a good idea at the time.'

Jeremy cackled and slapped the table before pointing a finger at him. 'I like you. So, what's Shelley gone and done, then?'

'How do you know her?'

'Just in passing, you know?' He waved his hand towards the expanse of the hall. 'You get to know a few familiar faces coming to the shelters. In summer, it's different. Some of the shelters aren't open, so you have to make do. Anyway, I spotted her a couple of weeks ago. I think she stood out because she was new. Like she had no idea what to do when she got here. Me and a couple of the women got her sorted out and signed up with a couple of the other charities, too, so she stands a good chance of getting a roof over her head at night.'

'Did she say where she'd been?'

'No, not really.' Jeremy's eyes softened. 'It's not like we're friends. I mean, if someone doesn't cause you any trouble then you look out for them. Doesn't mean we hang out together, like the youngsters say.'

He broke off as Laura walked towards them and set three steaming mugs on the table before divvying them out.

'Fabulous, lass. Cheers.'

'No problem. Got you some biscuits, too.' She grinned. 'Can't have tea without something to dunk in it.'

'You'll make someone a wonderful wife someday.'

'Jeremy was telling me he's seen Shelley a few times over the past couple of weeks,' said Gavin. 'Do you know what her surname is?'

'No. Never asked. One of the others might know.'

The man craned his neck. 'Can't see them here, so they must've left for the day. I can ask them tonight, though if you like? If they come here, that is.'

'That'd be great, thanks.'

Laura reached into her bag and pulled out the sketch of Ethan Archer. 'Do you recognise this man?'

Jeremy took it from her, then frowned. 'No, I've not seen him.'

'We think he was around three or four years ago. He might've come into Maidstone.'

'Ah, then no – I wasn't on the streets back then. He in trouble as well?'

'You could say that.'

Jeremy looked from Laura to Gavin, and then leaned back in his seat. 'Oh. Like that, is it?'

'Yes, unfortunately.'

'Right.' The man ran a hand over his chin. 'I wonder... There was a bloke Shelley mentioned. Sounded like she was close to him. She got right upset, and then clammed up. Didn't mention it again.'

'When was this?'

'Soon after she first turned up here. She wouldn't talk about it after that.'

'You've been a great help, thanks Jeremy,' said Gavin, and slid a business card across the desk. 'Do me a favour? Let me know if you see Shelley again, or know where we might find her.'

'She in trouble?' The man flicked the card between his fingers.

'Not with us. We're trying to protect her.'

'All right, then I will.'

'Thanks. And if you need anything, phone that number. I'll see what I can do.'

CHAPTER THIRTY-ONE

Kay ran her eye over the weary expressions on her team's faces, and vowed to keep the briefing as short as possible.

Attention spans were beginning to wane, and she knew from experience that it was vital to maintain their energy and focus. Mistakes would happen otherwise. Small errors, perhaps, here and there, but a vital lead could be missed if she wasn't careful.

'You know, if my old form teacher at school could see your faces, he'd have you all doing star jumps,' she said as she reached the front of the room.

A ripple of polite laughter filled the space, and she smiled. 'Let's get down to business, then. Barnes – how did you get on this morning with Stephen Halsmith?'

The detective sergeant pushed back his chair, buttoning his jacket as he stood. 'Halsmith positively identified our victim as Ethan Archer. He also provided me with a few names of places – shelters, drop-in centres and the like – that he remembers Ethan visiting from time to time before he disappeared. I'm working my way through that list to find out which ones are still open, and whether anyone is around who recalls the name.'

'Thanks, Ian. Gavin – you're next.'

'Guv. Laura and I have spent the day visiting as many of the shelters in the Maidstone and district areas as possible. We've learned that Shelley has been seen in recent days at one of the shelters there, and one of the blokes who uses the shelter has said he'll keep an eye out for her and ask her to get in touch. He's got a note of my number. We're trying to find out where she might be staying so we can interview her formally – unless you want to do that one?'

'I think in the circumstances, given how skittish she was yesterday morning, that I'd like to be involved,' said Kay. 'Good work, though. Anything else to report?'

Laura rose to her feet. 'We've spoken with one of the housing associations who work with vulnerable people and they've undertaken to provide her with somewhere to live for a while if we manage to get this case to court. It might only be for a few weeks, though. It's not perfect but——'

'It's something, at least. Thanks.' Kay gestured to two figures hovering at the fringes of the crowded space. 'Everyone, I'd like to introduce you to DS Colin Maxwell and DC Mark Weston, who will be joining our team for the duration of this investigation.'

Maxwell nodded in response, and held up his hand so the team members could see him amongst the throng.

'Colin brings a wealth of experience in dealing with modern slavery cases, and Mark has been with the Rural Crimes team for the past two years. They'll probably have some ideas about how we can angle this investigation and pursue lines of enquiry we might have overlooked. Debbie – could you spend some time this afternoon, please, bringing them up to date with what we have so far?'

'Will do, guv.'

'Colin, do you want to wander over here and we'll share what we've discussed prior to this briefing?'

'Thanks, guv.' Maxwell weaved between the rows of chairs until he stood in front of the whiteboard.

'I'll give a brief overview for those of you I

haven't met before. For the past six years, I've been leading one of the teams based out of Headquarters tasked with tackling the increasing modern slavery problem we're experiencing in Kent – both here in West Division, and working closely with East and North Divisions. We've had some breakthroughs in relation to the gangs operating between here and Eastern Europe, but with the UK leaving the EU we're seeing an increasing problem with domestic slavery cases as well. Through the initiatives we've been implementing with other agencies – especially Border Force – there's been a slight decrease in boat arrivals over the past year, but we're getting more reports of people falling into slavery or poor working conditions who are UK citizens. Having met with DI Hunter and DCI Sharp yesterday to discuss Ethan Archer's murder and the subsequent investigation to date, it's my view that what you have here is a clear case of someone being coerced into work, and then held against their will as a slave.'

'Thanks, Colin.' Kay waited until he retook his place next to Weston, and then continued. 'We also discussed the type of work Ethan – and Shelley – might have been made to do. Given the fact that they've been missing for over three years with no sighting of them by people they knew prior to that time, we have to assume that they've been kept somewhere that was under cover, and away from the public eye.'

'So we can discount nail bars, car washes, and places like takeaway food shops,' said Barnes, his pen pausing above his notebook.

'Exactly.' Kay gestured to the map of the crime scene. 'Based on Ethan's build, we can assume he was used for physical work. Shelley, being smaller, may have been used for vegetable or fruit picking. If they weren't working indoors, they could have been made to work at night to lower the risk of being seen.'

'It also lends itself to the fact that food and other supplies could be purchased for the workers without raising suspicion,' said Weston. 'A lot of farms provide meals and sometimes lodgings for workers, so it wouldn't seem out of the ordinary.'

'I'll liaise with uniform and organise a wider search of neighbouring farming properties,' said Gavin. 'We need to return to the three landowners we've already spoken to, but I'll arrange visits to any farms producing vegetables, fruit and then factor in animal producers such as dairy farms and chickens – anything that can be farmed inside a building.'

'Thanks, that's perfect. Mark – can you give him a hand with that?'

Weston nodded in response.

'Barnes – while they're investigating that angle, I want you to work with me to arrange another group of officers to monitor the markets over this weekend. Find out the location of the bigger ones, and let's monitor them to see if anyone's still trying to illegally recruit workers like Shelley alleged. If they're two workers down with Ethan's murder and Shelley's escape, they might be trying to find replacements.'

'Will do, guv.'

'Laura, your job is to find Shelley. Check CCTV images from Wednesday night between the Archbishop's Palace, the river and the town centre. Then do the same for Thursday morning. I've uploaded my reports of both incidents to HOLMES2 so you'll be able to get the descriptions of what she was wearing from those.'

'Guv.'

Kay jotted the new angles of investigation onto the whiteboard and then turned to the newest member of the team.

'I can't stress how important it is that we locate her, Laura. Ethan's killer is still out there, and if Shelley knows something she hasn't yet told us, then she's in grave danger.'

CHAPTER THIRTY-TWO

Laura zipped up her black quilted coat and stalked along Palace Avenue, gritting her teeth as a bracing wind whipped off the River Medway and smacked her cheeks.

Unable to shake the fug that clouded her thoughts since the briefing, she decided to get some fresh air and gain a sense of understanding of Shelley's potential points of egress before sitting in front of a computer screen for the rest of the day.

CCTV cameras would only show her so much – she wanted to walk the exact routes Kay had noted within her reports.

She tapped her foot as she waited for the pedestrian crossing lights to turn green, not willing to risk her life dodging the traffic as Kay had done on

Wednesday night. Mid-afternoon on a Friday was bedlam as the town ratcheted up a gear into an early commuter rush amongst the rumour of a rain-free weekend.

Hurrying across as soon as she heard the familiar *zap*, she slowed as she approached the entrance to the car park for the Registry Office and pulled out her phone.

Snapping photographs of the cameras fixed to streetlights above some of the vehicles, she narrowed her eyes and gauged the angle the cameras were able to view, and then moved onwards, tracing her DI's steps and making a note of each camera she spotted. A sense of unease seized her as she reached All Saints Church.

She lifted her head to the ornate architraves and buttresses that projected from the stonework, but could see no indication of security measures taken by the diocese.

Pacing back from the door until she stood under the yew trees, Laura used her phone to trace her footsteps from the direction of the Registry Office, past the church and onwards to the footpath.

Pausing the video she'd taken, she stood aside for a gaggle of tourists heading in the opposite direction, and then stood on the footpath leading down to the river. Turning her back to the waterway, she ran her gaze over the busy junction with Knightrider Street.

She snapped photos of the cameras she could see fixed to two of the streetlights in that direction, then turned back to the church, pulled out her notebook and wrote down the route she had taken so far.

Where she stood was where Kay had turned and watched Shelley's figure retreat into the darkness.

Laura sniffed to counteract the effect of the cold air, and walked down to the river before turning left and following the path.

Moments later, she stood at the edge of the amphitheatre and turned around. Facing the towpath that led along the back of the church and Archbishop's Palace towards the town centre, she had a clear view of Shelley's escape route the previous morning.

Kay had noted in her report that she hadn't seen the woman cross the pedestrian bridge, so Laura set out along the path.

A floating restaurant and bar bobbed forlornly on the current, deserted save for the crew who swarmed over the decks cleaning and preparing for the Friday evening crowd that would descend on the place come sundown.

Beyond that, she passed the brightly coloured

passenger boat that conveyed tourists up and down the River Medway, noting a cluster of people huddled against the elements while they waited for the rope across the gangplank to be lowered so they could board and shelter within the fibreglass awning, smart phones and digital cameras at the ready.

Passing a motley collection of abandoned picnic tables placed beside signs for ice cream that snapped in the wind, Laura headed towards the busy road bridge that loomed ahead.

A throng of stop-start traffic filtering into four lanes swept above her head prior to being spat out in all directions east and north of the town centre.

She paused beside the concrete pylon and once more lifted her phone at an angle to catch the CCTV cameras fixed to the streetlights above, then hurried up the footpath and crossed the road.

Back at the incident room, she set her jaw as she peered at the monitors in front of her.

Three computer screens ran simultaneously, all displaying a sequence of camera angles filmed at the same time on Wednesday night.

She watched as Kay left the police station and walked along Palace Avenue towards All Saints Church, then disappeared from sight under the trees as she used the shortcut through to the public car park in front of the Hermitage.

Time held as she waited for Kay to emerge from the other side, past the archway cut into the stone wall that bordered the footpath down to the river.

Checking the images she'd saved to her phone, she flicked back and forth while keeping an eye on the CCTV recording.

Eventually, Kay reappeared and moved towards her car.

Laura watched as her DI paused, then pulled her hand from her pocket and looked back towards the archway. She stopped the recording, wound it back and then peered at the screen once more, focusing on the churchyard.

Finding nothing and exasperated with her search, she stopped the recording and switched over to those from Thursday morning. Sure enough, there was Kay parking her car just before seven o'clock outside the Hermitage once more.

Laura changed to a camera angle that gave her a clear view of the amphitheatre on the river side of the building. She ran the recording forward until Shelley appeared in the bottom left-hand corner, and settled in to watch.

The woman paced back and forth, arms hugged

around her waist as she spoke with Kay, but Laura noted there was no hesitation in her movements when the DI handed her the coffee and sandwich.

She moved closer to the screen as the conversation between the two women drew to a close – reading Kay's statement, she knew roughly when to expect Shelley to turn tail and head for the towpath, but the speed at which the woman moved away from the amphitheatre caught her by surprise.

She hit the "rewind" button, then replayed the last few moments before clicking on a set of controls to bring up new CCTV camera angles.

Shelley disappeared from sight within a minute of leaving Kay, weaving underneath the main road bridge and then—

Nothing.

Nothing at all.

Laura swore loudly and shoved her mouse and keyboard across the desk away from her in frustration.

'Bloody hell. She knew where the cameras were.'

CHAPTER THIRTY-THREE

Kay spun around at a loud snap, then relaxed as she saw one of the stallholders manhandling a plastic tarpaulin that had broken free from an awning across from where she sheltered within the doorway to a derelict discount kitchenware shop.

The morning chill clung to her fingers and toes, creating an ache in her stomach and leaving her earlobes numb.

Barnes stamped his feet next to her, grumbling under his breath.

'How many do we have on surveillance?' she said.

'Ten, plus us. Six indoors, the rest out here.' He frowned. 'It's not enough, I know, not with covering the car boot fair as well.'

'It is what it is.' Kay rubbed at tired eyes and blinked.

Her alarm had gone off at five-thirty that morning, giving her enough time to shower and dress in the warmest clothes she could find before heading to the market when it opened to stallholders at six o'clock.

'Anything at the farmers' market yesterday?' she said.

'No – we were there too late. They start packing up after lunchtime, and Maxwell reckons that based on what Shelley told you, anyone after cheap labour would be around early, so they don't draw attention to themselves. He's planning to have a team wandering around that one next week, just in case.'

'We need to get some results before then.' Kay turned her back as the market trader attached the tarpaulin to the metal framework of his stall, and nudged Barnes. 'Come on. Let's have another walk around. My toes are numb.'

She ran her gaze over the gaudy-coloured signs and awnings that jostled for space on the concrete apron outside the cafés and shops that lined the street.

Olive oil suppliers traded alongside cheese merchants and winemakers, while the smell of fresh vegetables and baked goods soaked the air as she passed. Someone, somewhere, was frying sausages and as they turned the corner, she spotted the food wagons.

'I've died and gone to heaven,' said Barnes.

'Pia will never forgive me if I let you near that lot. Keep moving.'

He grinned, and then led the way down a narrow path created by two lines of stalls. 'I'm surprised this is so popular, given the usual Saturday market over at Lockmeadow.'

'I suppose traders might switch between the two – they'd get a different crowd of customers, won't they?'

'This isn't as well organised, though – look.' He paused and pointed at a pile of discarded burlap sacks and rope that cluttered the pavement beyond the stalls they walked past.

'Well, given Maxwell's feedback, this is the sort of place we might expect people like Shelley's captors to hang around. They're going to avoid the other market, aren't they? The council keeps a tight control on that one.'

'I think so. I sent over a team of four to that one anyway. I expect they'll have a quiet morning but I didn't want to leave anything to chance. Not while Shelley's still out there somewhere.'

Kay wrinkled her nose and cast her eyes over the

throng of people that swarmed between the different market areas, chattering loudly and laden with tote bags and cardboard boxes.

'I hope she's okay. I can't imagine what she's been through, or how on earth she's going to fend for herself if someone's looking for her. I just wish she'd told me more. I could've done something to help, or at least worked with Maxwell's team to put her somewhere safe until we'd cleared all this up.'

'You did your best,' said Barnes, his tone kindly. 'And she knows where to find you, right? She's already tracked you down once.'

'I know, but it worries me I haven't heard from her for two days now, Ian.' She paused when they reached the end of the row of stalls and ran her gaze over the expanse of awnings. 'We're going to have to split up the teams to tackle the smaller markets from tomorrow morning if we have no success here. What reports have we had in so far from the other markets in the area?'

Barnes pulled out his phone and scrolled through his messages. 'Three arrested for pickpocketing at Tonbridge, one twelve-year-old kid cautioned for misbehaviour in Tunbridge Wells who then got an earful from his mum when she turned up, and an arrest forty minutes ago – someone carrying a knife in Sevenoaks.'

Kay sighed. 'The usual, then.'

'Shall we circle back to where Maxwell and his lot are based?'

'Yes.' She fell into step beside her colleague, biting back her disappointment.

After a few moments of walking against the direction of the crowd, she spotted the other detective sergeant beside a newsagents, his phone to his ear.

'Tell you what, guv, I'll fetch us all some coffee,' said Barnes. 'I'll catch up with you.'

'Thanks, Ian. Sounds like a great idea. I can defrost my fingers at least.'

She watched her DS head over to a van selling hot drinks, and then waited until Maxwell had finished his call and wandered over.

'Any luck?'

He shook his head, and put his phone in his pocket. 'Nothing at this end, and I hear there's been no news from the other markets. It was a long shot, anyway. Whoever's been recruiting from the markets in the past might be keeping out of the way for the time being.'

'And we've only got Shelley's word for it that they were recruited from a market,' said Kay.

'It was worth following up,' said Maxwell. 'And it doesn't hurt to have a presence here – it might encourage others to come forward if they know we're interested.'

'That's a very charitable way of putting it. I hope you don't think today was a waste of your officers' time.'

'It's never a waste of time, guv. Not when people's lives are at risk.'

'Here you go.' Barnes joined them and handed out the hot drinks, placing the cardboard tray in a recycling bin outside a shop. He took a sip, and then frowned. 'Maybe we've got this all wrong. I mean, if people don't escape that often, they won't need to recruit more people, will they?'

'I suppose so. I wonder what stops them from escaping, though?' said Kay. 'I mean, it's an awful situation to find yourself in.'

Maxwell grimaced, his takeaway coffee cup halfway to his lips.

'Fear,' he said. 'The gangs instil terror in these people. The last thing on their minds is escape. They're simply trying to survive.'

CHAPTER THIRTY-FOUR

Kay spun her chair from side to side, leafing through the reports she'd printed out of HOLMES2 following that morning's surveillance of local markets, and bit back a sigh.

The last team members had returned to the incident room half an hour ago as the stallholders had packed away their wares at the market in Sevenoaks, and were now starting to gather by the whiteboard, their conversation a low murmur.

Exhaustion seeped into the atmosphere in the room, and despite her concerns for Shelley's safety, she knew she would have to take drastic action to ensure her team remained focused.

Dropping the last report to her desk, she pushed

back her chair and wandered over to where they congregated.

'Okay, let's do this briefing and then I'm splitting the team into two for the remainder of the weekend. Debbie, can you make the necessary changes to the roster for me?'

'Will do, guv.'

'It's three o'clock now, so we'll run a pared down shift this afternoon and evening, with the remainder of you to keep your phones on at all times. Just because you're getting an early pass doesn't mean you won't be called in. I want everyone on standby in case we get a breakthrough, understood?'

A mumble of consent swept through the room, and she waited for them to settle once more.

'Laura – any luck with that CCTV footage?'

The young detective constable shook her head. 'I ran through it again this morning while you were all out at the markets, and I obtained some new film from the council as well. Shelley knew where all the cameras were – she might've only been back in town a week or so, but she's street-smart.'

'Anything from the shelters?'

'Nothing, guv,' said Gavin. 'All the organisers and volunteers have been asked to keep a lookout for her, and we've let them know we think her life is in danger, but so far nothing at all.'

Kay leaned against the desk and peered at the whiteboard, her gaze resting on the photograph of Ethan Archer's mangled body.

'We can't give up on her,' she said. 'She's out there, somewhere. She'll be scared, paranoid – she just won't have the energy to stay ahead of these people if she doesn't get help soon.'

'Do you think she's left Maidstone?' said Barnes.

'I don't think so. If she's telling the truth about all this – and I'm inclined to believe her – then despite being held for three years or more, she's familiar with the town.' Kay began to pace the carpet tiles in front of her team, her eyes tracing the faded blue-tinged whorls of colour. 'Having said that, it depends how much money she's been able to beg off the streets since last week when she said she escaped.'

'If she's trying to keep out of sight for fear of being caught, then she might not have much money,' said Laura.

'True, but if she has managed to get some cash together, she's got two mainline train stations and a bus station to choose from.'

'I haven't seen her on the CCTV images I've

checked outside those, but I can take another look, guv.'

'Do it, please. And get two of our colleagues from uniform here to help you so you've got fresh pairs of eyes on that footage.'

'Thanks, guv.'

Kay nodded at her young protégée, pleased that Laura had taken the advice well. Having spent the past twenty-four hours looking at the same camera angles, it would be all too easy to miss something.

'Okay, that's it for today. Check the new roster with Debbie and if your name isn't on it, then I'll see you tomorrow.'

A flurry of activity swept through the room as officers moved away, and Kay bit her lip as she watched them begin to drift towards Debbie's desk.

After the assignments were handed out, some headed towards the door with a bounce in their step and others returned to their computers, resolved to make some headway over the rest of the afternoon.

Barnes wandered over to her and smiled. 'Go on, get lost, guv. You look dead on your feet.'

She smiled, and shook her head. 'Sorry – I was miles away for a moment there.'

'Like I said, get yourself home. I'll stay here until

six and then the night team can run the place. You're
no good to us if you're tired.'

'Cheeky. Isn't that one of my lines?'

'It's a good one.'

'YOU'RE WORRIED ABOUT HER.'

Kay's hand dived into the bucket of pellets Adam
held out before letting the feed run over her fingers.
'Yes.'

'If she's managed to survive for three years as a
slave worker and escape, perhaps she's just keeping
her head down. Maybe something scared her on
Thursday when she was talking to you, and she's
biding her time.'

'Maybe.'

'She knows where to find you, right?'

'Only in person. I never got the chance to give her
my card.'

Adam gave her a nudge with his elbow. 'Just as
well you came by here on the way home. You'd have
only sat there worrying about her. I know what you're
like. Being around this lot should take your mind off
her for a while.'

'That's what I hoped.' Kay tossed the pellets into the stainless steel trough and stood back as three miniature goats tumbled over each other to be first to the food. 'Christ, you'd think this lot hadn't been fed for a week.'

'I know – and this is the second lot today. Plus all the kitchen scraps we've been bringing in for them.'

Kay grinned and looked across the network of pens Adam had constructed at the rear of his veterinary practice when he'd first opened for business several years ago.

Beyond the goats' pen, two pigs snorted as they furrowed amongst a bed of straw that had been laid out under a wooden shelter, and a donkey raised its velvety nose as they moved along the paddock towards him.

'At this rate, you could open a petting zoo. You'd make a fortune,' she said.

'That's what Stephanie said earlier this week. I think if she had her way, she'd have the brochures already designed and on shelves at the tourist information office.'

Kay laughed.

Adam's receptionist was in her fifties and ran the front-of-house part of the business as well as an incident room manager. The owner of a smallholding with her husband and a qualified book-keeper,

Stephanie was referred to by Adam as his secret weapon against any competitors.

Kay reached out and squeezed his arm. 'You've achieved a lot here. I'm so proud of you.'

He grinned, then kissed her on the cheek.

'Oi, we'll have none of that lovey-dovey stuff out there,' came a shout from the back of the surgery. 'Not in front of the patients.'

Kay turned to see Scott Mildenhall peering out from one of the windows, a mock shocked expression on his face.

'Peeping Tom!'

The junior veterinarian grinned, and held up a four-pack of lager. 'It's beer o'clock. Want one?'

'On our way,' said Adam. 'Just got the pigeon to check.'

'Pigeon?' said Kay.

'Yes – he flew into someone's patio windows yesterday afternoon and completely stunned himself. We've just had him here overnight to keep an eye on him. He should be fine. You go inside – I'll be there in a minute. It's getting cold out here.'

Kay brushed pellet dust from her hands and traipsed along the tree-bark-lined path to the back of the surgery, thanking Scott as he held open the door for her.

'We haven't got any glasses,' he said. 'Sorry – we only tend to keep a few beers in the fridge for emergencies, and you look like you need one.'

'That bad, eh? I'll wash my hands and join you before we head home to feed those fox cubs.'

Moments later, the three of them were gathered on the sofas in the empty reception area, a dull glow from the back office lending a warmth to the room while they relaxed.

Kay picked at the label on the side of her beer bottle and then jerked up her head at the sound of her name.

'Sorry, I was thinking. What did you say?'

'I said, I'll bet that despite having a team that you can rely on, you'll be back at work in the morning.' Adam smiled. 'You're going to keep looking for her, aren't you?'

'I have to. I don't think she trusts anyone else.'

CHAPTER THIRTY-FIVE

Gavin tweaked the volume on the Airwave radio next to his computer monitor before cricking his neck, then ran a pencil over the black typed lines of the report he was halfway through reading.

A weak sunlight shone through the window on his left, and as his watch blinked half past seven the central heating system gave a half-hearted grumble before the radiator beside him attempted to warm up.

He'd arrived early, determined to make some headway on the paperwork that had been generated by the previous day's surveillance activities at the markets. He didn't mind pulling a twelve-hour shift if he had to, but he wanted some results to show for it.

Meanwhile, he listened in to the call-outs and the on-scene progress reports from his uniformed colleagues who were on duty around the smaller Sunday markets in the West Division area in case Shelley's name carried through the static.

Laura pulled off fingerless gloves as the temperature in the incident room rose above Arctic levels and chucked them onto her desk to the right of his, then pushed her hair out of her face before swivelling her chair around.

'Where's Carys, then?' she said, leaning forward and lowering her voice.

Gavin turned another page of the report and checked off a location point he'd already seen on the CCTV footage. 'I don't know.'

'But you two are usually like *that*.' Laura crossed her fingers. 'Surely she'd say something to you if she was going to disappear for four days. I mean, something like this, Carys would usually be in the thick of things, wouldn't she?'

Gavin tossed the report onto his computer keyboard, his brow furrowed.

The same thought had crossed his mind several times since the end of shift on Thursday when Kay had informed her detectives that Carys would be on leave until Monday.

He'd tried to phone her, but her mobile went straight through to the voicemail service – and she wasn't returning those messages, or the texts he'd sent her, asking if she was all right.

'Maybe it's, you know, women's stuff,' he said, heat rising to his cheeks. 'Something she doesn't want to talk about.'

'Trust me, if it is she'd make an appointment after this investigation was over. She wouldn't want to miss all this, would she? The waiting times these days for anything like that are horrendous, anyway.'

Gavin cleared his throat and began to stack the reports into a neat pile, uncomfortable with the way the conversation was heading. It was the same when his mother and his younger sister got talking at family barbecues – nothing was off-limits when it came to their health, and he often fled to do the washing-up with his dad.

'Have you finished making a list of all the other landowners we have to interview with uniform?' he said.

Laura gestured to her computer screen. 'I've run a title search encompassing a twenty-five-mile spread from where Ethan's body was found. We've already spoken to three, so that leaves us with a further eight.'

'That's a lot of landowners for that amount of land.' Gavin stuck his heels in the carpet and edged his chair closer to his colleague's desk and peered over her shoulder at the screen.

'Some of them are smallholdings, but I thought we should check them as well.'

'True. Good thinking. So, what have you come up with?'

'A chicken farmer, two orchards, a dairy farm and a mushroom producer. Those are the larger properties, and then there are two smallholdings – one outside Sevenoaks, and the other on the way into Hildenborough.'

'Okay. How did you get on with the CCTV for the train stations and the bus? Any sign of Shelley?'

'No-one of her description. I worked with Phillip and Debbie until we clocked off yesterday and none of us could see her. If we had a clear photograph of her, I could organise uniform to pop over there and ask around—'

'Something might turn up.' Gavin patted his colleague on the back. 'This is good work. At least when Barnes gets here you can give him a head start with that list of landowners and he can liaise with uniform to start the property searches.'

'Yes, I suppose so.'

Gavin wheeled his chair backwards and picked up his mobile phone.

Still no word from Carys.

He wondered whether he should mention her absence to Barnes when he arrived – and if the detective sergeant knew the whereabouts of their colleague. Surely she was fine, otherwise they'd have been told.

So, where was she?

Ever since he had joined the team two and a half years ago, he and Carys had been close. They watched each other's backs while on duty, teased each other remorselessly off duty, and shared a competitive streak that made for lively banter.

She was like an older sister to him.

So, why the silence now?

He glanced over the top of his screen as the incident room door opened and Barnes strolled towards them, his hands laden with paper bags, grease staining the sides.

'Bacon butties,' he said, grinning as he handed each of them a bag before heading over to his desk. 'Any news?'

'Not yet,' said Gavin, 'and thanks.'

'Cheers, Sarge,' said Laura. 'Where's Carys?'

'Had to take some time off,' said Barnes. 'She'll be back tomorrow.'

'Is she okay?'

'As far as I know.' He pointed at her sandwich. 'Now eat that, before it gets cold.'

Gavin caught his eye, but Barnes looked away before he could question him further.

Battening down his frustration, he devoured the warm sandwich and eyed the next list of tasks that the HOLMES2 database had allocated to him that morning.

His mobile phone vibrated on the desk as he was finishing his breakfast, and he frowned at the screen as the words "unknown caller" were displayed.

'DC Gavin Piper.'

'Detective, it's Jeremy. From the shelter. I need to speak to you urgently. Can we meet?'

CHAPTER THIRTY-SIX

Twenty minutes later, Kay waited alongside Gavin at the steps that led up from Earl Street to the Fremlin Walk shopping precinct.

He'd phoned her while she'd been traipsing alongside the river, her eyes sweeping the towpaths and alleyways as she'd walked a cross-section from there to the amphitheatre and back, desperately seeking the woman who held the answers to Ethan's murder.

She wore jeans and a sweater under a leather jacket to blend into the early morning crowds and stopped from time to time to check her messages. There were a number of uniformed teams at markets across the Division's area that she maintained contact with, but to no avail.

'What's he like, this Jeremy?' she said to Gavin.

'Friendly. Helpful.'

'Do you think he can be trusted? I mean, he's not the sort of person to make spurious claims just to get attention?'

'No, I didn't get that impression. He sounded genuinely concerned when we spoke.' He jerked his chin at a lanky forty-something who was hurrying towards them, a sports bag over his shoulder. 'Here he is.'

Kay waited while Gavin shook hands with the man, and then introduced herself. 'I hope you don't mind me joining you, Jeremy. I'm very concerned for Shelley's safety.'

'So I understand.' He peered over his shoulder, then back to them. 'Can we talk somewhere else? It's a bit exposed out here, isn't it?'

'I've heard the café down the road there does good coffee.'

'I'd rather not. What about the park around the back of the shopping centre?'

'I know the one. Lead the way.'

Kay let Jeremy head off in the direction of Brenchley Gardens, and followed after him and Gavin. Her first impressions of the man were that he was soft-spoken, and some of the bravado her colleague said he had demonstrated when he and Laura had met him at the shelter on Wednesday was noticeably lacking.

Instead he seemed reticent, on edge, and she wondered if it was his way of coping with life on the street – or something else entirely.

As they made their way up St Faith's Street and past the museum, Jeremy glanced over his shoulder, his gaze moving past Kay and beyond with such intensity that the fine hairs on the back of her neck stood on end and created an urge to look back and see what he might have seen.

Before she could, he turned left past the museum and followed the footpath into the gardens behind St Faith's Church, the two detectives in his wake.

Kay noticed CCTV cameras had been mounted on tall steel posts at the perimeter of the park, and made a note to ask one of her team to check those for signs of Shelley as well, in case the woman had sought shelter here over the course of the past three days.

The grassy expanse of the rest of the park was deserted, save for a few shoppers using the footpaths as a shortcut between the shopping centre and Maidstone East station or nearby car parks. Bare trees, their branches only just starting to show the early stages of new buds, cast skeletal shadows across the footpaths, adding to the desolate atmosphere.

The footpath went up a slight incline as they approached the ornate bandstand, and as Kay took in the iron framework she understood why Jeremy had suggested it.

Landscaped hedgerows surrounded the perimeter of the Victorian structure, straggly and unkempt following the winter months of disuse, providing a screen from prying eyes.

Gavin held back, waiting to speak until he was side by side with her.

'He's worried about something.'

'I guessed as much. I assume he was calmer when you last spoke?'

'Definitely. Much more laid back.'

'All right. Let's see what he's got to say for himself. Hopefully he won't get spooked like Shelley did and disappear before we've made some headway. You lead – he trusts you.'

'Guv.'

He broke off as Jeremy entered the bandstand, and Kay raised her eyes to the name of a classical composer inscribed between the spandrels below the awning before joining her colleague.

Inside, the soundboard fixed to the underside of

the roof was strewn with old cobwebs and dust – all of which would be swept away before the summer band season began. For now, the place held a winter dereliction and forlornness.

She shivered, and turned to the homeless man who paced the floor from one side to the other.

'What did you want to tell me?' said Gavin, stepping in front of him and holding up a hand. He kept his tone calm, unhurried. 'Is everything okay?'

Jeremy took a deep breath and seemed to force himself to stand still. 'No, it's not.'

'Have you seen Shelley?'

'No. Not since I spoke to you at the shelter. No-one's seen her. She's disappeared.'

'Any idea where she might have gone?'

'Haven't got a clue.'

'What's wrong, Jeremy? You seem nervous.'

'Do I? Yeah, I am.'

'What's happened? Is it something about Shelley? Has something happened to her?'

'I don't know.' The man tore the woollen hat off his head and scratched at close-cropped hair. 'Maybe. Look, I heard a rumour on Thursday night at the shelter that someone had been wandering around town, asking after her. Friday, too.'

Kay looked at Gavin, then back to Jeremy. 'I'm

sorry if that gave any of you cause for concern, but I'd tasked my investigation team with speaking to shelter volunteers and anyone they knew on the streets around here in case any of them have seen Shelley. She asked me to meet her at the amphitheatre on Thursday morning, but something spooked her and she took off. I'm worried about her, too and I've got no way of getting in touch with her.'

'Do your lot go around offering money for information?'

'What? No, I—'

'That's what I told the others. No – I'm not talking about police. Not your lot. You stick out a mile. This was a bloke on his own – heavy-set, about as tall as me, with a beard.'

Kay's mouth dried. 'When was this?'

'Yesterday morning. Round by the post office on the High Street. Showed me a photo of her, and said he was trying to find her. Said she might be in danger. Like I said, he's been asking others, too.'

'What was he wearing?' said Gavin, pulling his notebook from his coat pocket.

'Blue jeans, black jacket with a hood. He was wearing a baseball cap, too.' Jeremy's eyes found the wooden slats of the bandstand's ceiling, then he blinked. 'He had the hood of his coat up, but I could see part of a logo on the front of the cap – I can't remember what it was. Not one of those well-known sports ones.'

'That's helpful though, thanks. We might be able to spot him on CCTV.'

'Who else has he spoken to?' said Kay.

'A few regulars around here. They know I'm looking out for Shelley because I'm worried after our chat the other day, so they told me when I saw them. He's walking around with a fistful of twenties for anyone who'll tell him where she is.'

'Have you ever seen him before? Prior to knowing Shelley, I mean?' said Gavin.

'No – the others haven't either.'

'Jeremy, could you do me a favour?' said Kay.

'Go on.'

She handed him a business card. 'You've already got Gavin's number, so if you spot this bloke hanging around, or speaking to anyone, could you call one of us? It doesn't matter what time of day or night. Pop down to the station on Palace Avenue and ask for us at the desk if you can't call. We'll let them know you're helping us.'

He took her card and ran his thumb over the text. 'He's going to hurt her if he finds her, isn't he?'

'We don't know that for sure, but we do need to

talk to him,' said Gavin. 'If only to find out why he's offering money in return for information about her.'

Jeremy nodded, his face glum as he tucked Kay's card into his jeans pocket and then pulled his woollen hat back on.

'The problem is, this time of year it won't be long before someone takes his money and tells him where she is,' he said. 'Hunger beats solidarity most of the time in my experience.'

CHAPTER THIRTY-SEVEN

Barnes peered over his reading glasses as his mobile phone emitted a low buzzing sound, and smiled at the name displayed on the screen.

Flicking open the notification, he opened the app to find a new photograph from his daughter, Emma, alongside two of her university friends. The three girls were attempting to manoeuvre indoor go-karts through a slalom with little success, the caption underneath suggesting it wasn't going well, evidenced by the fits of giggles on the girls' faces.

'Is that your daughter?' said Laura. She paused at his elbow, dropping two manila folders into his tray.

'Yes. She lives with her mum when she's not at uni.'

'She's pretty.'

'Definitely takes after her mum.' Barnes grinned, then sent a brief message to Emma telling her he'd call her later in the week, and put the phone aside. 'Right, do you want to email me that list of landowners you've collated and I'll give Dave Morrison a shout to see if we can get some help from uniform to do the interviews? It'll probably be tomorrow morning by the time we get everything organised, but put yourself down on the roster for those.'

'Will do, thanks, Sarge.'

He spun his chair around as the incident door burst open and Kay and Gavin appeared.

'What's wrong?' he said.

'There's someone walking around town offering money in exchange for information about Shelley,' said Kay. She hung her coat on a peg outside Sharp's office and then came over to his desk and pulled out a spare chair as Gavin joined them.

'And you think it's Ethan's killer?'

'Has to be, doesn't it?' said Gavin.

'What if it's a relative of hers trying to find her?' said Laura.

Barnes snorted, unable to keep the bitterness from

his voice. 'They haven't bothered for the past three or four years, so why would they start now? They haven't even filed a missing person report for her.'

'Laura has a fair point, though,' said Kay. 'We need to move fast on this new information, because if it isn't a concerned relative, then Shelley is in more danger than we thought. Laura, can you make a start and find out what secondary schools are in the area? Shelley told me she struggled at school, so ignore the grammar schools. She has quite a broad Liverpool accent, and moved down here when she was thirteen. I'm guessing she didn't go on to study A-levels, so she would've left by the time she was sixteen.'

'Okay, guv. Most of the school websites have emergency contact details for holidays and weekends, so I should be able to get hold of them today.'

'Good, thanks. If you can find out her surname from them, that's a start. Ask them if they've got an address up in Liverpool for her mother, too – even if it's an old one, it'll give our colleagues up there a head start. Gavin – based on the description Jeremy gave us, work with Parker when he reappears and get your hands on CCTV footage for the High Street near the post office. See if you can spot the man he says approached him. If necessary, phone Andy Grey over in digital forensics at Headquarters – you know what he's like; he'll probably know about some additional camera angles that could help us.'

'Guv.'

'What about the landowner interviews, guv?' said Barnes. 'Do we still go ahead with those tomorrow, or wait to see what developments we have with this angle first?'

Kay tied her hair back, and then rested her arm on his desk and stared at his screen. 'I think we go ahead. Looks like you've got quite a list there from Laura, and it's going to take time to coordinate. Set it up with uniform, and if anything happens in the interim, we can reschedule as necessary.'

'Okay. What's known about the bloke who offered money to Gavin's contact?'

'Nothing except a description at the moment, but Jeremy – that's the homeless bloke who called Gavin – says he was offered a handful of twenties to tell him where Shelley was. He didn't take it, of course, and he's tried to tell as many of the others who use the shelters not to speak to the man, but, like he said to us, they're hungry and in need of warm clothes and a roof over their heads. If someone offers them money like that, it's not going to be long before someone talks.'

Barnes gestured to his colleague who now had her head bent over her desk, her phone to her ear. 'Laura went through the CCTV images near all the shelters from last night when Gavin headed out to meet with you earlier. There's no sign of Shelley near any of them.'

'I'm not surprised, given what we now know. She's probably sleeping rough somewhere, trying to stay out of sight.'

'That's what worries me.' He wiggled his mouse and opened the Internet browser. 'Look at the night-time temperatures that are expected this week. She needs to be somewhere warm, and safe.'

'I know, Ian. Hopefully we'll turn up something this afternoon, or maybe one of Jeremy's contacts will tip us off where we might find her.' She rose from her chair. 'I'd best head over to Headquarters. I'm meant to be meeting Sharp there at four o'clock. Will you be all right holding the fort?'

'No problem. I'll call you if we find her.'

'Thanks. Chat later.'

He watched her sweep from the room, coat over her arm and mobile phone already to her ear, then turned back to his computer and tried to batten down the thump of his heartbeat.

Shelley was only three years older than his daughter, and must be scared out of her wits.

He shook his head to clear the thought, and began to coordinate the house-to-house enquiries for the farms and smallholdings the next day.

CHAPTER THIRTY-EIGHT

Carys pulled the handbrake and slid her seatbelt off, her gaze settling on the two silver vans and three patrol cars that blocked off the entrance to an alleyway a hundred metres away.

Her phone had shrieked forty minutes beforehand, jerking her from a deep sleep.

She'd been wide awake within the first three seconds of hearing Kay's voice at the end of the line, and had hurriedly showered and dressed before driving across to the fringes of the town centre, battling the early morning traffic.

A wayward empty kebab wrapper tumbled into the gutter beside the car as she pushed open the driver's door, and her top lip curled at the pool of vomit that had been spilled in the middle of the pavement before she side-stepped it and hurried towards two uniformed police constables at the blue and white cordon.

Holding up her warrant card, she waited while they wrote down her details, and then signed where the taller of the two indicated.

'Who else is here?'

'Harriet's here with her CSI lot, and the pathologist turned up half an hour ago. We've got a second cordon at the other end of the alleyway.'

'What do you know so far?'

His colleague cleared her throat. 'No-one heard anything, ma'am. The nearest neighbour lives in the flat just past your car, above the fish and chip shop. The buildings that back onto this alleyway are service entrances for the shops on the streets either side. All closed up since four o'clock yesterday, if they bothered opening at all. We don't expect to see them open until nine o'clock this morning—'

'That's if we let them open at all,' added the other police officer.

'What've we got?'

'Female, deceased, mid-twenties by the look of it – perhaps younger. Her body was dumped in a skip halfway up the alleyway.'

'How'd it get spotted if none of the shops are open?'

'A homeless bloke was scavenging for food scraps and found her.' He aimed his thumb over his shoulder to the parked patrol cars. 'PC Harris is interviewing him at the moment. He was pretty shaken up, but says he didn't know her."

'Got a name for him?'

'Goes by the moniker of Spikey, apparently. He's off his head on something. Hopefully Harris will get more sense out of him once he's got some coffee down him. Do you want some gloves and bootees to put on?'

'Please, that's great.'

Carys tugged on the paper bootees and matching overalls, pulled the gloves over numb fingers then nodded her thanks and ducked under the tape, heading towards the nearest CSI technician who was crouching on the cracked asphalt near the entrance to the alleyway with a camera in his hands.

'Morning, Patrick.'

'Carys. How are you?'

'Okay, I suppose, given the circumstances. What do you know?'

He rose to his feet, groaning under his breath.

'Don't laugh – you're only a few years away from making noises like that when you stand up.'

She managed a smile, and gestured to the camera. 'Can I see?'

'Sure.'

'Carys!'

Turning at the shout, she saw Kay walking towards her, a purposeful stride to the DI's gait.

'Hang on, Patrick – the DI might as well see those at the same time,' she said. 'Morning, guv.'

'Just got here?'

'About ten minutes ago. Patrick was about to take me through the photos he's got so far.'

'Okay, go for it.'

Carys waited until Kay moved around to Patrick's left, and then he angled the viewing pane on the back of the digital camera so they could both see.

'I'll scroll past the first few – they're shots of the entrance to the alleyway, and then I've moved up through here and towards the skip where the woman's body was found.'

'Was she carrying any identification?' said Kay.

'None that we've found yet. Harriet's got a team of three there at the moment working through the contents. It'll be a while before we know for sure.'

Kay nodded, then gestured for him to continue through the images.

Carys winced at the first shot of the woman's twisted form within the folds of discarded takeaway wrappers, aluminium drink cans and other detritus.

All that was visible of her face was a pale cheek framed with dark-coloured hair that obscured her eyes and nose. She wore a grubby pale-pink spaghetti-strap vest top, and Carys spotted the waistline of denim jeans showing before these too were covered by old cardboard boxes and torn magazines.

'Thanks, Patrick,' she said as he reached the end of the photographs he'd taken so far. 'Is it okay if we wander over there?'

'It should be fine – just stick to the designated path we've marked out and clear it with Harriet before you enter the second cordon.'

Kay patted his arm before they walked away, and Carys knew from experience it was her boss's way of letting the photographer know she appreciated his diligence and care in such difficult circumstances.

'When did you get back from Bridgend?' she said as they passed a second technician crouching to one side of the alleyway, marking out another area of interest to the CSI team.

'About ten o'clock last night.'

'Did it go all right?'

'I think so. Hard to tell, isn't it?'

Kay's lips twisted into a sardonic smile. 'It is, you're right. When will they let you know?'

'One of the DCIs who interviewed me said they were going to make a decision by the end of the week.' Carys heard her DI exhale under her breath, and swallowed. 'I'll stay until the end of this one, guv. I won't let you down.'

'I know.' Kay jerked her chin towards the skip, now only a couple of metres away, and raised her voice. 'Harriet? Are we okay to approach?'

The lead CSI lowered her mask. 'Come on over. We're halfway through but we've processed all the ground here, so you're good to go.'

Carys followed Kay towards the small team of technicians, then took a step back in surprise as Lucas Anderson appeared from within the skip next to one of them, his body covered in a protective full-body biohazard suit.

'Still here?' she said.

'Hmmm,' he said by way of reply. 'Thought I'd better stay on. This one is almost as bad as the chap in the field the other week.'

'Why?'

Both detectives hurried forward, Carys's interest piqued.

'Hang on, I'll get a second stepladder,' said Charlie, another of Harriet's team.

She waited while he unfolded a spare ladder that had been propped up against the dark-coloured brick wall of one of the shops to the right of the alleyway and placed it against the skip for her, holding out his hand and steadying her arm as she climbed up to the platform.

'Thanks,' she said, then turned her attention back to the pathologist.

Beside her, Kay climbed the other ladder, placed her gloved hands on the side of the skip and let out a groan.

'Is it her?'

The DI nodded, sadness crossing her features before her jaw clenched. 'It's Shelley. We were too late.'

Lucas gave them a few seconds to absorb the revelation, and then cleared his throat. 'Whoever did this to her likely strangled her first. I'll be better able to provide an opinion about that after the post mortem, obviously.'

'Dammit.'

Carys heard Kay swear under her breath, and

knew she would be vowing justice for the dead woman and would find her killer, no matter what it took.

'There is one more thing,' said Lucas. He pointed to the woman's legs. 'Her feet have been hacked off.'

'What?' Kay failed to keep the horror from her voice.

'Probably post mortem, given the lack of blood in here.'

'Why would someone do that? Cut off her feet?' said Carys.

Kay narrowed her eyes against the dirt scuffed up in the wind that howled across the yard.

'It's like with Ethan, isn't it? They're sending a message to the others to show them what will happen if they try to run away.'

CHAPTER THIRTY-NINE

'Kay? Kay. A moment, please.'

Sharp's voice carried across the incident room as she and Carys entered, and she looked across to the DCI's office to see him peering out of the door, beckoning to her.

He waited until she was closer, and then turned and led the way inside. 'Shut the door.'

She did as she was told, moving towards his desk as he adjusted the back of his suit jacket and sat, gesturing to her to take one of the visitor chairs.

Kay ignored him, and stood before the desk, clenching her teeth.

'Are you all right? I heard the news.'

'We were too late to save her, guv. He mutilated her. Cut off her feet at the ankles.'

'We'll find him.'

'Bloody right I will, guv. I'll make sure he goes away for a long time for this. I'll—'

'Kay? Breathe. Take a minute. I know you're angry and upset. I would be too, but you did everything you could to try to find her.'

She flung her bag onto one of the visitor chairs, then moved across to the window and wrapped her arms around her waist as she watched the movement of other officers in and out of the building. 'I let her down.'

'The only person to blame for all this is the person who killed her.' Sharp pushed back his chair and joined her. 'Is Carys all right?'

'Yes, I think so. I should get out there and do the briefing, otherwise we're losing ground standing here chatting.' She forced a smile as she turned to face him. 'Thanks, guv.'

'It gets to me, too,' he said. 'It's because we're human.'

'Tell that to some of the reporters we have to deal with,' she said, swinging her bag over her arm and heading for the door.

Carys was cradling her phone between her ear and shoulder as she approached the group of detectives' desks, her voice a low murmur as she read her notes from the crime scene.

Barnes handed Kay a mug of tea as she sat. 'There's extra sugar in that. Carys looked like she could do with one when she walked in, and so do you.'

'Thanks, Ian.' She took a sip, blinked as the sugar hit her back teeth, and then ran her gaze over the crowded incident room. 'Everyone here?'

'Gavin and Laura are on their way back from Headquarters – they were working with Andy Grey late yesterday to try to find out who was talking to Jeremy about Shelley, and he phoned earlier to say he had some footage from a private security camera on the High Street that might help us.'

'Okay, good. We'll give them another ten minutes and then have the briefing.'

'Carys told me what happened. Are you okay?'

She nodded, exhaustion threatening. 'I will be, when we catch the bastard who did this.'

Five minutes later, the two detective constables had arrived and she'd moved to the front of the room, updating the whiteboard with the basic details of Shelley's murder, and photographs from the scene that Carys had downloaded from her phone for context.

As Kay turned to face her assembled colleagues, she straightened her shoulders.

'Despite our best efforts to locate Shelley before any harm came to her, I can confirm that the body found in a skip this morning is hers. Lucas was on scene, and has stated that she was strangled prior to her feet being cut off.' She ran her eyes over a message displayed on the front of her phone. 'At present, her feet haven't been found. They weren't in the skip.'

A shocked murmur rippled through the room.

'We'll keep the details of her death from the media at this time,' Kay continued, 'and I would ask that if you're approached by any members of the press, you direct them to DCI Sharp or myself in the first instance. We'll issue a formal statement later today. In the meantime, do we have any progress on the man Jeremy said approached him offering money in return for news of Shelley? Gavin?'

'Guv.' He walked over to join her as Laura handed out a two-page document to each member of the team. 'We had no luck with any of the council-operated CCTV cameras in the town centre, but when Andy's digital forensics team phoned around, they obtained footage from a licensed betting shop near the post office that was able to help. The images you see here are the four clearest ones we have.'

Kay peered at the photographs that had been captured and laid out two per page for the purposes of the briefing. 'Are these in HOLMES2?'

'Yes, guv. Andy updated it for us while we were on our way back. The first two photographs confirm the man on the left is Jeremy. On the second page, we have our suspect.' He paused as a rustle of paper filled the room. 'Obviously, we can't enhance the image given the restrictions of this being a fixed camera angle, but Andy was able to pick out some of the man's features.'

'Do any of you recognise him?' said Kay, holding the page closer.

A murmur of negative responses filled the room.

'All right, no messing about with this one. Get this photograph circulated across the Division. If we have no responses by the end of today, go nationwide with the request.'

'Will do, guv.'

Gavin retook his seat while Kay ran through the list of tasks that would come with the event of Shelley's murder, and then turned her attention to Barnes.

'Ian, are uniform ready to start doing the searches of the farms Laura identified?'

'Yes, guv. We've narrowed it down to five producers and two smallholdings.'

'Let me have the paperwork to sign off and we'll get those started this morning.' Kay updated the whiteboard with the new tasks, then turned back and surveyed her team.

'I don't need to tell you that we won't rest until this killer is found,' she said, 'and I know I can count on you to find him, and give Ethan and Shelley the justice they deserve. Dismissed.'

CHAPTER FORTY

'Ready, guv?'

Kay turned at the sound of PC Morrison's voice, and tugged a pair of protective gloves from her coat pocket. 'I'll let you brief your team, Dave. Just tell me where you want me.'

'Thanks.' He beckoned the six officers milling about at the entrance to Wiseacre Mushroom Suppliers, and waited until they'd formed a rough semicircle beside them. 'The warrant for this morning's search has been served on the owners, and DC Laura Hanway is currently interviewing them in the house with PC Phillip Parker in attendance. Our remit is to conduct a thorough search of the outbuildings and yard. The four individuals you can see over my shoulder near the house are the full-time workers they employ. Three are local, one is Romanian – and before you ask, his visa checks out. He's been working here since October and although he says the pay is lousy, my daughter's earning less than him on a hairdressing apprenticeship in Tunbridge Wells, so I reckon he should stop complaining.'

A ripple of good-natured laughter passed through the group, and Kay smiled.

It was typical of Dave Morrison to try to lighten a stressful situation. A lot depended upon the outcome of the searches being carried out today and they were all feeling the pressure, especially after the nature of Shelley's death spread through the police station.

Her murder had touched a nerve.

The previous night, Adam had taken one look at her face when she'd got home and marched her to the pub up the lane from their house before settling her into a quiet corner and placing a large tumbler of brandy on the table beside her. He'd listened to her quiet undertones as she'd told him what had happened, and held her hand while she'd wiped away angry tears with the other.

She'd left the house that morning with a renewed determination, a single thought going around in her head.

She would deliver justice for Ethan and Shelley, whatever it took.

As Dave ran through the search procedure for a pair of special constables new to the force and ensured they were paired with more experienced officers, she cast her gaze across the yard to where the mushroom pickers waited.

A steady stream of cigarette smoke curled into the air above their heads, and a wave of resentment pervaded from the group as they kicked at stones and cast sideways glances at the police officers who had forced them to stop work.

'Why are they so nervous?' said Kay. 'Anyone spoken to them yet?'

Dave looked up from his notes as his team dispersed. 'According to the owner, they're supposed to check the temperature and humidity three times a day. He's got twenty growing houses here, so they're worried the crops will perish if we hold them up too long. It's why I've started the search at the far end. Once we check each building, they can come back to work behind us.'

Kay ran her eyes over the arched buildings that had been built each side of a dirt track leading away from the farmhouse. 'What are the chances of us finding an aircraft in one of those, do you think?'

'They'd be a perfect hiding place. Do you want to join me and we'll take a look around?'

'Come on, then.'

She scuffed along beside the police constable, her boots sinking into soft mud that exuded a distinct aroma of composted waste, manure and chemical plant treatments. To each side, the large growing houses reared above them, creating a wind tunnel effect down the track that had her burying her face into her scarf to keep out the chill.

When Dave followed one of the teams into a building at the far end, she was relieved to escape the elements – and surprised at the warmth within.

Her jaw dropped at the sight of the rows of aluminium shelving that disappeared into the far reaches of the building some thirty metres away, the end of which was illuminated by the dull glow from low wattage bulbs hanging from steel girders in the ceiling.

'As winter jobs go, this has to be one of the better ones,' she said.

'It's why they were worried about how long we were going to take,' said Dave. 'This temperature has to remain at a constant.'

Twenty minutes later, she blinked as they exited the growing house into weak sunlight, and saw two of the farm labourers entering the building opposite as the uniformed officers completed their search there and moved on to the next.

'Let's wander along the rest of these,' she said. 'We can check for the aircraft or people, and your team can conduct a more thorough search in our wake. At least we'll keep this moving.'

'Sounds good, guv.' Dave grinned. 'It's too bloody cold to stand around out here, anyway.'

'My thinking exactly.'

She bit her lip as she followed in his wake, and pulled out her mobile phone.

It had taken DCI Sharp a series of phone calls to his superiors at Headquarters and coercion of two other detective chief inspectors within West Division to allocate enough officers to conduct the day's searches, and she knew he would be expecting an update soon – and results.

Dave pushed open the door to another building and stepped inside. 'I'll take the left, you take the right if you want, guv?'

'Meet you at the other end.'

She loosened the scarf at her neck and unbuttoned her jacket as the warmth from the growing house began to seep through the layers of clothing, then set off between the rows of fungi.

Moments later, she met Dave at the far end and shook her head.

'Nothing. No-one's hiding in here. You?'

'No. On to the next one, then.'

Frustration began to set in, as each building was investigated, that she would never locate the killer or the other victims of slavery. They had no idea how many others there might be, or how long they had been subjected to the horrors of enforced labour, and as their search efforts reached the end of the track close to the farmhouse she resigned herself to the realisation that there was no aircraft hidden on the property either.

Laura emerged from the front door of the house as they reached the yard, gestured to Parker to head over to one of the patrol cars, and then stomped towards Kay.

'Mr Clapperton and his workforce all check out, guv,' she said as she drew near. 'How did you get on?'

'No sign of anyone, or a light aircraft. They'll probably be here another couple of hours concluding the search, but I think we're done.'

'We can definitely cross this place off our list,' said Dave, disappointment colouring his words.

Kay checked her watch. 'I guess we just have to

hope we get a breakthrough at one of the other properties, then. Thanks, Dave – I'll see you back at the incident room.'

Walking back to her car with Laura at her side, she dug her fingernails into her palms and tried to ignore the dread that was clawing at the back of her mind as her thoughts tumbled over each other.

What if they were too late?

What if the killer had destroyed the evidence?

What had happened to the others held in captivity with Ethan and Shelley?

CHAPTER FORTY-ONE

Laura jumped in her seat as a ferocious gust of wind rattled the glass next to her, rain lashing against the panes.

Recovering, she took a sip from a mug of tepid coffee and scowled at her computer screen as she typed in her notes from the day's searches.

The incident room door swung open as another group of uniformed officers traipsed in, pulling off sodden stab vests and hats or running hands through wet hair having been caught in the deluge between the car park and the police station.

Exhaustion and dejection peppered mumbled conversations, snippets of which carried across the room to where she sat, slouching, avoiding eye contact with any of them.

She tried to ignore the embarrassment that had been nipping at the edges of her confidence like an irate terrier since she and Kay had returned from the mushroom farm.

One by one, the team leaders responsible for each property search had radioed in their progress, and Laura's confidence dissipated with each update.

The door to DCI Sharp's office opened, and Kay and Barnes appeared, their faces grim.

Apart from a handful of minor vehicle offences, the extra manpower assigned to the searches had turned up nothing, and she had no doubt that her superiors were now receiving the Chief Superintendent's thoughts on the matter.

She cleared her throat as they walked over to where she sat next to Carys and Gavin – both of whom had phones to their ears.

'Can I get either of you something to drink?' she said, then blushed. She sounded desperate.

Barnes shook his head. 'No, thanks. We'll get the briefing underway and then let everyone go – it's been a long day.'

He seemed to force a smile, and then wandered over to speak with a pair of police constables who had arrived, their faces drawn and tired.

To her surprise, Kay pulled out a spare chair

beside her and dropped into it before resting her elbows on her knees and lowering her voice.

'I know what's going through your head, and I'm telling you to stop it right now.'

'Pardon, guv?'

'The fact we found nothing at any of the properties we searched today isn't your fault.'

Laura blinked, angry that her eyes began to sting. 'But it was me who identified them, guv. It was me who gave the list to Ian and you based the searches on that.'

'Yes, and if anyone else had been tasked with that job, they'd have probably come up with the same list. I've told you – we don't get a result with everything we do.' The detective inspector straightened, and gestured to the reports Laura had been entering into the system. 'All of this, all of these hours we spend searching through pieces of information, helps to build up the bigger picture. Any of it could provide the breakthrough we need, but if we don't do the work and tick off the things that aren't relevant, we'll never get to the truth.'

Laura jerked her chin towards Sharp's door. 'What about the DCI? Does he feel the same way?'

Kay winked, then rose to her feet. 'Who do you think trained me?'

As she watched Kay move through the incident room, calling to the team to join her for the briefing, Laura exhaled.

'Hurry up, Hanway, you won't get a seat near the front,' said Gavin. He jostled past her, closely followed by Carys who paused at her desk while she gathered up her notebook.

'Everything okay?'

Laura smiled. 'Yes, thanks. Lead the way.'

'Okay, everyone,' said Kay, as they found somewhere to sit, 'I'll keep this short and we'll regroup in the morning. As you're probably aware, we've had no results today after searching the five farm properties and two smallholdings, although we did identify a handful of minor infringements for our colleagues to follow up at a later date.'

She paused and rapped her knuckles on the bullet points written on the whiteboard. 'Let's revisit why we believe Ethan and Shelley's killer to be linked to agriculture rather than another industry. One, manual labour is a requirement and modern slavery represents a cheap resource. Two, the fact that properties are spread out over several acres means that workers can be kept hidden for long periods of time – in outbuildings, or other temporary accommodation. Gang masters have the ability to buy supplies of food in large quantities without raising suspicion locally.'

Kay dropped her hand and paused for a moment, staring at the carpet before raising her gaze to the team once more, her expression hardened. 'Finally, and most importantly for our interests, agriculture represents an opportunity for modern slaves to be kept in isolation, and if they're isolated from others then it's easier to create an atmosphere of fear and control. Ethan and Shelley broke the rules. They managed to escape, but paid for it with their lives. Shelley risked everything to try to help the ones who might still be held captive. We owe it to her and Ethan to find them. No, we didn't get the results we wanted today, but we're not giving up. Get yourselves home, get some rest, and then be here at seven-thirty tomorrow morning because we're going to find the bastard who did this.'

Laura pushed back her chair as the gathered officers began to disperse, her heart racing after Kay's words.

The DI was right.

They would find who murdered Ethan and Shelley, whatever it took.

CHAPTER FORTY-TWO

Gavin shovelled another chopstick-laden scoop of noodles into his mouth, then swallowed and resisted the urge to yawn.

The incident room had finally emptied an hour ago, DCI Sharp walking past Gavin's desk to check he was all right before heading home, and now he was relishing the unusual peace and quiet.

His gaze flickered to Kay's desk as her phone began to ring, and he wiped his hands before answering the outside line.

'It's Lucas,' said the voice. 'I wondered if some of you were still around. Kay not there?'

'She headed off a little while back. She'll be on her mobile if you need her, though.'

'That's all right. I was just going to give a quick

update about the post mortem on the young woman who was found in that skip this morning.'

Gavin frowned, and reached for his notebook. 'That was quick – I don't think the guv was expecting that until later this week.'

'In the circumstances, my staff and I thought we'd reschedule some of our less pressing cases. Least we could do.'

'That's good of you, thanks. What can you tell us?'

'As I suspected, Shelley was strangled, but someone used their hands, rather than a ligature.'

'Prints?'

'Gloves, I'm afraid. No indication that she was sexually assaulted. Actual cause of death was heart failure, caused by the strangulation.'

Gavin ran a finger under his collar and swallowed. 'What about— what about her feet?'

The pathologist sighed. 'They haven't been found. I had a conference call with Harriet and her team earlier, and despite working their way along the entire length of the alleyway and a search of litter bins in the area, they've got nothing.'

'Were the feet removed—?'

'After death, as I first thought. Going by the state

of her legs, I would think two to three blows with a blade such as a cleaver.'

Gavin winced. 'That'd take some doing.'

'You'd certainly need strength. I suppose we have to consider that her killer was quite possibly in a rage, too.'

'And bigger than her. Do we need to look for another crime scene?'

'No – myself and Harriet are of the opinion that her feet were removed in the skip.'

Gavin tucked the receiver under his chin and leaned across to his computer, refreshing his emails. 'We haven't got Harriet's report through yet.'

'She mentioned she was going to finish it tonight and send it over first thing,' said Lucas. 'I'll have mine to you by mid-morning tomorrow, too.'

'Did Harriet mention whether Shelley was carrying any belongings?'

'There was nothing noted apart from two five pound notes and a bit of loose change. She had no distinguishing features such as tattoos or skin discolouration. If Kay hadn't recognised her—'

'We wouldn't have been able to identify her.'

'Something that was consistent with both Shelley and the body of Ethan Archer is the paleness of skin tone, as if they suffered from a lack of sun exposure.'

'Kay said Shelley told her that they'd been made to work indoors all the time they were held captive,' said Gavin. 'I'd imagine whoever did this to them couldn't risk having them seen outside.'

'Well, that would be consistent with my findings.' Lucas covered the phone and spoke to someone at the other end. 'I've got to go, Piper – we've just been requested to attend an incident in Dartford.'

'Thanks for calling – safe travels.' Gavin placed the receiver back in its cradle, then gathered up the remnants of his takeaway and wandered into the kitchenette.

As he waited for the coffee to percolate, he sorted out the food scraps from the recycling and then heaped sugar into a large mug of coffee and wandered over to the highlighted tasks on the whiteboard at the end of the room.

They were almost two weeks into investigating Ethan's death, and they were still no closer to finding out who was responsible for his and Shelley's brutal slayings.

He placed his coffee mug on a desk close by, his gaze falling to the map spread out across an adjacent table.

Brightly coloured sticky notes indicated the properties that had been searched that day, the boundaries between each farm marked with a yellow highlighter pen and a red tick across the middle to show that the owners were in the clear – for now.

He spun around the map until it showed Hildenborough in the bottom right-hand corner and Sevenoaks at the top.

Somewhere within that area west of the two towns, there might be others like Shelley and Ethan, desperate to escape horrific working conditions.

But where?

He shoved the map aside, and reached across the table to a stack of aerial photographs that had been printed out from a well-known app and arranged into separate bundles for each of the properties. Slipping the paperclips from each bundle, he laid them out on the table until he had a view across the whole of the western fringes of Kent, and crossed his arms over his chest as his eyes took in the landscape.

The field where Ethan's body had been found was marked with a silver dot, making it easier for him to get his bearings. To the north of that, he could see the woodland where Barnes had found the tread marks that might have been left by the van Peter Winton said he had heard in the lane outside his house. South of Maitland's farm were the properties owned by Hugh Ditchens and the Peverells, the Ditchens' orchards blending seamlessly into a wide paddock on the edge of the Peverells' rabbit farm.

Further away from the properties, the nature reserve that included the reservoir provided an even greener expanse, the angle of the aerial shot catching the water glistening in the sunlight.

Gavin yawned, wrapped his fingers around his coffee mug, and then stopped.

Ever since Laura had returned from the searches that morning, she'd been quietly embarrassed at the lack of a breakthrough based on the intelligence she'd gathered, but he and Carys had both agreed that her logic had been sound.

He flipped through the pages in his notebook, trying to find his notes from the pre-search briefing that had been held, in which Kay had reiterated the parameters.

Somewhere isolated.

Somewhere people could be hidden.

Somewhere a light aircraft could be stored.

He looked at the photographs once more, his gaze falling on the property belonging to the mushroom farmer. The precise placement of plastic roof coverings identified the growing houses, and he traced the line of buildings with his finger before tapping the photograph, a memory clutching at the corner of his thoughts.

As it began to take shape, he scrambled for his mobile phone, only checking his watch and realising the late time when the number connected.

A sleepy voice answered. 'Piper?'

'Sorry to wake you up, guv. We need to extend the searches. I think I might know where Ethan and Shelley were being held.'

CHAPTER FORTY-THREE

A bitter stench of animal waste and death clung to the air as Kay walked beside Adrian Peverell towards a corrugated iron-clad shed, her stomach churning with dread.

'Why rabbits?' she said.

The man beside her shrugged, and rubbed his hand over a sprinkling of red sores covering his cheeks. 'Helen did some research and found out how much rabbit meat was being imported from the EU for pet food. She figured we'd be able to fill a gap in the market and provide in-country supplies and save retailers money on those import costs.'

'Is it going well?'

'Really well.' He blinked, as if surprised at his

own success. 'We can hardly keep up with demand, to be honest.'

Kay gestured to the taller of the buildings in front of her. 'Do you have any other buildings on your land?'

'No – just these. There was an old barn around the back of those when we first bought the place, but the roof had collapsed and the supporting timbers were rotten – it was cheaper for us to have it pulled down.'

As she passed she nodded to Gavin, who, after phoning her to share his theory that the outbuildings at the rabbit farm met the same parameters set for the other properties searched the day before, was now leading the interviews and speaking with the Peverells' team of part-time workers.

She tried to ignore the blood-spattered apron of the smaller man in the group of four who milled about in the yard waiting for their turn to be questioned, and instead concentrated on what Adrian Peverell was telling her.

'We have a few thousand rabbits here at any one time. They're kept in cages from the day they're born until we slaughter them.'

'How long are they in the cages for, then?'

'About eighty days. We separate out the males and

keep them away from the females so we can artificially inseminate those and control the number of litters they have each year. Obviously, the more the merrier for us.'

Kay grimaced, took the protective bootees and gloves he held out, and slipped them on while he lifted the latch on the door to the first building.

'Ready?'

'Yes, thanks.'

'All right, well – I should tell you that you'll probably find this confronting if you haven't been on a farm before, but just remember it's the same process for chickens.'

She took a deep breath, and then followed him inside.

Her first impression was that the layout was similar to the mushroom farm, except that instead of rows of shelves containing fungi in various stages of growth, this building contained rows of cages, each half a metre square and stacked four cages high.

A terrible squealing came from the far side of the building before falling silent, and she turned to Peverell, unable to keep the shock from her face.

'What was that?'

He shrugged. 'They fight from time to time.'

Swallowing down her retort, she wandered a few metres further into the battery farm, her boots scuffing through waste that coated the floor in a slick of manure and old straw. Her eyes widened in horror as she paused next to one of the cages.

Eight rabbits blinked up at her, their mouths open as they panted in the stagnant air.

'Don't they need more room than this?'

'They're fine.'

'Where's their water supply?'

'In that bottle there. It's drip fed.'

'How is the building ventilated?'

The farmer jerked his thumb upwards, and she raised her eyes to the ceiling to see a line of battered vents.

Frustrated, she gritted her teeth, then turned and followed him through the bowels of the building then back towards the main door.

The search team was waiting to start on the battery farm having already checked the slaughterhouse, and she had no desire to stay inside any longer.

'I can't help noticing that these cages haven't been cleaned out in a while,' she said.

Peverell paused and glared at her over his shoulder, his eyes hardening. 'We clean them out every day.'

'There's a dead rabbit in that one.'

'It's a fact of life – and this business, detective. Do you want to see the slaughterhouse next?'

Kay wrinkled her nose as a handful of flies launched into the air above the cages before descending on the next row, the drone from their wings creating a horrific white noise she was sure she would hear for days. She'd rather do anything but see the other side of the farming operation, however, professional interest made her nod in agreement.

'Lead the way.'

Half an hour later, she tugged off the gloves and plastic bootees and tossed them into a dustbin Peverell indicated outside the slaughterhouse.

He had been matter-of-fact during the tour, describing the butchering process, showing her the enormous walk-in cold rooms where the meat was kept until shipped out to the pet food companies, and extolling the fact that his business only used a third of the space of other commercial meat enterprises.

She'd been taken aback at the scale of what he and his wife were doing.

'Like I said, there's a demand for the meat,' he said as he shut the door and tore his gloves off. 'If that's everything, I've got paperwork to do. Will your lot be much longer?'

Kay peered past him to where the search teams

were beginning to congregate in the yard for a debrief, their faces stoical.

'Thank you, Mr Peverell. I think we're done here. We'll be in touch if we need anything else.'

He nodded, then turned his back on her and stalked towards the house.

'Jesus.' Kay exhaled, checked that Gavin had the debrief under control, and then moved away from the yard towards a grassy track that began at the side of the slaughterhouse building.

She took deep breaths as the stench from the farm subsided with a fresh breeze whipping through a paddock to her left, and gulped the sweet aroma of freshly cut grass while she walked.

The track widened, the ground under her feet levelling out between an avenue of coppiced trees and neatly cut hedgerows of blackthorn and damson, and the stress of the past few hours began to subside a little, allowing her to focus her thoughts on what angles of enquiry she'd have to follow up next.

When she glanced over her shoulder, she was surprised to see how far away from the rabbit farm she'd strayed.

Beyond her position, she spotted the tell-tale tangled branches of fruit trees and wandered closer to take a look. After a hundred metres or so, she found her way blocked by a single chain that had been stretched across the track at knee height, a simple hook attaching it to a wooden post on the right-hand side.

Tugging her folded-up copy of a map of the area from her pocket, she eased out the creases with her fingers, traced her progress and realised she was standing at the border with the Ditchens' land. Surprised at the lack of boundary markings or other signage at the fence line, she refolded the map and then set off back towards the Peverells' yard.

The cloud cover broke for a moment, bathing the landscape in a warm sunlight that promised better weather ahead, and she squinted in the sudden contrast from the gloom that had cloaked her surroundings a moment before.

As she drew closer to the rabbit farm, the now familiar stench wafted towards her. She took a final, deep lungful of fresh air and then plunged onwards as a uniformed officer stumbled away from the group dispersing from the yard and rested her hand on the side of the slaughterhouse.

Kay took one look at the young police constable's face, and waved her towards to a patch of undergrowth beyond the open door of the outbuilding.

'There's a breeze around that side of the building. It helps.'

'Thanks, ma'am.'

Kay turned away from the police constable as Gavin sloped towards her, his face glum.

'Guv, I'm sor—'

She held up her hand to stop him. 'Like I said to Laura yesterday, we have to follow up these leads. As it is, I want you to give the council and the Department for Environment, Food and Rural Affairs a call. Ask them to inspect this place to check on their farming practices. I can't imagine they're going to be too impressed with the conditions in that outbuilding.'

His shoulders straightened as he pulled out his phone. 'Thanks, guv. Will do.'

Satisfied the rest of the team could manage without her, she made her way over to where she had parked, swapped her boots for shoes, and shoved the silage-covered wellingtons into a plastic bag that she sealed and placed in the back of the car to wash when she got home.

Reversing into the lane, she stomped on the accelerator.

As the countryside passed by in a blur, she tried to temper her frustration. Two searches in as many days turning up nothing did little for her relationship with the Chief Superintendent, but she stood by her decision to listen to her detectives.

She was sure that they were close.

'Dammit.'

She checked her mirrors before braking, then slewed the car into a lay-by, yanked the handbrake and slapped the steering wheel.

What the hell were they missing?

CHAPTER FORTY-FOUR

Carys sat with her pen poised over her notebook as Kay strode to the front of the incident room and stood in front of the whiteboard, her face grim as she crossed out the tasks relating to the property searches.

She'd heard from Gavin about the rabbit farm on his return, and was at once glad she didn't have to go and see the poor creatures, and sorry for her colleague that the hunch he'd been so sure about had eventuated in another frustrating day for the team.

Raising her eyes above the computer screen, she watched as her colleague sat slumped in his chair while he typed out his report, dark circles under his eyes from the late night he had had before an early morning start.

She bit her lip and opened up a web browser,

typing in the name of one of the nearby villages and enlarging the map that appeared in the results.

The maps spread out on the table near the whiteboard were no good to her – all the mark-ups and highlights would cause a distraction and serve to embed the opinions that had been discussed since Ethan Archer's body was discovered.

She needed a clean slate to work from.

At some point, she had to tell Gavin about the call she'd received this morning as well.

Her hands had started to shake when she'd seen the number displayed on her mobile phone screen, and she'd raced out into the corridor, speaking to the man from South Wales Police in hushed tones while keeping an eye on those who passed her by in case they suspected what was going on.

Afterwards, she couldn't recall what had been said – words such as "congratulations", "start date", and "notice period" were mentioned, and she was sure she had made the appropriate noises, but as the man had ended the call and confirmed an offer letter would be emailed and posted to her by the end of the afternoon, she had at least remembered to thank him.

Her elation at the news contrasted bitterly with the atmosphere in the incident room when she had returned to her desk, and it was then that she resolved to help her colleagues find Ethan and Shelley's killer before leaving them.

She swallowed, the corners of her eyes prickling, and she blinked to refocus her thoughts.

'You all right?'

Laura walked past with an armful of manila folders as she headed towards Debbie's desk.

Carys nodded. 'I'm fine, thanks.'

'You looked miles away there.'

She gestured to the documents and photographs strewn across her desk. 'Just trying to see if I can find another angle on all of this.'

Laura smiled then moved away, and Carys breathed out.

She couldn't tell them – not until she'd spoken to Kay first.

She owed her that much, and more.

A mobile phone rang at the front of the room, and she peered over her shoulder to see Kay deep in conversation.

The DI's face fell as she listened, and for a fleeting moment Carys thought someone had beaten her to her news, until Kay ended the call and headed towards them.

'That was Merseyside Police,' she said. 'They managed to trace Shelley's mum with the information

Laura gleaned from the secondary school here in Maidstone, and broke the news to her about her daughter's death an hour ago.'

'Bloody hell,' said Gavin. 'I can't imagine what she's going through.'

Kay's lips narrowed. 'I'd imagine it's going to get worse when the media get wind of the news. Our colleagues up there have provided a Family Liaison Officer for her and I'll have Phillip liaise with him to keep her and Shelley's stepdad up to date with our progress down here.'

Carys watched as she hurried back to her desk as another phone began to ring persistently, and heard Kay greet the Chief Superintendent when she answered.

Dropping her gaze back to the photographs, she tapped her finger against the back of the one she held and frowned as an idea began to form.

She bit her lip – they had already wasted valuable time pursuing leads and conducting searches to no avail; would she be faced with the same disappointment as her colleagues if she was wrong?

'Hey, Piper – got a minute?'

'What's up?'

'Come and take a look at this.'

He sighed, locked his computer screen and wandered around to where she sat.

Holding up two of the aerial photographs, she turned to face him. 'This rabbit farm you went to. They told you and Laura they don't have an aircraft, right?'

'Yes.' His brow puckered. 'I thought they might've been lying. That's what I thought we might find in the outbuildings. They're big enough.'

She smiled, pushed back her chair, and nudged his arm. 'I don't think you were too far off the truth. Come on.'

Leading the way between the desks, she crossed to where Kay sat while she tried to sort through the paperwork piling up in her in-tray.

'Guv?'

'Yes?'

'When you were at the Peverells' rabbit farm this morning, did you by any chance take a look around outside the buildings?'

Kay's eyes narrowed at the pair of them. 'Why?'

Carys put the aerial photograph on Kay's desk and jabbed her finger at the boundary line. 'What's this?'

The DI pulled the image closer, then leaned back in her chair and shrugged. 'A trackway. It must've been an old bridleway or something back in the day –

I had a walk along it, and it goes from the back of the building they're using as a slaughterhouse and leads into Ditchens' orchards. There's just a chain separating the two properties.'

'How wide is it?' said Gavin.

Kay cocked her head. 'About three car lengths, I suppose. Why, what are you thinking?'

Carys grinned.

'I think someone's using that track as a landing strip.'

CHAPTER FORTY-FIVE

Kay shifted gears and slowed the car as the thirty-mile-an-hour speed limit signs flashed into view, then looked across at Carys who held her phone and read out directions from the maps app as they weaved through the village streets.

The hastily convened briefing had ended forty minutes ago, with the instruction that an audit of existing witness statements and evidence be undertaken before anyone approached the Peverells.

It was going to be a late night for all of them, but Kay wanted to be sure.

If she allowed any of her team to go back to the rabbit farm, it would alert the owners to the premise now driving the investigation given that the property had already been searched, and she didn't want to have to explain to the Chief Superintendent a second time why time and costs had been wasted on a fruitless path of enquiry.

Despite Sharp's best endeavours at shielding her from the conversations taking place at Headquarters, her ears were still ringing from the reprimand she'd received earlier that afternoon.

Instead, she'd taken it upon herself to join the team in pulling apart everything they had to date, which was why she was now driving towards the house of Luke Martin, the man who had discovered Ethan Archer's body.

'The turning's coming up here on the right, guv – just past the infant school.' Carys pointed through the windscreen as a low brick wall topped with metal fence palings appeared, and then enlarged the map on her phone. 'Number sixty-three is about two hundred metres up on the left-hand side.'

'Ta.'

She found the address quickly, braking to a standstill at the kerb and peering at the house beyond a low privet hedge that framed a garden that had been landscaped to within an inch of its life, with decorative gravel where a lawn had once been and shrubs of varying heights providing a splash of colour.

'They're in,' said Carys, and checked her notes. 'His wife's name is Sonia, and they've got no kids at home. One son at boarding school near Guildford. Luke's forty-eight and runs a painting and decorating business.'

'Okay. At least with no kids at home, it'll make it a little easier turning up on the doorstep unannounced. Let's go.'

Kay had opted not to phone ahead to speak with Luke Martin because she wanted to gauge his reaction face-to-face – not that she believed that he had anything to hide, but she found that sitting with a witness and going over their statements provided more insight if she could watch their facial expressions.

People gave away more than they thought with the way their eyes and hands moved, and she wanted to know if Luke's subconscious had taken in more detail about the farm where Ethan's body was found than was contained in his current statement.

Leading the way up the short driveway, she heard a television through the front window, the light flickering against curtains that had been pulled almost completely shut. A gap at the top provided a view of the living room ceiling, nothing more, and she moved to the front door.

At the sound of the bell ringing, the television was muted and she could hear the undertones of a conversation as the inhabitants wondered who was calling at this time of night. Eventually, the hallway light was switched on, a chain rattled against the wooden surface, and then the door opened and Luke Martin peered out, confusion in his eyes, and his mid-length brown hair sticking up on end as if he'd been reclining on the sofa.

He rested a hand on the doorframe and frowned. 'Detective—?'

'Kay Hunter. We met at Dennis Maitland's farm a few days ago. This is my colleague, DC Carys Miles. Can we come in?'

She moved forward, not giving him a chance to come up with an excuse as a voice carried through from the living room.

'Who is it, Luke?'

'The police.'

A shocked silence met his response, and then his wife appeared, her mouth open in surprise.

'What are you doing here?'

'Shall we sit down somewhere and stop this cold air getting in?' said Kay, aware that the front door was still open and keen to press on with the interview.

'We've just got a few questions we'd like to follow up with you if that's okay.'

Luke blinked, then moved aside as Carys stepped over the threshold and shut the door. 'But I gave you a statement.'

'I know. We've been working through a number of lines of enquiry though, and so we wanted to clarify a few things.'

'I suppose so – best use the kitchen; Sonia's got her studying spread out all over the sofa.'

His wife gave a slight shrug. 'I'm trying to finish my degree before I hit fifty – I figured I wanted to learn something new.'

'What she won't tell you is that it's her third degree,' said Luke as he led the way down the hallway, a note of pride in his voice. 'Needless to say, our son takes after her, not me.'

'I understand from your statement he's at boarding school at the moment,' said Kay as the couple busied themselves clearing the kitchen table of interior design magazines, paint catalogues and paperwork.

'Just outside Guildford,' said Luke, closing a laptop and pushing it to one side. 'Take a seat. Do you want a coffee or anything?'

'No, that's fine, thanks. We won't keep you long.'

Kay waited until he and his wife sat opposite, checked that Carys was ready to take notes, and then turned her attention back to Luke. 'The farm where you were metal detecting – how long have you known Dennis Maitland?'

'About four years. I painted his kitchen, got chatting with his wife about how I liked history and things like that, and she mentioned I should ask him if I ever wanted to explore some of the land around the farm. She'd been researching the place on and off since they got married and was interested in what might be there. Me and Tom didn't get into the metal detecting until about a year ago, and it wasn't until now that Dennis could let us on the land. We only had a window of a few days anyway, because he was keen to plant the first of this year's crop.' His face fell, and he dropped his gaze to his hands. 'I wish I'd listened to Sonia and taken up golf now.'

His wife reached out and squeezed his fingers. 'Luke won't tell you, but he's been having nightmares ever since he found that man's body.'

He blushed, and raised his chin. 'I'll get over it eventually.'

'It's nothing to be embarrassed about. You must speak to your doctor if it's affecting your sleep,' said Kay. She gestured to the invoices and bills that had been pushed to one side. 'After all, you've got a business to run. Our officers often find talking to someone helps.'

Luke nodded, but said nothing.

'Have you been back to the farmhouse recently? Since painting the kitchen?' said Kay.

'No – no need to, really. That day at the field was the first time I'd been back there.'

'Did you see anyone else between leaving the main road and getting to the field?'

'No. Dennis was working in the adjacent field, and it was just me and Tom. The track leading to the field hadn't been used in a while, either. I thought I was going to get my vehicle stuck in the ruts before I even got there.'

Kay recalled the way Barnes had struggled to reach the crime scene, and couldn't argue with the man.

'When you did the decorating for the Maitlands, did you see anyone else around the farm?'

Luke frowned, and drummed his fingers on the table for a moment. 'Only a couple of workers – I think they'd been with them for a while. They seemed friendly enough.'

'Have you had any contact with Mr Maitland since the day you found the body in his field?'

'He phoned to check how I was doing about three days ago, which I thought was good of him. He said he hoped I hadn't been put off by what happened – I think his wife is still keen to find out if there's anything of historical interest on the land.' Luke shivered. 'I won't be helping her though. I'm never going back there again.'

CHAPTER FORTY-SIX

'What do you think, guv?'

Carys peered over the roof of the pool car at her, her breath fogging in the cool air that cloaked the village.

A light fog was beginning to appear, creating soft balls of light where streetlights shone from sporadic placements along the street.

'I want to speak to Dennis Maitland again.'

'Tonight?'

'Yes. Jump in.'

She twisted the key in the ignition and pulled away from the kerb while Carys fastened her seatbelt, and accelerated as she reached the main road. 'When you spoke with Maitland, did he say anything about hearing an aircraft going overhead in the days leading up to finding Ethan's body?'

'Only that he didn't hear one. I asked him whether he knew if his neighbours owned a light aircraft too, but he said he didn't know.'

Kay tapped her fingers on the wheel and kept a keen eye on the deep verges either side of the road in case a large animal decided to run out in front of the car. This time of night, she wouldn't spot a deer until it was too late, and she'd been to enough accident scenes in her days as a police constable to know what the aftermath of an impact like that could be.

After twenty minutes, she turned the car into the Maitlands' farmyard, the tyres rumbling over the iron cattle grid before she braked in front of the farmhouse.

A security light blinked to life above the front porch as she climbed from the car, but the front windows remained dark, with no sign of life.

Rapping the brass knocker fixed to the oak panelled door, she held her breath.

Hopefully the farmer hadn't been in bed for long.

Muffled footsteps sounded from the other side, followed by a muttered curse before a man's voice called out.

'Who's there?'

'Detective Inspector Kay Hunter, Kent Police.'

A bolt shot back. Seconds later, keys jangled and the door was wrenched open.

Dennis Maitland stared out at them, tightening the sash of a thick dressing gown, worn slippers on his feet and an equally fatigued expression on his face.

'Detective, it's half past eleven, and I'm due to be up in six hours. What do you want?'

'I'm sorry, Mr Maitland, but I have some urgent questions that won't wait until the morning. Can we come in?'

'Hang on.' He rummaged in the deep pockets of his dressing gown, and then placed his fingers to his ears. 'That's better. Hearing aids. Can't hear properly without them.'

'Then how did you—?'

'I woke him to see who was at the door.' A woman's voice floated down the stairs before Maitland's wife appeared, looking none too pleased. 'We were asleep.'

'I'm sorry,' said Kay, 'but like I said to your husband, we're at a critical point in our investigation.'

'Liz, go and light the wood burning stove in the sitting room,' said Maitland. 'It's too cold to be standing here, and the heating went off hours ago.'

His wife rolled her eyes, then beckoned to Kay

and Carys. 'Come on, then. I'm not putting the kettle on, though – he'll never get back to sleep if he has caffeine at this time of night.'

Kay caught Carys's expression as they traipsed after her, and gave a small smile.

She knew she would annoy the Maitlands with the late visit, and if she could have waited she would, but she desperately needed some answers.

She took a seat on the sofa the farmer's wife indicated and waited while the woman coaxed flames to life before placing a couple of logs in the stove and closing the iron door.

A warm glow emanated through the glass, and soon she could feel the heat filling the room.

'I'll be as brief as I can,' she said once the Maitlands were settled in armchairs on each side of the stove. 'When Carys here spoke to you in the days following the discovery of Mr Archer's body in your field, you stated that you didn't know if the landowners of the properties joining yours owned a light aircraft – is that correct?'

Maitland frowned. 'That's right, yes.'

'Mrs Maitland—'

'Call me Liz.'

'Liz, are you aware of any aircraft owned by your neighbours?'

'No, but then we don't really have much to do with them. We don't socialise with them, and I've never been to their properties. I've got no reason to.'

'Where were you in the days leading up to Mr Archer's body being found? I see from your husband's statement that my colleagues in uniform took that day that you weren't around and had been away for five days.'

'I was visiting a supplier,' said Liz. 'We're about to start growing lavender for the oil, and I needed to make sure we were going to get the seeds in time. I'm importing them from Europe, and I've had all sorts of issues with the paperwork. The suppliers tend to put their long-term clients' needs before ours as well.'

'I told her she should've gone for one of the common varieties already grown around the county,' said Dennis. 'It would've been easier.'

'I don't want "common".' Liz pouted. 'That's the whole point.'

'When did you get back?' said Kay.

'Thursday morning. After Dennis phoned to tell me what happened, I was in two minds whether to drop everything and come back, but he persuaded me not to.'

'She'd invested so much time into building up a relationship with the suppliers, I didn't want her to ruin her chances of getting a good price,' he said, reaching out and patting his wife's knee.

Kay glanced at the stove as one of the logs crackled and popped before settling against the glass door with a shower of sparks, and then turned back to the farmer.

'How long have you worn hearing aids for?'

'I blame all these years operating loud machinery,' he said with a rueful smile. 'I can't hear a thing without these. Mind you, given the choice of what's on the television, I don't think it's so bad. At least I can read my book in peace.'

'Why on earth would you want to know that?' said Liz.

Kay ignored her. 'And do you remove them every night?'

'Yes. We tend to go up at about nine-thirty and I'll read for half an hour or so before we put the light out.'

'Nothing wakes him,' said Liz, 'not even his own snoring. More often than not, he doesn't hear the alarm go off unless he remembers to turn up the volume if I'm away.'

Kay sat back against the cushions, noting Carys's look of wonder.

'Then, Mr Maitland, could I put it to you that if a light aircraft went overheard at a low altitude at night that you wouldn't hear it?'

CHAPTER FORTY-SEVEN

Kay sipped from a takeout coffee cup and peered through the windscreen at the entrance to the Ditchens' fruit farm a few hundred metres down the road.

The fog had lifted from the countryside in the past half an hour, bright sunshine piercing through pockets of cloud casting shadows onto the lane. A damp chill clung to the inside of the pool car, and she wiggled her toes within her ankle boots to try to keep warm.

Beside her Carys spoke into a radio, coordinating with the Force Control Room as they waited for a patrol car to join them.

She flicked her wrist, her gaze catching the dials of her watch.

Eight o'clock.

'How far away are they?'

'Ten minutes.' Carys put the radio in its cradle on the dashboard. 'They've got Harriet's team on standby as well.'

'Okay. Where are Barnes and Piper?'

'Parked about a mile from the Peverells' rabbit farm, just the other side of this lane. There are two cars on the way to support them, but they won't do anything until you give the word.'

Kay drained her coffee and put the empty cup between the front seats. 'Have you told Gavin that you're leaving?'

Her colleague sighed. 'Not yet. I'm not sure how to.'

'Well, don't leave it too long. You don't want him finding out from someone else – you know what the station can be like once a rumour starts.' A flash of white appeared in the door mirror, and she gestured to Carys to start the car before opening the radio channel. 'Barnes? You're good to go.'

Carys checked her mirrors, then pulled out in front of the liveried Kent Police patrol car and accelerated along the lane towards the Ditchens' farm.

Kay gritted her teeth as Carys swung the vehicle into the driveway, her foot hardly touching the brake, and unclipped her seatbelt as the car stopped.

The patrol car braked beside them, the two occupants springing out before walking towards the farmhouse.

Carys tapped her on her elbow. 'That's the office over there.'

'All right. Check it – make sure there's no-one inside and then seal it until the search teams are ready to go through.'

As Carys walked away, the front door to the farmhouse opened and Kay saw a man in his fifties take a step back in surprise at the two uniformed officers standing on his doorstep.

She turned at the sound of another car engine.

Moments later, a second patrol car pulled up beside her, PS Harry Davis at the wheel, his face grim.

'Morning, Harry. Didn't know you were joining us.' She nodded to PC Phillip Parker as he climbed from the passenger seat and closed the door.

'Thought you could do with an extra pair of hands, guv.' He glanced over his shoulder towards the farmhouse. 'Have they served the warrant?'

'Just now. Do you want to coordinate with them? I'll have a quick word with Mr Ditchens before I take a look around.'

'Sounds good, guv.'

Kay wandered across the muddy yard to the farmhouse, where Hugh Ditchens was standing on the threshold to his home, his eyes wide in shock.

'Are you the detective in charge of all this?' he said, his arms crossed over his chest. 'What's going on?'

She held up her warrant card. 'Detective Inspector Kay Hunter, and yes – I'm in charge. My officers will search your property in relation to a murder we're currently investigating.'

Ditchens' mouth opened and closed before he found his voice again. 'That's preposterous. Is this about the chap who was found dead in Maitland's field? What has Maitland been saying about me?'

'What can you tell me about the track between your orchard and the Peverells' rabbit farm?'

'What?' He blinked. 'It's an old drover's track. We keep it as a fire break between the properties.'

'Are fires a big problem here?'

'Look, it's a safety precaution – that's all. The track helps to space apart the tree varieties to aid propagation as well. We grow specific varieties for London markets, local restaurants, that sort of thing so we can't afford those to cross-pollinate.'

Kay narrowed her eyes at him. 'All right, Mr Ditchens. If that's how this is going to be. Make sure you stay here where one of my officers can see you, and please refrain from using your mobile phone.'

Turning away, she stomped across to where Carys waited beside the low outbuilding used as an office, the door closed and a criss-cross of blue and white police tape sealing the entry until the uniformed search team were ready to enter.

'What did he say?'

'A lot of hot air about the track being a fire break, or a way to stop cross-pollination of trees.'

'Fancy a walk then, guv?'

Kay grinned. 'I think we could do with some fresh air, so why not? Which way is the track from here?'

'Behind that machinery shed with the tractor outside it.'

She set a fast pace, her shorter colleague a few steps behind as she made her way past the corrugated steel structure.

A wooden five-bar gate separated the yard from the first orchard, and as she opened it she lifted her gaze to the tops of the trees to see the first blush of pink cherry blossom.

On any other day, the walk between the fruit trees would have been idyllic, but her thoughts kept returning to Ethan and Shelley and the conditions they must have endured.

She waited while Carys caught up.

'There are no buildings here,' she said, 'so where were Ethan and Shelley kept?'

'I can't see any sign of anyone camping here, either,' said Carys. She pointed ahead of their position. 'There's the start of the track – you can see where the trees begin to thin out.'

Kay set off once more.

Here and there, the longer grass between the trees had been trampled, and she gestured to Carys to move away. 'This path through here has been used recently. Can you use that tape to form a barrier between these trees until we've got an idea of how the search at the farm is going?'

She took the end that Carys held out to her, tied a knot and waited while her colleague did the same, and then moved forward once more, skirting around the area they'd cordoned off.

She paused at the edge of the track, her heart lurching as her eyes swept the ground. 'Phone Harriet – we're going to need her here.'

'What've you got, guv?'

'Look.'

She waited until the detective constable was at her side, and then pointed to the deep parallel ruts a few metres from where she stood.

The two lines disappeared along the grass track, the markings becoming fainter as they passed underneath the chain that separated the two farms, and heading in a straight line towards the Peverells' property.

'Something heavy dropped here, then continued onwards along this track. I didn't see any deep lines at the other end.'

'An aircraft landing,' said Carys. 'Bloody hell, guv. You found it.'

Kay peered into the distance. 'But we haven't, have we? There was nothing at the rabbit farm. And I haven't heard anything from our team here. They'd have come to find us if their search had turned up an aircraft.'

'Well, it definitely landed here.' Carys walked across to the trees that lined the left-hand boundary, then stopped. 'Guv, the ends of this branch have been broken off. Clipped by a wing, perhaps?'

'It'd take some balls to land here, wouldn't it? I mean, it's wide enough but you'd have to know what you were doing.'

'Maybe that's why the ruts are so deep here. We've always assumed that the plane was being flown at night, so that would make it more difficult, even for a pilot who was used to landing here.' Carys moved back to where Kay stood and shielded her eyes from the low morning sun. 'Is this track long enough to taxi and take off from?'

'When Harriet arrives, ask her to get one of her team to measure the length, and then check that with one of your contacts from the airfields you spoke to.'

'Will do. Do we arrest Ditchens?'

Kay peered through the orchard towards the house. 'Take him in for questioning. I'll head over to the Peverells' rabbit farm to see how Barnes and Piper are getting on.'

CHAPTER FORTY-EIGHT

'I'm never eating rabbit again.'

Barnes tore the protective gloves from his hands and dropped them into the biohazard waste bucket one of the uniformed officers held out to him, and scowled at the cages he could see through the open door to the outbuilding.

'These aren't for human consumption. They're for dog and cat food. The proper rabbit farms around here that supply restaurants are much more humane,' said Gavin. 'This place is a disgrace.'

'Did you get in touch with DEFRA?'

'Yes, and the council.' His colleague scowled. 'They said they were understaffed and struggling to deal with the complaints they already had in the system about various places in the county but that they'd send someone out at some point.'

'Unbelievable.' Barnes shook his head and pulled out his mobile phone as it emitted a beep. 'The guv is on her way.'

'God, I hope we find something. She won't thank us if this is a waste of time again.'

'It's never a waste of time, Piper, you know that. Now, do you want to show me that slaughterhouse? Might as well take a look while we're here. Where are the owners, anyway?'

Gavin gestured towards the house off to the far side of the outbuildings. 'Uniform have Helen Peverell inside. Her husband isn't here – she says he should be back in a couple of hours.'

'Where is he?'

'The post office in Tonbridge, apparently.' Gavin pulled open the door to the slaughterhouse. 'They've sent someone over there to find him.'

Barnes reached for his handkerchief and covered his nose. 'Christ, it stinks in here.'

'I suppose if they're selling the meat for pet food, they don't have to worry so much about hygiene.'

'I'll bet the council will say otherwise. This place is huge, isn't it? I mean, they're only using a third of the space in here.' He pointed at the solid doors at the end of the building. 'Are those the freezers?'

'Yes. They kill the rabbits over in that corner, butcher the meat at those galvanised tables at the back there, and then the meat is stored in the freezers until it's collected for distribution to the pet food suppliers. It's like a production line, isn't it?'

Barnes grimaced at the description, but could see why his colleague described it in such a way. He turned at movement next to the door and a uniformed constable peered in.

'All right if we start the search in here, Sarge?' she said.

'Be our guest. We'll get out of your way in a minute.'

'Thanks, Sarge.'

He pushed his handkerchief back in his pocket and squared his shoulders. 'All right, I'm going to have a quick look around, and then we'll head outside to wait for the boss.'

'Okay.' Gavin wandered away, his shoes echoing off the concrete floor as he crossed to the far side of the open space, his head bowed as he read through updates from other members of the investigation team on his mobile phone.

Barnes shoved his hands in his coat pockets and

began to work his way along the wall, his gaze taking in the sharp knives and cleavers lined up beside the workstations and the chopping boards propped up in a galvanised sink.

Flies buzzed around a large covered bin directly behind the workstations, and he lifted the lid off one, instantly recoiling.

Scores of rabbit skins filled the steel container, the matted fur bloodied and stained with urine.

He dropped the lid back into place, a shiver crossing his shoulders as he progressed towards the freezers, and then wrapped his handkerchief around the steel handle set into one of the doors and peered inside.

A cloud of icy air escaped, chilling his face and sending the hairs on the back of his neck standing on end.

The stench lessened in here, although the sight of all the small frozen pink bodies lined up in neat rows turned his stomach.

There were so many of them.

'Ian – get over here!'

Gavin's shout echoed across the slaughterhouse.

Barnes slammed shut the freezer door and hurried past the search team who paused in their work, an expectant look in their eyes.

He found the detective constable crouching beside the front of the building in the far corner, his excitement palpable.

A row of sacks containing hay and food pellets for the rabbits had been propped against a row of empty shelves, and Gavin was staring at the wall.

'What've you got?'

'These shelves were full when we were searching the place on Tuesday – sacks like those on the floor there were stacked along them. The team looked between the sacks as part of their search, but they didn't see this.'

Barnes tweaked his suit trousers and crouched beside his colleague, pulling his reading glasses out of his pocket before peering at the timbers between the shelves.

A faint set of scratch marks had been cut into the wooden surface with a sharp blade depicting a rough approximation of a parachute between open wings that had been carved with an unsteady hand.

He held his breath as he read the words inscribed underneath.

Help me.

'Bloody hell. That's Ethan's tattoo, isn't it?'

CHAPTER FORTY-NINE

'Ready?'

Gavin tapped the edge of the manila folder against his thigh, his jaw set as he eyed the door to interview room two, then exhaled. 'I think so. Thanks, guv.'

Kay smiled. 'No problem. I'm going to be relying on you even more in future, you realise that, don't you?'

'I know.'

'When did Carys tell you?'

'Just after you both turned up at the Peverells' place. I can't believe she's leaving us so soon.'

'They're keen for her to start as soon as possible. I'm sure she's just as keen to get on with it.'

He frowned. 'I wish she was staying here. Are there no DS roles available in Kent, guv?'

'Believe me, I checked. So did Sharp. There's no budget for promotions at the moment in the area – all the funding has been allocated to train new police constables as soon as possible to meet the targets set by the government. Hope you weren't expecting a pay rise this year, either.'

She winked, then pushed open the door and crossed to the table and four chairs set against the far wall.

Helen Peverell sat with her hands in her lap, her head bowed. A thick strand of hair hung over her face, and she'd been crying. Mouth downturned, she lifted her eyes to the two detectives as they sat opposite, and wiped a streak of watery mascara from her cheek.

Her solicitor, a skinny man in his late fifties with close-cropped hair and a pinched expression, glared at the detectives as he passed across his business card.

'Thank you, Mr Brackenridge,' said Kay, and then waited while Gavin pressed the record button on the machine beside his elbow and read out the formal caution.

That done, he opened the manila folder and extracted three photographs of Ethan Archer, placing them on the table in front of Helen. 'Do you know this man?'

The woman bit her lip, then shook her head.

'Answer for the purposes of the recording, please, Helen,' said Kay.

'No.'

'Are you sure?' said Gavin. 'Take another look.'

'I don't know him.'

The detective constable reached into the folder and selected a fourth photograph. 'Do you recognise this tattoo?'

'No.'

'Really? Here's another image of it. Looks similar, doesn't it?' said Gavin. He leaned forward and tapped it with his finger. 'This photograph was taken in your slaughterhouse three hours ago. It's on the wall, behind the shelving units. What's it doing there?'

'I don't know. I've never seen it before.'

'I'll bet if you had, you'd have had it removed, wouldn't you?'

Helen said nothing.

'Who's in charge of restocking the shelves, Helen? You, or one of your workers?' said Kay.

She shrugged. 'The workers. That's what they're paid for.'

'Are we talking about the part-timers you have on your payroll, or someone else?' Kay leaned back and folded her arms. 'Because someone moved the bags after our last search on Monday, didn't they? Did someone hope that we'd come back, and that we'd notice?'

Helen swallowed, but held her tongue.

Gavin turned another photograph around to face Helen. 'The writing is different under this tattoo in your slaughterhouse. Can you read out what it says?'

The woman glared at him, then at her solicitor, who gestured to her to answer the question.

'It says "help me",' she said, her tone petulant.

'Who might have wanted help?' said Gavin. 'Why would someone carve that into the wall?'

'I don't know.'

'Why were the shelves empty today?' said Kay.

'There's a new delivery of food coming this afternoon,' said Helen. 'We need to rotate the stock so the older food pellets get used first so they don't rot. The new sacks get placed under the old stock, that's all.'

'And why was the work abandoned in such a way that this drawing was exposed?'

'I don't know.'

'You've provided us with details of the part-time workers you employ, but looking at your payroll it seems that you're extremely generous with their pay compared with other farms in the area. Why would that be?'

'It's difficult work. It's hard to find good people,' said Helen. 'We pay them well in the hope that they'll stay. We haven't had anyone quit in four years, so that shows we're doing something right.'

Gavin pulled a sheaf of witness statements from the folder and ran his eyes down the text. 'Not one of them has a bad word to say about you or your husband. Are you paying them to keep quiet about your other workers?'

'What other workers?'

Kay clasped her hands on the table. 'Helen, we've spoken with similar agricultural businesses and we're of the opinion that the number of workers you legally employ isn't enough to keep up with the supply levels you've been maintaining for the past three years. You'd need at least another half a dozen full-time people to manage the battery farm on top of those you employ in the slaughterhouse. Where are those other workers?'

'I've got no idea what you're talking about. My employees are incredibly hard-working and diligent, that's all.'

Gavin turned to Kay and raised an eyebrow. 'Bet

they're having to work even harder, now two of the unpaid workers are dead.'

'Exactly my thoughts, DC Piper. And in hellish conditions.' Kay turned back to Helen. 'Who killed Shelley? You, or Adrian?'

'I didn't kill anyone!'

The woman's sudden outburst took Kay by surprise, and she leaned back. 'Where is your husband?'

'I told the policeman at the house – he went into Tonbridge. He had to go to the post office.'

'Helen, local police went to the post office. They haven't seen your husband. They didn't recognise his photograph at all. Where is he?'

Helen dropped her head and bit at the corner of her thumbnail. 'I don't know.'

CHAPTER FIFTY

Laura eyed the man on the other side of the table, and wondered why someone with such success in life would become caught up in such a heinous scheme as enslaving defenceless and vulnerable people.

Carys sat beside her, chin in hand while she nonchalantly flicked through Hugh Ditchens' original statement as the man sat opposite her, a trickle of sweat dribbling down the side of his face.

They had started the interview recording a few minutes before, and after reciting the formal caution Laura had fallen silent, expecting her colleague to start the questioning.

She worried at first that Carys had perhaps lost track of time, but then realised the more experienced detective was making Ditchens wait.

So, instead, she watched with fascination as the farmer first shifted in his seat, then cleared his throat, and finally looked to his solicitor for help.

'Detective Miles, if you've got something to say to my client, then please do.' The legal representative glared at them both. 'He's a busy man.'

Carys finally lifted her gaze from the witness statement and smiled. 'Yes, he *has* been busy, hasn't he?'

A few more moments passed while she jotted down some notes, and Laura bit the inside of her cheek as she glanced across and realised her colleague was writing her shopping list for the evening.

'Detective Hanway, do you have those aerial photographs please?' she said eventually.

'Here.' Laura slipped her hand into the manila folder under her elbow and picked out two clean copies of the photographs that she'd printed out for the interview.

None of the mark-ups used during the investigation were visible, and so when Carys placed them in front of Ditchens and his solicitor, the two men had a clear view of the farmer's property and the surrounding countryside.

'Do you own a light aircraft, Mr Ditchens?'

He pulled a handkerchief from his pocket and dabbed at his forehead. 'No, no, I don't. I told you that when you asked me the other day.'

'This isn't a test, Mr Ditchens. If you feel the need to change your previous statement, now is the time.'

'I don't own a light aircraft.'

'Do you have a pilot's licence?'

'No.'

'Are you aware of any private airfields in the area?'

'No, I'm not.'

Carys pushed the aerial photographs closer to the farmer, and indicated the wide track leading from his land to that belonging to the Peverells. 'What's this?'

'I told you. It's an old drover's track. It acts as a firebreak these days, and helps me avoid cross-pollination with the tree varieties.'

'Again, Mr Ditchens, I'll advise you that you can change your previous answers to my questions if you wish.'

Laura watched as the man's Adam's apple bobbed in his throat.

An aura of desperation hung in the air around him as his jaw worked, and she wondered what truths he was grappling with.

She held her breath as he opened his mouth to speak, then changed his mind with a slight shake of his head.

'Can I have the photographs taken at the Peverells' property earlier today, please, DC Hanway?' said Carys.

'Of course.' Pulling the series of six images from the folder, Laura laid them on top of the aerial photographs and waited.

'For the purposes of the recording, we are showing Mr Ditchens photographs taken on the ground at his property and at Helen and Adrian Peverell's farm,' said Carys, her voice clear and steady. 'Specifically, these images show the track leading from their property to yours, a measurement taken of the width of that track depicted with a tape measure, and a third photograph that shows deep indentations in the ground at the far end – on Mr Ditchens' land – of what appear to be wheel ruts. Any idea what might have caused these markings, Mr Ditchens?'

'I'm not sure.'

'But they're on your land. Surely you would want to know what caused them. There's quite a lot of damage to the ground there, isn't there? Didn't you tell us that you were worried about fly-tippers?'

He didn't respond.

Carys picked up a close-up photograph that had been taken of the trees at the side of the track. 'What caused this damage to your trees, Mr Ditchens?'

The farmer frowned. 'I don't know. I haven't seen that before.'

'What? Don't you check the trees in your orchard on a regular basis? Surely if some of your crops were damaged, you'd want to find out who did it?'

Misery swept across the farmer's eyes and he ran a hand over his mouth before speaking. 'Look, I just didn't want to cause a fuss, that's all.'

'Cause a fuss?' said Carys, her expression incredulous. 'We're dealing with two brutal murders, Mr Ditchens. And at the present time, you're a suspect in those murders.'

'But I had nothing to do with that man's death.' His face paled. 'Who else is dead?'

Laura shoved another photograph across the table to him without waiting for a cue from Carys. 'Shelley Yates. Twenty-five. Strangled, before she was dumped in a skip in Maidstone. And then, her feet were cut off.'

'Oh my God.'

'Now, Mr Ditchens,' said Carys. 'Perhaps you would like to tell us what you know about a light aircraft using the track that goes through your orchard to take off and land?'

He glanced at his solicitor, who nodded and gestured for him to continue, and then turned back to the two detectives, his whole demeanour that of a defeated man.

'Look, I'm sorry about that woman, but I had nothing to do with her death – or the man who was found in Maitland's field. The track in the orchard… you're right, it is used occasionally as a landing strip for a light aircraft, but it's not mine.'

'Whose is it?' said Carys.

'Helen and Adrian's.' He shrugged, his mouth downturned. 'Look, I didn't want to get into trouble, that's all. I tag along with them sometimes.'

'Tag along with them to where?' said Laura, her curiosity piqued.

'Well, mostly to France. They've got friends with a vineyard over there, so – and this is only once or twice a year, mind – we fly over and stock up on wine,' said Ditchens, his face miserable. His gaze moved to the table and he picked at a dent in the veneer with his fingernail. 'We – I – sometimes bring over cigarettes or tobacco for my employees. You know, to thank them. It's the same with the wine. Some of it I keep, some of it I might sell on. I think

Helen and Adrian might do the same. We don't mean any harm by it. It's just a bit of a jolly, to be honest.'

Carys held up her hand to stop him. 'Hang on. Are you telling us that all you use the aircraft for is to get from here to France to stock up on wine and tobacco every now and again? And am I right in presuming that the reason you've been lying to us is because you've been doing so without reporting the duty tax on excess purchases when you get back here?'

'I told them we'd get caught if we weren't careful.'

'Who's the pilot?'

'Helen, of course.' He smiled. 'Adrian doesn't have the patience – he's all brawn and muscle, that one.'

'Mr Ditchens, you should have told us this when we first interviewed you,' said Carys, unable to keep the frustration from her voice. 'You should have told us the truth.'

'I realise that now, and I'm so sorry. I just didn't want to get them into trouble,' said Ditchens. 'They're such a lovely couple. So hard working.'

CHAPTER FIFTY-ONE

Kay shoved open the door so hard the handle bounced off the plasterboard, and both Helen Peverell and her solicitor jumped in their seats.

She dropped her collection of manila folders onto the table, clenching her teeth as Gavin started the recording equipment and provided the required verbal confirmation that they were continuing the previous interview.

'Where's the aircraft, Helen?'

The woman kept her hands flat on the table, but her eyes widened. 'What?'

'The light aircraft you use to fly to France a few times a year. Where is it? It's not in any of the outbuildings on your farm – that much is certain given the number of searches we've carried out in the past few days, so where the hell is it?'

'I don't—'

'Don't, Helen.' Kay took a deep breath to maintain her calm, and then exhaled. 'Enough lies. Did you kill Ethan Archer?'

'No—'

'Did you tie his feet together, and then push him out of the aircraft while he was still alive?'

Helen's pallor turned a sickly shade of grey, but she remained silent.

'What about Shelley? Whose idea was it to hack off her feet?'

Blinking, Helen gripped the edge of the table, and then looked at her solicitor.

'The whole truth, Helen,' said Kay. 'Now.'

The woman swallowed. 'It was Adrian's idea.'

'To do what?'

'To kill Ethan.'

Hearing Gavin's sharp intake of breath at the admission, Kay sat back in her seat and folded her arms, relief coursing through her as she studied the woman. 'All right, Helen. Let's hear it. All of it.'

'It... it wasn't meant to end up this way. When we first bought the farm and did our research into the rabbits, it seemed so simple. Hardly anyone was doing it in the south of England – farming them for pet food, I mean. A lot of pet food companies were importing the dead rabbits in bulk from France, or Belgium. They don't have such stringent controls over there about how the rabbits are housed. Then, the political climate changed, and there were rumblings about lack of supply and delays at the ports. Can I have a drink of water?'

Kay waited while Gavin went to the door and signalled to a uniformed constable outside.

Moments later, he returned with two plastic cups and placed them in front of Helen and her solicitor, who, Kay noted, drained his water in three gulps before returning to his note taking.

Helen took a sip, and clasped her cup between her hands, her gaze remaining on the photograph of Ethan's prone body.

'Carry on,' said Kay.

'I saw a gap in the market, and said so to Adrian. We positioned ourselves as a better alternative to the pet food companies, pointing out that we wouldn't be affected by anything that was going on politically and that we could guarantee an uninterrupted supply. I mean, you've heard the term "breeding like rabbits", right?'

Neither Kay nor Gavin smiled.

'Anyway, within six months we were struggling. We couldn't afford to pay for more workers – we had four people helping us, but we'd agreed to some stupid terms when we first negotiated the supply contracts because we wanted to give the customers a reason to change to us, and so they wouldn't even think of paying us until at least ninety days had passed.' She moved the cup to her lips with a shaking hand, then changed her mind and lowered it to the table once more, water slopping over her fingers. 'That's when Adrian said we could get cheap labour. When I asked him how, he said we could get homeless people to come and work for us in return for a roof over their head and free food.'

'How very noble of you,' said Kay, unable to keep the sarcasm from her voice. 'Take the homeless off the streets, and turn them into modern-day slaves.'

'It wasn't like that!' Helen's face fell. 'Not at the beginning. I really did think we were doing them a favour. Then we got busier, and Adrian said we had to keep them, that we could turn a bigger profit if we found some more. It was his idea to pay more to the four employees we had in return for their silence. They could work part-time on a full-time wage, as long as they didn't tell anyone. Well, they weren't going to, were they? They had it easy, too.'

'What went wrong?'

Helen snorted. 'Everything. The customers renegotiated the contracts, we had to supply half as much meat again, and – I don't know – Adrian took it really badly. He started hitting the people we were housing—'

'The slaves, you mean,' said Gavin.

'He said that we could never risk them leaving, and that if anyone found out how we'd been treating them for the past three years, we'd be in a lot of trouble.' Helen pushed the water away. 'He said that the only way to make sure that happened was to make them too scared to want to try to escape. He would beat anyone who tried to get away, and make the others watch.'

'What about you, Helen? Did you ever try to escape?'

Kay watched as the woman bit her lip, then closed her eyes and gave a slight nod.

'Yes,' she said. 'Only once.'

'What did Adrian do?'

Helen opened her eyes, and it was then that Kay saw she was terrified.

'What did Adrian do to you, Helen?'

'I can't – he'll kill me.'

'Helen, he can't get to you in here. What did he do?'

The woman's shoulders heaved as tears spilled over her cheeks. 'He held a knife to my throat. One of the boning blades you saw in the slaughterhouse. He said he'd skin me alive if I tried to leave him, or if I tried to tell anyone about the people that we kept there.'

Kay gave her a moment to compose herself, and waited while she blew her nose.

'When did you learn to fly?'

'In my early twenties – before I met Adrian.' A watery smile crossed her lips. 'I'd wanted to learn to fly since I was a teenager, so my parents paid for lessons on my twenty-first birthday.'

'Where?'

'In Shropshire, where I grew up.'

'Are you allowed to fly at night?'

Helen shook her head, then remembered the recording equipment. 'No.'

'So, what happened the night Ethan Archer was murdered?'

'Adrian burst into the kitchen at about ten o'clock on the Friday night in a hell of a temper. He said there had been a breakout, and one of the workers had escaped. Said she'd disappeared up the lane before he could stop her, but that he'd caught the bloke who had helped her. Then, he said he was going to teach them a lesson that they wouldn't forget.'

She stopped, and took a few more sips of water.

'He made me go outside with him, to the slaughterhouse. He had chained Ethan's wrist to one of the supporting timber posts in the middle of the floor. It looked as if they'd been fighting – Ethan's nose looked broken—'

'Hardly a fair fight,' said Kay. 'Was your husband injured in any way?'

'Not that I could see.'

'Go on.'

'When I asked him what he was going to do, he… he changed. There was this look in his eyes that I've seen before, when he threatened me that time and I think Ethan saw it, too. Adrian didn't say anything – he got some plastic ties that we use to secure the food pellet sacks and wound one around Ethan's wrists before he unchained him. He told me to start up the plane – I'd flown it down from my parents' place that morning—'

'Stop there,' said Kay. 'You *own* an aircraft?'

'No – my parents own it. I just fly it now and again. I either drive up or get the train and then fly back. We were going to go over to France the next day.'

Kay scribbled a note to contact West Mercia Police in Shropshire to seize the aircraft for a forensic examination as she realised that Helen's story explained why they'd been unable to find any such aircraft registered or hidden locally.

'How did you get Ethan into the aircraft?'

'Adrian… He threatened to kill the others if Ethan didn't do what he was told. I think he knew he was going to die, but he was too weak to run away by then…' She broke off, and dabbed the tissue at the corner of her eyes.

Kay clenched her jaw at the abject cruelty of what she was hearing. 'Keep going.'

'When Ethan got in the aircraft, Adrian put the other plastic tie around his ankles, and then hit him.' Helen swallowed. 'He kept hitting him, beating him around the head until he passed out. Then he told me to get in and get the plane up in the air. I was terrified – I've never flown at night before, but Adrian said all I had to do was get us up high enough over the reservoir so he could push him out. He said it would be a fitting end for a paratrooper.'

'You knew what Ethan did?'

'Yes. I overheard him telling the others one day. I didn't put two and two together at the time – I didn't know he would try to use what he knew back then to help them escape.'

'Would you have told Adrian if you did?'

'I don't know. I suppose so.'

'What happened once you were up in the air?'

'It's only a small aircraft. Adrian was sat between me and Ethan, who was passed out and leaning against the passenger door. I was trying really hard to get my bearings and read the instruments – taking off was a nightmare. Adrian got out his mobile phone – he said he was going to film the moment he pushed Ethan out the door so he could show the others, to show them what happens to people who try to escape. We were only up a few hundred metres when suddenly Ethan came to – he lashed out at Adrian before he had a chance to react, and I screamed. I thought I was going to lose control. Adrian somehow managed to lean over Ethan while he had him in a headlock, and opened the door. He – he pushed him out.' She closed her eyes. 'He managed to twist around and cling to the door frame, but Adrian kicked his hands so he lost his grip. I can still hear him screaming. I… I can't sleep at night.'

Kay heard Gavin shift in his seat next to her, and turned to see the detective constable's face paler then she'd ever seen.

'Helen, what happened after you landed the plane?'

The woman used her shirtsleeve to wipe at her eyes. 'Adrian was angry – he said that Ethan should have been dropped over the water so his body wouldn't be found. He took one of the vans we use to get around the far side of the property – we don't use it on the roads, so it isn't registered. He said he knew of a track north of Maitland's place and we were sure that Ethan had dropped somewhere near there. He was gone for nearly two hours, but when he came back he said he couldn't risk trying to move the body. He left him there, and told me to fly the plane back to Mum and Dad's first thing in the morning. I got the train back the next day.'

'Where's the van, Helen?'

'He said he took it somewhere on the Isle of Sheppey and set light to it so it couldn't be traced back to us. It wasn't registered anyway – he only used it to transport stuff around the farm.'

'Who killed Shelley?'

'Adrian, of course. He was livid that having to deal with Ethan meant that she'd got away. He spent days hunting her down, going back to Maidstone where he'd first convinced her to come and work for us. He said she didn't have anywhere else to go, and we couldn't risk her talking to anyone.'

'Why the hell did he hack off her feet?'

'For the same reason he killed Ethan. To warn the others.'

'How many more slaves are you holding at the farm?'

'Four now. There were seven originally, but one man got too sick to work about six months ago. Adrian took him away.'

Kay shivered at the woman's words. 'You said he chopped off Shelley's feet "to warn the others",' she said. 'What do you mean? What did he do?'

'He threw them down the cellar steps and told them that's what happened to people who ran away.'

'What cellar?' said Gavin. 'Where have you been keeping these poor people?'

'Under the slaughterhouse,' said Helen. She ran a hand through her hair, defeated. 'It's an old nineteenth-century grain store, you see. There's a hatch in the floor under one of the boning tables. Saves us having them ever leave the slaughterhouse and being seen by anyone.'

Kay pushed back her chair. 'Interview suspended at seven forty-five. Gavin, with me.'

She rushed from the room, pulling out her mobile

phone as she ran along the corridor, the detective constable at her heels.

'Where are you going, guv?'

'Back to the farm, Piper. There are four people trapped under a barn without food or water, and Adrian Peverell will know by now that his wife is in custody. He's got nothing to lose.'

CHAPTER FIFTY-TWO

Kay lowered her mobile phone to her lap, and watched the darkened countryside pass the speeding car's window.

Since Helen's confession, she'd been liaising with DCI Sharp and Headquarters to provide sufficient manpower to go to the Peverells' farm and apprehend Adrian – and locate the rest of the slaves he and his wife were keeping in captivity.

Uniformed patrols had already visited the homes of their four employees, carrying out the arrests as the men and women had been having dinner or watching television in comfort while their unpaid counterparts tried to survive in squalor, starving.

Helen's solicitor was already working to ensure his client received more lenient charges than her husband, arguing that she had lived in fear of her life.

Kay was having none of it.

She wanted both of them to be incarcerated for as long as possible, to know what it was like to have their freedom taken away. Even then, they would be living in better conditions than the people they enslaved.

'Are you all right?' said Barnes, shifting up a gear and guiding the car around a sharp bend. 'You've been quiet ever since you finished that last call.'

'I should've put two and two together when I saw Adrian this morning,' she said. 'The sores on his cheeks, I mean. I put it down to acne or something like that, but it's an allergic reaction, isn't it?'

Barnes choked out a sardonic laugh. 'Bloody hell, you're right. I didn't realise either. It's the glue, right? The glue he used to fix the fake beard to his face when he was approaching those homeless people in Maidstone. It's why we didn't recognise him when we saw him on the CCTV footage talking to Jeremy.'

'Exactly.'

Her detective sergeant slowed the vehicle as they approached the Peverells' farm and glanced over. 'It wouldn't have saved Shelley, guv. She was long gone by the time we heard from Jeremy.'

'I know.' Her eyes snapped to the radio clipped to the dashboard as it spat to life and the drivers of the patrol vehicles called in their positions. 'God, I hope we're not too late to save the others.'

'Adrian's car was found an hour ago out on the main road between Sevenoaks and Hildenborough, guv – do you think he's still in the area? He could be anywhere by now.'

'He's violent, and vindictive, Ian. I don't think he's going to let those people go free. He could've made his way back to the farm by any number of footpaths that cross this countryside, and he knows the area better than us. At least we've got patrols out at the Maitland and Ditchens farms in case he turns up there.'

'Do you think he'll threaten them if he does?'

'Yes – it's why I authorised the use of Tasers if necessary. I'm not taking any chances with this bastard.'

'Here we go.'

Barnes swung the car into the entrance to the farm behind a patrol car travelling from the opposite direction, and parked next to the house as floodlights blinked to life around the farmyard.

'If we were anywhere else, I'd think he was overcautious with his security,' he said.

'Helen said there are cameras all over the place, too – on the back of the outbuildings as well, in case any of the slaves try to make a break for it over the fields.'

'Bloody hell. They're monsters,' said Barnes as a uniformed officer crossed to the house and began to hammer his fist against the front door.

Moments later, two more officers joined him, brandishing a ram that they smashed through the lock before all three disappeared into the building.

'Put your stab vest on,' said Kay. 'I'm not taking any chances given those knives he's got in the slaughterhouse.'

She fastened her own over her jacket, then got out of the car, her eyes sweeping the floodlit yard.

Save for the six uniformed officers and Barnes, the farmyard was deserted.

The wind caught her hair and sent a blue plastic tarpaulin tumbling over the concrete hardstanding outside the outbuilding that housed the rabbits.

She held her breath as she scanned the yard for any sign of life.

The doors to the slaughterhouse were wide open, a padlock lying on the ground beside the right-hand one, its metal surface catching in the light. The space beyond the doors was pitch-black, and as the wind direction shifted, she caught the stench of something that sent a chill crawling through her veins.

She peered over her shoulder at a shout from the house.

'He's not in here, ma'am.'

'Guv, that's petrol,' said Barnes as he moved to her side.

Kay lowered her chin and murmured a command into her radio. 'I want everyone to spread out around the slaughterhouse – move slowly, stay in the shadows where you can. Suspect is believed to have spilled petrol, and is considered a threat.'

She turned down the volume as the responses were called back, and greeted PC Dave Morrison as he joined her.

'Ma'am, you should move back. With the dust from the food and straw that's stored in that building, it's highly combustible.'

'There are at least four people trapped in the cellar underneath the building,' said Kay. 'I'm not going anywhere. Get onto control and tell them we're going to need the fire brigade here just in case.'

'Will do, guv.'

Morrison moved a short distance away and relayed her message while she contemplated her options.

If she had her team rush into the building, Adrian could harm the captives before they had a chance to reach them.

She could smell petrol, but they had no idea where it had been spilled, or in what quantity.

Until she knew where he was, she couldn't contemplate staging a rescue in case he attacked a member of her team.

She had to assume he had armed himself with the knives used to butcher the rabbits, and she had no idea whether he had access to firearms as well – Helen had clammed up shortly after telling them about the cellar, and her solicitor was holding out until he knew what sort of charges were going to be brought against his client before persuading her to talk any further.

'Kay – it's him,' said Barnes.

Her attention snapped back to the doors of the slaughterhouse as a figure emerged from the gloom.

Adrian Peverell cast a formidable figure as he moved forward, brandishing a long blade in his right hand that he pointed at her.

'You stand back,' he shouted. 'All of you, stand back.'

'Calm down, Adrian,' said Kay, holding up her

hands. 'We just need you to let us see that those people are alive and well.'

In response, Adrian started to laugh. As he raised his left hand, two of the officers emerged from the shadows, battens raised, each shouting at him to drop his weapon.

Instead, his left hand twitched, and the flare from a naked flame illuminated his face.

'Shit,' said Barnes. 'He's got a cigarette lighter. He's going to burn the whole bloody place down.'

'Adrian, please – let's talk.' Kay heard her voice shake, desperation clawing at her nerves.

Behind the farmer, buried within the depths of the slaughterhouse, she heard a woman scream.

'What do we do?' said Barnes out of the side of his mouth.

'Keep him talking. Dave, are you still there?'

'Yes, guv,' said a voice behind her.

'Can any of your officers get between him and the barn?'

'I'll see if they can try.'

'Do it. Slowly and quietly. Use whatever force necessary.'

'Guv.'

Kay exhaled, hoping her height would go some way to mask the actions of the police sergeant behind her as he relayed her instructions under his breath.

She focused on the man moving from one foot to the other only a few metres away from where she stood.

'Adrian, we know what happened here. We know what happened to Ethan and Shelley. Don't make it worse for yourself.'

He waved the flaming cigarette lighter towards her. 'That bitch. I knew she wouldn't keep quiet. I knew I should've dealt with her years ago.'

He kicked at a pile of empty sacks in front of the doors, then threw back his head and screamed at the night sky.

The cigarette lighter wavered before the flame went out, and Kay heard the scratch of metal before fire shot out from the end once more.

'He's lost it,' said Barnes. 'You're not going to talk him down from this. Is he on something?'

'Helen didn't mention drug use.'

'Great, we've got a psychopath on our hands, then.'

'Adrian, can you put out that lighter?' said Kay, keeping her voice even despite her colleague's prognosis. 'Can you show us those people inside are all right?'

The man cackled and moved a few steps closer towards her. He thrust his hand behind him, using the lighter to point at the slaughterhouse, his face glistening with sweat under the floodlights.

'I'll burn the lot of them! That's what I'll do.' His face lost its manic expression for a moment, his mouth downturned. 'It's all over, anyway. All gone.'

'Let them go, Adrian. Please.'

The lighter went out again, and she saw anger and frustration flit across his features in the glare of the floodlights.

His thumb moved, but it was several moments before the spark wheel worked and a flame appeared.

'His hands are sweaty,' said Morrison. 'He can't keep a grip on the spark wheel properly.'

'Where the hell are your men?' Barnes hissed.

'Adrian, put that out,' said Kay. 'We can work through this, trust me. Let's get those people to safety, and then we can talk.'

'No!' Adrian took a step backwards, thrusting the leaping flame in the direction of the barn while he kept his eyes locked on her. 'They'll tell you everything. Just like that bitch, Shelley. I warned her, don't tell anyone, I said, otherwise you'll pay. I told her!'

A shadow moved behind him, moments before

Kay realised it was one of Morrison's officers advancing from his position beside one of the open doors.

She held her breath.

If Adrian turned around – if he took another step backwards – he would see the constable and panic, or worse.

'Adrian!' Barnes held up his hands. 'Come on, please. She's right, you're only making this worse. We don't want you to get hurt. Put out the flame and walk over here.'

The man snarled, began to turn towards the barn – and then dropped the cigarette lighter, his whole body convulsing.

He dropped to the floor, unable to break his fall, twitching in agony where he lay.

Within a few seconds, it was over.

'Get that away from him!' Kay rushed towards the open doors and kicked at the cigarette lighter, sending it flying towards the concrete expanse of the yard, and away from the slaughterhouse.

Turning to the police constable, she saw the Taser he held outright in front of him, ready to discharge it once more if he had to.

She stepped forward, addressing the prone man on the ground. 'Adrian, you have been Tasered. If you threaten my officers or try to harm anyone, my officer will discharge the Taser again. Do you understand?'

Peverell nodded, his face still contorted as he rubbed at his arms.

At the sound of running feet, she spun around to see Barnes and Morrison running towards her.

'Get this bastard into custody, and make sure there's a twenty-four-hour suicide watch placed on his cell.' She glared at the man who was now getting to his feet, aided by another officer. 'I want him put away for a long time.'

CHAPTER FIFTY-THREE

Kay's grip tightened on the handle of the umbrella as a vicious wind whipped off the town and buffeted the group of mourners clustered around the open grave.

Beside her, Adam kept his arm around her waist, both of them fighting a wave of emotions at being only a few metres away from where their baby daughter lay in a tiny plot decorated with fresh flowers.

DCI Devon Sharp and his wife, Rebecca, stood to her left, heads bowed as the church minister intoned the final blessing while Ethan Archer's coffin was lowered into the ground by six men wearing the distinctive uniforms and berets of the Parachute Regiment.

Janice and Andrew Crispin from the veterans'

support group stood side by side nearest to the church minister, hands clasped together, their lips moving with the words of prayer that carried over the sound of rain pelting against Kay's umbrella.

As soon as she had been able, she had telephoned them with the news that her investigation was at an end, and that Ethan could be laid to rest.

The couple had swept into action, locating Ethan's old commanding officer and organising a fundraiser to ensure the man received a burial fit for a hero.

'Amen.'

Kay let out a sigh as the six Paratroopers stepped away from the graveside and saluted their comrade, then turned and marched a discreet distance away.

'All right?' Adam murmured.

'It's over,' she said. She turned away from the grave as the minister shook hands with the Crispins and made small talk.

The day before, she had spoken with Jeremy and two of the shelter volunteers about the arrangements for Shelley's funeral.

The woman's mother had telephoned from Liverpool, suggesting that as her daughter had always had more of an affinity with the Kent county town than her family's northern home, she should be buried in Maidstone. She would travel south when a date had been arranged.

Kay and Adam had contributed to the funeral costs as soon as they became aware that Shelley's mother was struggling to make ends meet, wanting to ensure that her daughter was laid to rest properly, when possible. They knew what it was like to lose a child, and Kay had wiped away tears as she'd listened to the woman break down with relief and thanks at the other end of the line.

'Got a minute?' Sharp raised an eyebrow and gestured away from the graveside.

'Sure.'

She gave Adam's hand a squeeze, passed her umbrella to Rebecca and then ducked under Sharp's as he began to walk up the hill away from the gathered mourners.

'Harriet's team finished processing the cellar under the slaughterhouse late last night,' he said. 'They found the girl's feet in a corner under an old pillowcase. We think one of the people we rescued from the farm covered them up after Adrian threw them down there.'

'Jesus,' said Kay under her breath. 'According to Helen's statement, Adrian said it was to serve as a warning to anyone else who was thinking of trying to escape.'

Sharp hissed through his teeth. 'And you say there's video of him pushing Ethan out of the aircraft?'

'Yes. He thought he'd deleted the file off his phone, but Andy Grey over at digital forensics managed to retrieve it. You know what he's like – nothing stays hidden for long. Another of the captives we interviewed told us they were shown that video, again to frighten them into never trying to escape.'

'Has he told you what he did with the other body? The man who Helen said disappeared when he got sick?' said Sharp.

'Not yet. I've put in a request for more manpower so we can get the underwater team to search the reservoir north of the farms, and there are two search teams working through the undergrowth in the nature reserve for any disturbed areas of land. We'll find him.'

'What about the aircraft?'

'We've had a phone call from West Mercia Police this morning. They located it at Helen's parents' property in Shropshire. It hadn't been taken out of the hangar since she flew it back there after Ethan was killed. West Mercia's CSI team managed to find trace evidence of him being in the cockpit, and they found a fingernail lodged in one of the rivets on the wing – the poor man was clinging on until the end.'

'What a way to go.' Sharp faced the car park at the bottom of the hill while the mourners began to disperse, then sighed. 'He tried his best to help them escape. He really was a hero, wasn't he?'

'He was, guv. That he was.'

KAY WALKED BACK into the incident room an hour later, craning her neck to see past the stacks of archive boxes piled high on desks and chairs.

Shouted instructions passed between officers on each side of the room as paperwork was gathered, reports signed off, and quality control checks completed to ensure that every single part of the investigation was correctly catalogued ready to begin the process of taking the case to court with the help of the Crown Prosecution Service.

It would be months, maybe a year or more, before the boxes were retrieved in their entirety but the time-consuming procedure would mean everything could be located when the legal experts required it.

The team had already diminished in size, a skeleton crew remaining where once an entire side of the building had been crawling with officers and administrative staff. Now, they had taken on other casework, other duties, and dispersed around the police stations of West Division.

She paused next to her desk, checked her phone messages and then worked her way between two teetering piles of boxes towards the front of the room where a group of people gathered.

Colourful balloons hung from the whiteboard below streamers that criss-crossed the ceiling tiles, and a variety of greetings cards lay unopened beside a selection of gift bags on a desk off to one side.

Two tables had been dragged across the carpet and it appeared that Debbie had found a tablecloth left over from the Christmas party at the back of the stationery cupboard, along with the secret supply of beer, wine and soft drinks that was rumoured to be kept in a filing cabinet in Sharp's office.

The police constable had evidently paid a visit to the supermarket up the road as well, given the variety of party snacks that were laid out on paper plates and already half demolished by the hungry officers who turned to her as she approached.

'Don't stop on my account,' she said, smiling as

she helped herself to a plate and piled it with a selection of cheese, mini sausage rolls and sushi.

'Where's Sharp, guv?' said Gavin, receiving a slap on the wrist from Laura as his hand hovered next to a pile of chocolate eclairs.

'Oi, let someone else have some,' she said with a laugh.

Kay smiled. 'On his way. He said he had to do something first. I'm sure he won't be long.'

'Are you having a beer, guv?' said Barnes. He held up an unopened bottle of lager.

'Can't, I'm afraid. I'm on call until eight o'clock tomorrow morning. I'll grab an orange juice in a minute, don't worry.'

'Guv, you made it!' Carys walked over, a glass of wine in her hand. 'How was the funeral?'

'It was okay, you know – as much as those things can be. The Parachute Regiment did him proud, and it was a nice service.'

She paused as Sharp appeared at the door to the incident room, an enormous bouquet of flowers in his hands.

'There she is,' he said as he joined them, handing the flowers to Carys. 'A small gesture from Rebecca and myself. Make sure you stay in touch, otherwise I'll get into trouble with her.'

'They're lovely, thanks, guv,' said Carys, her eyes glittering. 'Oh my God, I'm off again.'

'She's been like this all afternoon,' said Gavin. 'You should've seen her when she was packing up her desk.'

Carys wiped at her eyes, and smiled. 'You promised you wouldn't tell them.'

'I lied.' He laughed, and took her wine glass from her. 'I'll get you a top up.'

'I daren't read those cards until I get home,' she said to Kay. 'I knew I should've worn waterproof mascara.'

An hour later the leaving speeches had been made, Sharp striking a balance between honouring Carys's contributions to the team and regaling everyone with some of her early exploits as a probationary detective, while Kay favoured a retrospective speech that had the incident room erupting with applause as Carys held up her hand at the demand that she now talk.

'Thanks, everyone,' she said, her voice wobbling. 'I don't know what to say. I'm going to miss you.'

'Give them hell!' someone called from the back of the crowd.

'I hope they know what they're in for,' said Barnes, enveloping her in a hug.

'Just don't go running out in front of any more trains,' said Gavin. 'And let us know how you're getting on.'

Laura stuck out her hand. 'Thanks for everything, Carys. I know I only worked with you for a little while, but I've appreciated you looking out for me.'

'Oh, come here,' said Carys, and hugged the probationary detective constable. 'You're going to be absolutely fine, and you're going to smash those exam results. Phone me if you need me, all right?'

Laura nodded, and sniffed.

'Shall I give you a hand with these?' said Kay, picking up four tote bags laden with cards and gifts.

'Please – oh God, there's so much stuff,' said Carys, juggling the bouquet and an archive box with the personal items from her desk.

It took another thirty minutes to reach the car park, as every uniformed officer and administrative staff member in the building stopped the detective constable on the way through to wish her well in her new role.

Finally, and to the taxi driver's obvious relief, Carys climbed into the waiting vehicle while Kay stacked the bags on the back seat next to her.

'Oh, Adam asked me to give you this.'

She handed her an envelope, and watched as Carys turned it over in her hands, her face quizzical.

'What is it?'

'He found the details of a local animal rescue place near you,' said Kay. 'That's the adoption papers they ask everyone to complete. He figured that once you've settled into your new place, you could give them a call and perhaps find a cat – or another gerbil – to keep you company, and he said you can phone him if you've got any concerns.'

Carys grinned. 'I'm going to miss all the animals he brings home.'

'You don't have to live with them,' said Kay, and rolled her eyes. 'Okay, go on, otherwise you're going to make me cry.'

'Thanks, Kay. For everything.'

As the taxi pulled out of the car park and under the security barrier, Kay waved until it was out of sight.

She sniffed and then shook her head as she turned towards the police station. 'That's the end of an era, Hunter.'

Her phone began to ring in her jacket pocket, and she glanced at the screen.

'Detective Inspector Kay Hunter.' She listened to the voice at the other end, and then began to run to her car. 'Tell them I'm on my way, and make sure they secure the crime scene.'

A sardonic smile crossed her lips as she twisted the key in the ignition.

Life went on, and so did the need for justice.

THE END

ABOUT THE AUTHOR

Rachel Amphlett is a USA Today bestselling author of crime fiction and spy thrillers, many of which have been translated worldwide.

Her novels are available in eBook, print, and audiobook formats from libraries and retailers as well as her website shop.

A keen traveller, Rachel has both Australian and British citizenship.

Find out more about Rachel's books at: www.rachelamphlett.com.

Made in United States
North Haven, CT
31 May 2023

37188078R00243